HEAVEN PRESERVE US

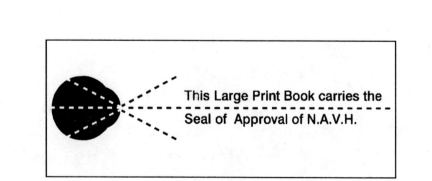

This Large Print Book carries the
Seal of Approval of N.A.V.H.

A HOME CRAFTING MYSTERY

HEAVEN PRESERVE US

CRICKET MCRAE

WHEELER PUBLISHING
A part of Gale, Cengage Learning

GALE
CENGAGE Learning

Detroit • New York • San Francisco • New Haven, Conn • Waterville, Maine • London

12/08 *Pub.* 26.00/19.47

GALE
CENGAGE Learning

LIBRARY OF CONGRESS CATALOGING-IN-PUBLICATION DATA

McRae, Cricket.
    Heaven preserve us : a home crafting mystery / by Cricket McRae.
    p. cm. — (Wheeler Publishing large print cozy mystery)
    ISBN-13: 978-1-59722-837-4 (pbk. : alk. paper)
    ISBN-10: 1-59722-837-0 (pbk. : alk. paper)
    1. Women artisans—Fiction. 2. Soap trade—Fiction. 3. Washington (State)—Fiction. 4. Large type books. I. Title.
PS3613.C58755H43 2008b
813'.6—dc22   2008032226

Published in 2008 by arrangement with Midnight Ink, an imprint of Llewellyn Publications, Woodbury, MN 55125-2989 USA.

Printed in the United States of America
1 2 3 4 5 6 7 12 11 10 09 08

For Kevin

ACKNOWLEDGMENTS

I'm grateful to so many people for their aid and support as I wrote this book: Jacky Sach, agent extraordinaire; all the fabulously helpful and efficient folks at Midnight Ink, including Barbara Moore, Connie Hill, Courtney Kish, Lisa Novak, and Donna Burch; my writing buddies Bob and Mark; Kevin for encouraging me even when I got snarky; my parents; and Mindy and Jody and everyone else, too many to name, who wanted to know what happens next.

ONE

"You don't have to fix any of the callers' problems; you just pass them on to someone else who can."

I nodded. "Got it."

"Okay, babe. I'll leave you to it. I'm going out back to have a smoke."

Smiling through gritted teeth, I tried to ignore the acrid stench of cigarettes that permeated his clothes. Philip Heaven could spend the whole evening toasting his lungs in the alley if it meant I wouldn't have to listen to him call me "babe" one more time in that gravelly, know-it-all voice. I'd handle every incoming call to the Heaven House Helpline if I had to. I mean, how hard could it be?

"Take your time," I said, aligning my list of referral numbers with the edge of the blotter and lacing my fingers together on top of the cheap laminate desktop. I glanced hopefully at the multi-line phone.

"Thanks, babe." He pointed his finger at me and made a gun-cocking sound with his tongue.

Yuck. Thank God, the phone rang. I reached to answer it.

After I referred a nice-but-scared-sounding lady to the next AA meeting in the basement of the Cadyville Catholic Church, the phone was silent for several minutes. The whooshing of tires across wet pavement on the street outside filtered into the spacious old building where I sat, a comfortable, lulling sound. I'd worked my way to forty-two across on the *Seattle Times* Tuesday crossword only to puzzle over a six-letter word for an exclamation of annoyance when the phone rang again. This time I gave a runaway boy an 800 number he could use to find a safe place to stay down in Seattle. I was pretty satisfied with the whole volunteer gig after that one and picked up the next call, feeling helpful as all get-out.

"I have the knife against my wrist. It shines in the light. And it's cold. I bet this thing is so sharp I won't even feel it slice through my skin."

Uh oh.

I struggled to remember what I was supposed to say, but Philip's meager training hadn't prepared me for anything like this. Where was he? He couldn't still be working on that cigarette, could he? After all, I hadn't really meant that about him hanging out in the alley all night. It was my first night manning the Helpline at Heaven House, and Philip Heaven was supposed to be mentoring me. Sheesh.

So I said the only thing I could think of: "Wait!"

"Why should I wait? I've been waiting my whole life to die."

Oh, brother. A philosopher. And a melodramatic one at that. "So have I," I said.

"What?"

I looked at the caller ID, so I could jot it down on the call sheet. It read *Private Call*. Great.

"I've been waiting my whole life to die, too," I said.

"You have?"

Yeah. Right along with all us other mortals.

Hush, Sophie Mae. He may be a moron, but he sounds pretty serious.

"But I'm not going to die today. And not tomorrow, either, at least not if I get a vote in the matter," I said.

Silence.

11

"And neither should you. What's your name?"

"It's . . . just call me Allen."

"Okay, Allen, listen, I'm going to —"

"What's yours?"

"What's my what?"

"Your name."

"Allen, I need you to write down a number. This is someone who knows how to help you."

"I don't want another number. I want to talk to you. Tell me your name."

"Sorry, it's against —"

"I told you mine."

No, you didn't, I thought, but stopped myself before I said it out loud. Just call me Allen? That's not how you tell someone your name, for Pete's sake.

"Call me Jane."

"No! I want your real name. Tell me."

An icky feeling crawled up my spine. I put some steel in my voice. "Allen, take down this number: 555-2962. There's someone there who's trained in how to help you deal with your suicidal thoughts."

"You're trying to foist me off on someone else? All I want to know is who I'm dealing with."

My resolve wavered. It was against the rules of Heaven House to give out our

12

names to the people who called the Help-line. For that matter, I shouldn't still be talking to this guy. Volunteers were armed with a long list of experts who dealt with all sorts of different problems, from teenaged runaways to unplanned pregnancy, depression to spousal abuse, alcoholism to . . . suicide. If Philip had been honest enough to list Heaven House as a Help *Referral* Line in the phone book maybe this guy wouldn't be so angry about having to call someone else.

Still. There was something about him that gave me the creeps.

"I'm not going to tell you my real name. That's against the rules here. I'm here to help you find someone to talk to. Are you going to let me do that?"

"No! All I want to know is who —"

A finger came down on the disconnect button. I went from staring stupidly at the phone to staring stupidly up at Philip. His cousin, Jude Carmichael, stood slightly behind him. I hadn't heard either of them come in.

"Should you have done that?" I finally managed.

"I could hear him yelling. He's a crank," Philip said.

I licked my lips, ambivalent about the

13

intense relief I felt at the timely rescue. "But what if he really needed help?"

Jude, his coat collar still turned up around his ears, shuffled his feet and looked at the floor. In the brief time I'd known him, I'd noticed that he did that a lot. When he spoke, I leaned closer so I could hear his soft voice.

"Then he should have taken it. You don't have to put up with abuse, Sophie Mae. Philip should have told you. Sometimes people call in just to call in. They're lonely." He shuffled his feet again. I had the feeling he knew about lonely. "Or they're weirdos. Like this guy. His next call will probably be heavy breathing and obscene language. He's just bored."

"Well, he better not call back here, then."

Philip bent toward me. "Tell you what, babe. It's your first night. Your shift's almost over. Go ahead home."

"You sure?"

"Yeah. It's fine. My boy here can start his overnight shift early."

"That okay with you?" I asked Jude, since Philip hadn't bothered.

Jude shrugged and tried a smile. "Sure. I forward the calls to my cell and keep it on my night stand. It hardly ever rings." He pulled a phone out of his pocket and started

14

pushing buttons on the one on the desk.

"I hope that guy didn't scare you off," Philip said.

"No, I'll be back," I said. "Friday, right?"

"That'll be great. We'll need your help. Friday night'll be hoppin'!" He made it sound like great fun, taking all those desperate phone calls from people in horrible situations.

Woo hoo!

So that was volunteer work, I thought as I drove home a little after nine. Not that Heaven House was likely to be the best example. Philip Heaven, grandson of the famous, or more accurately, infamous, Nathaniel Heaven, had started Heaven House in Cadyville over a year ago. Funded with money granted to the project by the foundation created after the old man's death, it was a nonprofit organization devoted to the community of Cadyville. What that meant in practical terms was yet to be seen.

So far there was the helpline and a bunch of empty rooms. Philip had programs planned for teens and the elderly, for job training, for low-cost childcare and helping the housebound, and even for the environment. It was a vague hodgepodge of good intentions. I'd heard several months before

15

that he'd brought in his cousin to help, but from what I could tell they needed more help than Jude could provide.

The name was misleading, too, as most people assumed it was a religious organization. But Nathaniel had been a died-in-the-wool agnostic, and while the foundation didn't actually ban religious activities altogether, it was clear in the informational packet provided to volunteers that the board would not grant funding to any activity that wasn't open to people of any and all denominations or belief systems.

I pulled to the curb in front of the house I shared with Meghan Bly and her eleven-year-old daughter, Erin. Jumping out of my little Toyota pickup, I ran up the sidewalk. Rain spattered down for the twentieth day in a row, and the temperature hovered around forty-two degrees — typical weather in the Pacific Northwest in February. The damp air smelled of rotting leaves and wood smoke.

In the foyer I shook like a dog, scattering the stray drops I hadn't managed to avoid in my mad dash from the street. I waved at Meghan as I passed the doorway to the kitchen on my way to the stairs, breathing in the scent of freshly baked bread.

"Back in a sec," I called over my shoulder

16

and climbed to the second floor.

I poked my head into Erin's room. "How's it going?"

Meghan's daughter sat in bed, wedged in on one side by a stuffed platypus and on the other by a big purple hippo. Brodie, Erin's aging Pembroke Welsh Corgi, lay on his back, legs splayed open as he slept by her feet. His right eye cracked open so he could peer at me upside down, then squeezed shut again. A textbook lay open on Erin's lap, and she looked up from scribbling on loose-leaf notepaper when I spoke. Her elfin features held pure disgust.

"I hate math. I hate algebra, I hate geometry, and I plan on hating trigonometry and calculus as well." She squinted blue-gray eyes at me and shook her head of dark curls for emphasis.

"Trig? When do you start that?" Could be next week for all I knew. She was in an advanced class and last year had blown by everything I'd retained from my English major's admittedly pitiful math education. But trig? In the fifth grade?

"And proofs. I hate proofs, too."

I had no idea what proofs were. I went in and looked at what she was working on. Drawn on the wide-ruled paper was a y-axis. And an x-axis. Lines connected some of the points in the grid. I still had no idea what proofs were.

"Looks like a graph," I said. "What are you supposed to be proving?"

The look she gave me was full of pity.

"Okay. Well, I'm going to change my clothes and go talk to your mom. So, er, g'night."

She sighed. "Goodnight, Sophie Mae."

I smiled to myself as I went down the hallway to my room and changed into my flannel pjs. Erin was a drama queen. It would only get worse as she morphed from tween to teen, but at heart she was such a great kid I knew she'd make it through okay.

I just hoped Meghan and I made it through okay, too.

Two

Downstairs, I sliced a hunk off the loaf cooling on the counter and grabbed a jar of peanut butter and some homemade raspberry freezer jam out of the fridge. Meghan raised one perfectly shaped eyebrow at me as I settled in at our butcher-block kitchen table and began slathering a thick layer of peanut butter on the warm bread.

"What? I didn't eat dinner."

"Okay," she said, and turned back to the lunch she was packing Erin for school. Meghan and Erin looked even more alike than you'd expect from a mother and daughter, with identical glossy dark hair, delicate bone structure and short, slight frames. Meghan's eyes were a little brighter blue. I, on the other hand, had little in common with the Bly girls. My hair was straight and blonde and hung in a practical braid down my back; I'd been told my green eyes were pretty, and sometimes I believed it; I was a little taller, and a little heavier. But who wasn't? Meghan couldn't have weighed much more than a hundred pounds.

I sighed at that thought, then noted with triumph there was already a peanut butter and jam sandwich on the counter beside Erin's lunch bag. Ha! If it was good enough for her kid, it was good enough for me.

"Is Erin doing her math?" Meghan asked, completely unaware of my covetous feelings about her waistline.

"Yep. And loudly hating every minute of it."

"I don't care, as long as she's doing it. She's been so obsessed with studying for that spelling bee coming up that she's been neglecting it."

"There are worse problems than your child avoiding her math homework because she's studying spelling words."

Meghan threw me a glance over her shoulder and turned back to the big fat brownie she was encasing in cling wrap. "I know." She shrugged. "I think I'd feel better about the bee if she weren't doing it just because she's got a crush on Jonathan Bell."

I eyed the brownie. "Who's he?"

She turned around and rolled her eyes. "You are so clueless sometimes. He's been over here studying almost every day after school. They're spending too much time together."

"Meghan, they're eleven."

"Eleven is the new fifteen," she said.

"I don't get that. Then how can twenty-six be the new twenty-one, with kids living with their parents until they're practically middle-aged?"

She cocked her head. "Good point. We should talk to someone about that."

"Damn straight," I said.

"How was the Helpline?" she asked.

"Um. It was okay. A little sad. Kind of boring. Until the end, at least. This creep called and said he was going to kill himself, but then seemed more interested in finding out my name than in slicing his wrists."

"Sophie Mae! You can't make fun of people who call in to the Helpline."

"No, really, he was creepy. Philip hung up on him. He even sent me home early. I think he was afraid I'd quit right then and there."

"Did the man who called get the number of someone to help him?"

"I gave it to him, but I don't know if he wrote it down."

"Oh, that poor soul. I hope he's okay."

"Um, yeah. Me, too." Which was true, of course. Never mind that the main reason I volunteered at Heaven House was because

21

Meghan had talked me into it.

I changed the subject. "Have you decided what we should take to the preserves exchange?"

"Oh, God, I'd forgotten. It's tomorrow night, isn't it?" She walked to the pantry, opened the door and peered in. "We pickled extra asparagus last spring; it's cured almost a year, so it'll be just right."

"Okay, but leave some for us."

She turned around and gave me a look. "We'll make more in May, you know."

"But a year, Meghan. You said it yourself — it's better after it sits a while. And it's only February."

A ghost of a smile crossed her face, and she turned back to the open doorway. "We have a ton of watermelon pickles."

"Watermelon pickles," I moaned. "I love watermelon pickles."

"We can make more of those next summer, too."

"Keep a few jars. Please, please, please?"

"God, you're worse than Erin. Of course I'll keep a few jars, if only for you children."

"Hey."

"Do you think we should whip up another batch of wine jelly in the morning? Everyone loves to eat that with beef and lamb, and it's done in a jiffy."

But I wasn't really listening. I was thinking about all the good stuff we were about to have added to our pantry. The preserves exchange was another project at Heaven House, though it was designed less to aid the community and more for the volunteers. It was based on an old Cadyville town tradition. During the Depression, Cadyville High School had sponsored a preserved food contest for the senior girls. They canned and pickled and jellied frantically for weeks; whoever canned the most food won the recognition of their peers and the kudos of a grateful town. It probably didn't hurt much in the search for a husband, either.

And Cadyville *was* grateful because most of the food preserved for the contest went straight into the kitchen of the local hospital to feed the patients all year long. It sounded like a perfect setup — the hospital won, and the girls had a chance to compete in something meaningful, both in terms of charity and in terms of learning how to preserve food for their future families. Though, truth be told, most of them were probably old hands at such things by the ripe old age of eighteen.

Thirty is the new eighteen . . .

Anyway, the preserves exchange at Heaven House worked in much the same way, except we only exchanged among ourselves. So many of the volunteers at Heaven House were great cooks, and this way we got to sample each other's home-preserved specialties.

Thaddeus Black would bring brandied peaches. Nothing like those eaten with a little vanilla-bean ice cream in front of an apple-wood fire on a cold snowy night. Yum. I hoped his niece, Ruth Black, would bring her famous blueberry conserve, perfect baked as a tart filling in a shortbread crust. There would be dilly green beans and bread-and-butter pickles and homemade sauerkraut for the best Reuben sandwiches in the world or to stew with lamb sausage in the slow cooker all day. I'd heard rumors of relishes, beets, marinated mushrooms and corn. If everything went as planned, everyone would have well-stocked and varied pantries.

Mmmm . . .

"Sophie Mae! What are you doing?"

I looked down to where I was about to double dip into the peanut butter jar with the biggest spoon in the silverware drawer.

"Mmmph." I said. Which meant, "I have no idea how this happened, but I require milk this very instant."

I headed to the refrigerator, bending just

a bit under Meghan's look of mild repri-
mand.

"No drinking out of the carton."

I poured the milk into a tall glass and
swigged it. Once again able to talk, I said,
"Jeez. One little faux pas with the peanut
butter, and you act like I'm going to start
eating like a guy or something."

"Don't you dare," she said.

I grinned. "I'm off to bed. See you in the
a.m."

"Uh huh. Don't forget the phone,
'Honeybunch.' "

"Shut up," I said and walked out, snagging the cordless phone off the hall table as
I passed by. Behind me, Meghan laughed.

"It was okay," I said, repeating what I had
said to Meghan about my evening of volunteer work to Barr Ambrose. "I'm not so sure
I like the kind of clientele you get to talk to,
though."

"Hell, Sophie Mae, the point is to help
people in trouble who don't have anyplace
else to turn. Those folks tend to be a tad
less refined than you or me."

"That's not what I mean. I talked to a
couple of people who probably fall a lot
higher on the social scale than I do. But
there was a kind of scary guy this evening,

25

and I bet he's only the first. It's not because they're bad people or anything. It's just that desperation makes you do things you wouldn't otherwise do. Like I did last October. And that's a little . . . frightening."

He was silent for a moment, and I knew he was thinking about the fact that I'd burned someone quite badly the previous fall, trying to keep Erin safe. That was okay, though: the silence. I liked Barr's silences. Rather, I liked the silences that fell between us. They felt full, not empty. Comfortable. I hadn't felt that with anyone since my husband had died five years before.

"What did the scary guy do?" he asked. Trust him to zero in on the one thing I wished I hadn't mentioned. Barr was a detective, make that *the* detective, on the Cadyville police force, and while that was nice in many ways, he did have a way of blowing the idea of me being in danger all out of proportion.

"It was nothing," I said.

"Sophie Mae."

"No, really. Just that desperation I was telling you about. Made me a little uncomfortable. I'll get used to it. And I really like the idea of helping people out. Maybe I can make a difference in somebody's life. You know, like in a big way."

"You're already making a big difference in somebody's life, just by being your sweet self."

And that was why I took the phone to bed with me, whether Meghan teased me about it or not. Because that was the kind of thing I liked to hear right before going to sleep every night. Not big statements, but the little bits of sugar he'd slip in now and again. That and the fact that he really wanted to talk to me every night when we were apart. Even when he was working. In his gentle, understated way he made me feel special.

"Aw," I said. "Ain't you sweet."

"Yes, I am. But I do have to go. I have at least two hours of paperwork to plod through before I can leave, and I'm working in the morning."

All the overtime Barr had to put in wore him out and tried my patience. "When are they going to hire another detective? Or at least make the uniformed officers do more of the investigative work?"

"When they get the funding," he said. "The Chief is working on it. And there's only so much the uniforms can do."

"I don't understand. How much crime is there in a little town like Cadyville, any-way?"

"More than I'd like to tell you about. I spent most of this evening interviewing a woman who was attacked walking to her car after work. It happened right downtown. I want you to be extra careful, Sophie Mae. We haven't caught the guy yet."

"When you say attacked . . ."

"He didn't rape her. But he might have if some high school kids hadn't cut through that alley and scared him off. He left her bruised and shaken, but that's all."

"That's enough."

He murmured his agreement. "Just be careful. Goodnight."

" 'Night. Sleep tight. You know, when you get a chance to sleep at all."

We rang off, and I lay in bed thinking. We weren't to the I-love-you stage of things yet. That was okay. We'd been seeing each other for over three months, and I liked moving slowly after years of relationship hiatus. Not that everything was moving that slowly, mind you. But I got the feeling when Barr Ambrose said "I love you," there would be a whole lot of strings attached. I was getting to like the idea of those strings, but I was still a little gun-shy. He knew that. I hoped that was why he was being so reticent. I sure didn't want it to be because he didn't know how he felt about me.

The phone rang. I pushed the talk button quickly, afraid the shrill sound would wake Erin and Meghan, both of whom had turned out their bedside lights down the hall.

"Forget something?" I asked.

"Sophie Mae Reynolds."

Oops. Not Barr. "Yes?"

"Sophie Mae, Sophie Mae, Sophie Mae." The man on the other end of the line softly sang my name.

All snug in my flannel pjs, under my mountain of down comforter, I suddenly felt very cold. "Who is this?"

"I found out your name after all, Sophie Mae. And that's not all I found out."

"Allen?" I knew it wasn't his real name, but I didn't know what else to call him. Correction: I knew what else I wanted to call him, but that seemed like a bad idea at the moment.

"I'll call you again, soon. I'm looking forward to talking more." And he hung up.

I beeped off the phone and lay there for a few moments, trying to think. I could call Barr back. But what could he do? Just worry. And I'd already caused him enough worry. I'd figure out how to deal with this Allen jerk myself.

THREE

A gentle rain pattered gently on the roof the next morning. Eventually, I got around to opening my eyes enough to peer at the clock on my nightstand. Six fourteen a.m. and still dark as night outside. My hand crept through the cool sheets to the other side of the bed before I really thought about it, but no one was there. Barr and I only spent a couple of nights a week together, always at his place, but I loved waking up with his tall, lanky form wrapped around me.

I missed it more than usual this morning. Why was that?

Then I realized: waking up with Barr made me feel safe, and the mysterious Allen had me thoroughly freaked out.

Well, thank heavens I'd remembered *that,* I thought as I let out a whoosh of breath and threw back the covers. No more lolly-gagging around. I had work to do, and then I needed to find out from Philip whether they'd ever had problems with callers suddenly taking it into their pea brains to stalk the volunteers at Heaven House.

At nine o'clock, after mixing a batch of lemon verbena soap and catching up on the wholesale invoicing for my handmade toiletry business, Winding Road Bath Products, I took a break and drove the few blocks downtown. In the daylight, Heaven House looked less than inviting. Just one block off the five-block length of First Street, it was a large brick cube, as wide and high as it was deep. Owned by the Heaven Foundation, for years the top floor held an apartment and office space, and the ground floor had been leased to a large antique "mall" where locals would bring their old crap and sell it to tourists on consignment. As soon as the lease expired, Philip Heaven had moved his personal brainchild into the building.

One large room took up most of the main floor, with the big cheap desk I'd been sitting at the night before located near the front door. Along the back wall was a smaller room, empty so far, and to the left a larger one we all referred to as the game room, though it only had one game in it, and no furniture. The entrance to the unisex bathroom was at the rear of the building, by the back door. To the right were the stairs to the second floor. The whole building was old, with layers of paint and a persistent odor of musty mildew.

Philip was big on vision, but from what I could tell so far, not so great with detail or implementation. Luckily, he had a full-time assistant named Maryjake Dreggle. When I walked in she was sitting at the desk, peering at her computer monitor with a frown. Beside her, the pungent smells of chili and garlic wafted from a cardboard take-out container of Thai food.

Her pale brown eyes brightened when she saw me. "How'd it go last night?"

"Okay, I guess. Hey, I've got a question for you."

"Yeah?"

"Ever have someone, you know, fixate on you before? A caller, on the Helpline?"

"Fixate? Not really. I've had repeat callers. But mostly they just needed someone to talk to." She shifted in her chair and put a booted foot up on the desk, displaying a heavily muscled leg between the top of her wool sock and the hem of the hiking shorts she insisted on wearing year round.

"Did you refer them?" I asked.

She pushed a chunk of her fuzzy dishwater-red hair behind one ear. "Sure. There was one woman, though. She and I seemed to connect, so I just let her spill her guts. I know it's not what we're supposed to do, but it seemed to help, and I referred her to a therapy network, too. She was going through a horrible divorce, and I've been there, too."

A completely different situation than the one I had with Allen.

"Philip up in his office?" I asked.

Her frown returned. "He was. Not feeling so hot, though, so he may have given up on working, gone back into his apartment. But take a look."

I crossed the large open area and climbed the narrow stairs to Philip's office and the apartment he'd taken over with the rest of the lease.

A short hallway at the top of the stairs revealed two doors, one of them closed. I strode to the open doorway and stopped, looking into the small office. The high ceiling sported beautifully carved molding, but the plain white walls remained unadorned, and fluorescent track lighting gave the space a stark quality. An ashtray on the windowsill betrayed Philip's sneak smoking, and the brisk tone in the air suggested he'd recently closed the window. Unfortunately, the room still smelled of stale cigarette smoke . . . and something else. I wrinkled my nose.

Philip's heavy oak desk, situated at an oblique angle to the door, completely dominated the room. Good feng shui, he'd told me. I had no idea whether he was right, and furthermore didn't understand why anyone who ran a nonprofit organization funded entirely through a family foundation would care about situating his office to make money. But what did I know? Maybe it was actually more about success than money.

In which case he might have been holding his book on feng shui upside down when he'd decided how to place the desk, because Heaven House didn't exactly qualify as a successful enterprise. The only thing that would solve that problem was a director with more focus than Philip would ever possess.

I hesitated, not sure if I was interrupting his work, but after several moments I realized he wasn't really reading anything on the computer monitor in front of him so much as staring a hole in it. The harsh light reflected from his scalp under the sparse sweep of a bad comb-over. I cleared my throat and stepped into the room. When he looked up, I was shocked.

Philip Heaven looked like hell.

"Hey, babe! How's it going? Just couldn't stay away until Friday, huh?" The words fit his usual persona, but they slurred together as if he were drunk. His eyes looked like two holes burned in a blanket, their muted hazel coloring eclipsed by red-rimmed lids. His nostrils flared over a two-day stubble, and his naturally pale complexion had taken on the moist appearance of newly risen bread dough.

"Holy crap. You should be in bed," I said.

"That an offer?"

Oh, good Lord. Fine. Not my problem if he didn't have the sense of a gnat. But I stepped back in the doorway. Whatever he had, I didn't want any of it.

I told him about Allen calling me at home the previous evening.

"He called you at your house? How'd he get your number?" He didn't look pleased. In fact, he acted like it was my fault "Allen" had decided to harass me.

"I was hoping you could tell me."

"Well, I didn't give it to him," he said.

"He shouldn't even have known my name."

"Well, I didn't give him that, either." He sounded defensive. "You're the only one who talked to the guy." He coughed, then gasped for a couple breaths as if he couldn't get enough air.

My brow wrinkled. He sounded like he

had pneumonia. "Listen, I'm not blaming you. I just wondered if this had happened before. You know, see if there's a protocol to follow."

"No. Never before. No protocol." More gasping.

I couldn't help it. "Philip, are you okay? I really think you should lie down. Or maybe go to the clinic down the street."

He waved his hand at me, dismissing the idea. "It's just something I ate. I don't know what to tell you about this guy, babe. I'd go beat him up for you, but we don't know who he is."

As if Philip could have beaten up a kitten right then. "I'll figure it out. Thanks for your help." More like thanks for nothing.

He licked his lips. "You know, I get threats all the time."

I paused in the act of turning toward the door. "Really? Why would anyone threaten you?"

He shrugged. "Most of them don't come to anything."

I squinted at him. "What do they say?"

His Adam's apple bobbed as he swallowed hard. "Various things. Most of them reflect wishes for unpleasant things to happen to me."

I wondered if I'd stumbled into something. Maybe Allen was less interested in me than in getting to Philip somehow. "This has happened recently?"

He looked away and rubbed his fingertips across his lips. "Yeah."

"Somebody threatened you — did you tell the police about it?"

"Sort of. Sophie Mae, it doesn't have anything to do with that caller."

"How do you know?"

"Because my latest threat was not exactly anonymous." He looked back at me, and I saw his Adam's apple work again as he tried to swallow. "Have you ever had your lips go numb?"

"Numb? No," I said. "Philip, is there some reason you're not taking this last threat seriously?"

"It's just someone letting off steam. Are you still coming on Friday?" His skin had taken on a weird grayish tinge.

"You look terrible. Go to bed."

"Friday?" he repeated.

I counted to ten. "Yes. I'll be here on Friday. I said I would, and I will. Okay?"

"You should call the police about this Allen character," he said.

"Maybe. I'll think about it." Of course, calling the police in my case was the same thing as putting my boyfriend on high alert.

I wasn't sure if that was a good idea or not.

"He probably followed you home from the parking lot," Philip said.

An involuntary shiver tickled my shoulder blades. "Oh, that's very helpful. Thank you for that thought. I'm going to go now."

"Maybe he's been following you for a while. Maybe it has nothing to do with the Helpline. Call the police, babe. I mean it."

"Sounds like you might want to do the same," I said.

He turned and threw up all over the wall.

"Holy shit!" It just sort of slipped out before I could stop it. I mean, I wasn't trying to make the guy feel bad; he obviously felt pretty bad as it was. His head lolled back and he slid off his chair.

"Maryjake," I called, hurrying around the desk. And then again, louder. "Maryjake!"

FOUR

Philip's mouth opened and closed like a beached fish now, but he wasn't making much noise. With rigid fingers, he clawed at the side of the desk. I was on the phone with emergency services when Maryjake hit the doorway. She saw Philip's feet sticking out from behind the desk and rushed around to join us. Now there were three of us in that tiny space, and I stepped back against the wall to make room, urging the 911 operator to send an ambulance as soon as possible.

"Oh, God! Philip, honey, what happened? Oh, God. Ohgodohgodohgod." She dissolved into a puddle by his side.

Honey? I spared the briefest of moments wondering what Maryjake's husband, James, would think of *that.*

"I don't know what's wrong with him," I said into the phone. "He can't seem to breathe, and he threw up." All over the wall.

Which I was leaning against. I shut my eyes, trying to remember how high the splatter had gone, and instinctively put a few inches between myself and the plaster. I suspected it was too late, though.

Ew, ew, ew.

"Yes. Thank you. I hear them now," I told the operator, and hung up.

The sirens got louder as I maneuvered around Maryjake sobbing all over Philip, now eerily quiet, his eyes closed.

"Maryjake, they're going to need to get to him. Come on. Let's move the desk to the side."

"Oh, Phillllllllip." Her voice quavered like Laura Petry's on the old *Dick Van Dyke Show* as she stood and ran out of the room.

Great.

I bent to try and move the desk by myself. Philip grabbed my arm and pulled me down toward him. Eyes open again, his gaze slid blearily around the ceiling. His mouth worked as he tried to speak. He smelled like cigarettes and vomit, but I forced myself to lean close to his lips.

"Threat. Meant it." He breathed the words against my ear.

"Who did?" I demanded.

But his lids fluttered down, and the grip on my arm loosened. Putting my ear to his chest, I tried to determine whether he was still breathing. Barely, and his heartbeat sounded way too loud.

I heard voices downstairs and called out, "Up here."

Boots pounded up the old wooden stairs. Maryjake darted in with a damp washcloth in her hand just before the bevy of uniformed men began filing into the room. She knelt over Philip and put the cloth on his forehead. It seemed an odd way to address an emergency medical situation, but what did I know?

If I'd thought there were too many people in the room before, now it turned into a how-many-people-can-you-fit-in-a-phone-booth thing. I struggled through the paramedics, which was not nearly as unpleasant as it sounds, and out to the hallway. Behind me Maryjake shrieked, whether because of the thoroughly uncharacteristic hysteria that seemed to have grabbed her, or because of anger at the paramedics asking her to move or leave, I didn't know.

One of the uniformed men followed me down the short hall. We paused outside the closed door to Philip's apartment, and I turned to him.

"Why so many EMTs?" I asked.

He shrugged. "Everyone at the station was

41

available. Plus, we're training."

The last time I'd called for paramedics only two had shown up. Of course, the man I'd called them for had been dead. But still.

Tall, blond, and cute-as-a-button spoke again. "You're the one who called?"

I nodded.

"Tell me what happened."

"We were just talking. He didn't look so hot. In fact, his assistant —" I pointed toward the office to indicate Maryjake, and he nodded his understanding, "— told me before I came up that he wasn't feeling well this morning. His speech was slurred, he couldn't seem to catch his breath, and then he threw up. After that he kind of turned gray and collapsed." I craned my neck to try and see if I had Heaven barf on my behind, then realized how strange my contortions must look.

He had a few more questions, but I couldn't really shed any more light on the situation. When he'd finished, Mr. Paramedic gave me a smile and thanked me.

As I noticed his pretty white teeth, the little voice that lived in the back of my brain noted ironically that having sex on a regular basis seemed to have a kind of ripple effect; getting more, I wanted more. It then reminded me not to leer, and I complied. I did, however, continue to stand with my back to the wall as he walked away so I wouldn't inadvertently show any unsavory smears that might be on my backside.

"Is he going to be okay?" I called.

The paramedic turned. "I don't know." And this time he didn't smile, not one bit.

Suddenly my calm didn't seem so laudable. Suddenly I felt like a horrible person. Philip was obnoxious and silly and rude and terribly inefficient, but I didn't want anything truly bad to happen to him. I mean, so he called me babe all the time. It was kind of cute, really.

Wasn't it?

I leaned against the wall and covered my face with my hands.

They took Philip off to the hospital, and I sent a hysterical Maryjake home. I stayed to answer the Helpline, until Ruth Black showed up for her volunteer shift. I practically wept on her shoulder when she walked in the door, I was so grateful to be able to leave. Ruth, seventy and sassy with her spiked white hair and an elaborate quilted cardigan that looked more like a work of art than something to wear, accepted my enthusiastic welcome with good grace, though the look she gave me wasn't exactly sympathetic.

The morning had evaporated. What had started as a quick break had turned into three traumatic hours. At home Meghan greeted me with a frustrated, "Where have you been?"

She'd had to begin the process of making wine jelly without me, and obviously wasn't very happy about it. Two dozen squat jelly jars sat waiting on a towel on the counter, still steaming from the sterilization process. On the stove, the huge black canning kettle roiled with boiling water. Meghan slowly stirred the beautiful deep red liquid in the double boiler, melting sugar into the hot cabernet sauvignon before adding the pectin that would cause it to gel.

"I'm sorry. I have a good excuse, though." I poured a cup of coffee and took over stirring, filling her in on the excitement at Heaven House.

"Oh, my God. Is he going to be okay?" she asked when I'd finished.

She'd added the pectin to the mixture while I'd been talking, and now I skimmed a little foam off the top while she fitted the pouring funnel into the first jar.

Grimacing as I ladled out the hot wine jelly, I said, "I don't know. That paramedic didn't look very happy."

"I'm calling the hospital." Meghan left to get the phone, wiping her hands on a well-stained floursack dishtowel.

I continued ladling until all the jars were filled and began fitting the lids on and affixing them with the screw-on metal bands. I heard Meghan murmuring in the other room. I had just placed the first set of jars in the boiling water canner, replaced the lid and set the timer when she came back in.

"Philip's in the ICU."

"Do they know what's wrong with him?" I asked.

Meghan bit her lip. "This isn't official information, by the way. They don't just give that out. But I called someone I know over there. Apparently it could be a ton of things, maybe even a stroke, but they're thinking it was probably something he ate."

I leaned against the counter and stared at the runnels of collected moisture making vertical worm tracks on the steamed-up window over the sink.

Threat. Meant it.

Had someone poisoned Philip Heaven?

"Are you okay? It must have been awful," Meghan said.

"Well, it wasn't fun."

"Why'd you go over there this morning

anyway? Forget something last night?"

I turned and looked at her. "I went over to find out from Philip whether there had been any other instances of a caller to the Helpline focusing on a particular volunteer."

"Is this about the suicidal man last night?"

"Mm hmm. Did you hear the phone ring after you'd gone to bed?"

She nodded, her head cocked a little to one side. "Wasn't it Barr?"

"Nope. It was Mr. Just-Call-Me-Allen. He wanted to let me know he knew who I was. And my phone number." Her eyes widened a fraction. "And probably where I live," I added, almost against my will.

"Does Barr know?"

"I'll call him. I'm sure it's nothing to be concerned about, but I'll call him."

Meghan looked worried.

"Listen," I said. "I still have a ton to do yet today. A gazillion retail orders to fill, and I have eight dozen Saltea Bags to make for that company in North Carolina that took all those samples at the Handmade Toiletries Trade Show."

I was a soap maker. Well, to be more accurate, soap was only a part of my repertoire — I designed, produced, and sold a variety of handmade toiletries in my workroom in the basement of Meghan's house. I lived in

46

the house, too, and paid rent. We'd been housemates since shortly after my husband died and she divorced that son-of-a-, well, you know . . . her ex. Richard.

Dick was pretty much out of the picture now, living in California with his mother, the Wicked Witch of the West, waiting out his parole and no doubt whining like the dickens the whole time.

Anyway. Meghan and I both worked out of the house, which made it handy Erin-wise, especially because we could coordinate our schedules. I'd been so busy lately that I'd been really bad about my side of coordinating things, though. Luckily, Meghan was pretty understanding about that. She was a massage therapist, and she had her busy times, too, when I tried to step up more on the domestic front.

"You look tired," she said. "Need any help?"

"Kyla and Cyan are coming after school this afternoon, so they can help me package up the wholesale order if I mix it up right away. And I should be able to knock out the retail orders either before they get here or after they leave, and then send those out first thing tomorrow. Besides, don't you have clients today?"

She was wearing her work uniform: a soft

white cotton T-shirt and loose gray yoga pants folded down to expose a narrow strip of her tiny waist. This woman had had a child? I sighed and tugged my sweater down.

"I do," she said. "Two this afternoon, starting in half an hour, and then I'm going by the hospital to work on a couple of physical therapy patients."

She'd recently branched out to work in the Caladia Acres Nursing Home and the hospital in the neighboring town of Everett. No wonder she knew someone who would tell her what was going on with Philip.

"I'll be here at three when Erin gets home from school," I said.

She looked relieved. "Good. I didn't have a chance to talk to you before I committed to the hospital thing. I'll finish up this jelly so you can get to work. And by the way, the Chase boys are going to be working on the chicken coop today. Luke said they'd be setting the corner posts in cement."

Luke and Seth Chase, both in their early twenties, had moved into the house two doors down with their father. The previous fall Walter Hanover, our local handyman, had died. We were thrilled when both our clay artist friend Bette and Walter's former landlady, Mavis Gray, told us about the Chase brothers starting up a handyman

48

business. They'd put new vinyl in Bette's tiny kitchen, and Mavis told us they'd done a nice job cleaning her roof and gutters. When we decided to keep a few laying hens in the back yard, we contacted them to see if they'd take on the job of building their quarters.

I bolted my coffee and poured another cup to take downstairs to my workroom with me.

"Sophie Mae?"

I paused mid-pour. Something in her voice. "Yeah?"

"Did you see Kelly O'Connell when you were at Heaven House this morning?"

"Who?"

She flapped her hand at me. "Never mind. Go. Work." The timer dinged, and she began lifting steaming jars of jelly out of the canner.

"Okay." I'd find out what that was about later. Right now I wanted to call Barr and tell him what had happened. Was I completely off-base, thinking someone had intentionally slipped Philip something lethal? Fear had shown from his eyes as he whispered those words to me. Or was I projecting that onto him? I was quite frightened myself at the time, I had to admit.

Maybe Barr could put things into perspective.

Downstairs, I looked out at the back yard and alley from the large windows that ran the entire length of my spacious workroom. I liked to have as much natural light as possible while I mixed and packaged and labeled my various Winding Road bath products. I watched a pair of stellars jays chowing down at the bird feeder as I waited for Barr to answer his cell. No luck. I left a message. He'd get back to me when he had a chance.

Outside, the sky was a smooth, even gray, dark enough to make me wonder whether dawn had given up rather than bother trying to break through the muck above. I opened the back door and took a deep whiff of the winter air of the Pacific Northwest, a mix of green moss, red cedar, and yellowed leaves. The combination calmed me. The moisture in the air was palpable against my exposed face and the backs of my hands.

Luke and Seth came around the edge of the house, each carrying a four-by-four post. Now I identified the scent of cedar as coming from the pile of posts stacked near the house and covered with a bright blue tarp.

"Hey, Sophie Mae," Luke said, nodding

in my direction as he walked past. With his dark hair, dark eyes, strong jaw and high cheekbones, he walked with the cocky confidence of someone who knows they're good looking. His brother Seth's eyes flashed up to meet mine for a split second. His mouth turned up in a quick, nervous smile, and then it was gone. Without a word he took his post over and laid it by one of the holes they'd dug the day before. The younger boy had received the toned-down version of his brother's looks, and apparently a toned-down version of his personality, too.

"Hey," I said. "You're going to be setting those this morning?"

He nodded.

"What if it rains?"

Luke answered. "Won't hurt anything. Mostly taking advantage of the mild temperature. Can't do cement work like this in the winter where we come from."

"And where would that be?" I asked.

"Kansas. Wichita."

"What on earth brought you out to our little corner of the universe?"

"Dad transferred. Boeing."

"Ah."

I'd heard their mother was dead, and Mavis Gray said it had happened recently. No doubt Mr. Chase was ready for a fresh start. I was a little surprised the boys had come with him, as old as they were. It was nice to think they'd remained intact as a family.

Luke turned back to his post, a hint, no doubt, for me to let him get on with his work. I took it and went back inside to face my own to-do list.

Three hours later I'd mixed the salts, soda, citric acid, green tea, herbs and oils for four kinds of Saltea bags — rosemary, citrus, lavender, and spearmint — and made a bit of headway on filling orders from my website. Kyla and Cyan Waters would be arriving any moment to put in a couple of hours of work, and Erin was due home from school. I'd called Barr again and left another message, but he hadn't called me back yet. I was a little surprised. It wasn't like I made a habit of calling him when he was working.

But a barrage of other phone calls had interrupted my task-filled afternoon. Word was getting around about what had happened to Philip, and the HH volunteers were trying to decide whether or not to go ahead with the preserves exchange that evening. Finally, I tracked down Jude Carmichael, and he said that since he hadn't been able to reach all the participants, we'd go ahead with the exchange as planned. I had mixed feelings about that, but agreed.

Upstairs, I opened the front door, and Brodie charged out of the house, rushed to the side yard, and lifted his leg. Poor guy; I should have taken a break sooner. As I waited for him to finish, I kept seeing Philip's gray face and the desperate look in his eye as he tried to pull oxygen into his lungs. Being in the intensive care unit didn't bode well, but surely they'd bring him around. Wouldn't they? And then he'd be able to share the name of whoever had threatened him.

The little guy finished his business and trotted arthritically back to the front porch where I waited. I looked up and down the street, thinking about what Philip had said about Allen following me home. I pictured him as a dark, shadowy figure waiting in the dark parking lot of Heaven House, watching as I ran through the rain to my pickup. Following me through Cadyville to my street, my home, and watching me hurry inside to get out of the rain.

Wait a minute. That was silly. Following me wouldn't give him my name. It wouldn't give him our phone number. Philip was full of crap. Bless his heart, I amended.

I needed to think.

And that meant . . . chocolate.

Brodie followed me into the kitchen, his nails clicking rhythmically on the wood floor. But we seemed to be out of the chunks of dark chocolate we bought on a regular basis at Trader Joe's. I rooted around in the cupboard and came up with a box of hot cocoa mix. When life gives you lemons, make lemonade. When it gives you a box of hot cocoa mix, make it triple strong and use half water, half coffee.

It only took two sips of that mixture before my brain kicked in. Two more swallows for fortitude, and I ran back out through the drizzle to my Toyota. My unlocked Toyota. The only time I ever locked it was when there was something to steal in it, and that was, well, pretty much never. It didn't even have a decent stereo.

The glove box was open.

FIVE

Why do they call them glove boxes, still? Did they ever hold gloves? I mean, really? Because all mine ever held was my car registration and insurance card and a pile of napkins and straws dutifully collected from my rare forays to fast food restaurants.

It was all still there, just as I'd arranged it.

I straightened up and rested my hand on top of the open door. Okay, I was stumped. How had Allen figured out my name? Had he read my registration or not? A thought made my breath catch in the back of my throat: could he have known it all along? Before he ever called the Helpline?

A flutter of white snagged my attention. I turned my head. A piece of paper was tucked into the steering wheel. With a bad feeling, I grabbed it.

Allen had left me a note.

Great.

The penmanship was atrocious, and I had

a hard time making out what it said. But with a little squinting in the artificial twilight of the day I managed:

> "Dear Sophie Mae. It was nice to talk to you on the phone. I'll call so we can do it again. I'm looking forward to that. We can have lots of conversations. About life. And about Death. I have a lot to say about Death. I want to hear more about what you think about it, too."

My head jerked up, and I scanned up and down the street. He'd been in my truck in the short time since I'd been home. Was that blue car across the street new to the neighborhood? The cocoa curdled in my stomach. I cursed myself for not paying closer attention to my surroundings.

I shook my head. "Get it together, Sophie Mae." The thought crossed my mind as I muttered that someone could be watching my strange performance. I didn't really care. Maybe Allen would think I was crazy and leave me alone. And the neighbors wouldn't be seeing anything they hadn't seen a dozen times before. You work alone enough, and you get in the habit of talking to yourself even when you're not alone.

But for some reason I didn't feel afraid

anymore. What a little creep. I didn't like someone trying to scare me. It was beyond irritating, and not only about me. This spilled over into the lives of Meghan and Erin, too.

And it didn't look like this guy was going away any time soon.

I had managed to get things set up in my basement workroom for Kyla and Cyan to package the Saltea Bags when I heard a cupboard door bang in the kitchen. I clomped up the narrow steps and opened the door at the top.

"Hey. How was school?" I headed for the fruit bowl on the counter.

Erin sat at the big butcher block table, shoving a cookie into her face and reading . . . what? I looked over her shoulder while peeling a banana.

"Odoriferous? Paleethnology? *Quacksalver?* What the heck is that?"

"That," she said, "is a spelling word."

"Well, duh. I kind of figured that out. But what does it mean?"

"I don't know. I just know how to spell it."

"But what good is that?"

"Ask me that after they give it to me in the spelling bee next week." She exuded smugness.

"Well, sure. But what's it worth if you don't know what it means? Isn't that what words are for, after all? To communicate?"

"God. You're so . . . literal." The doorbell rang and she tossed back the last of her milk. "That's Jonathan. We're studying."

"Okay. Bring him in. I'd like to meet him."

She looked less than happy at this prospect, but dutifully brought in her visitor. He walked right up to me and stuck out his hand. "Hi. I'm Jonathan Bell."

He was a little shorter than Erin, which was saying something. Smooth brown hair, bright blue eyes. His expression was far more sardonic than any eleven-year-old has a right to. This kid was going to get his growth spurt any second and start breaking girls' hearts left and right.

"Hello, Jonathan. I'm Sophie Mae."

"Did you guys buy any Coke yet?"

I raised my eyebrows. "How about some orange juice?"

"Sorry, Jonathan." Erin sounded truly contrite that we didn't have any sugary soda to give this kid. Apparently, he'd already started in on the heart-breaking. I wasn't pleased to see him practice on Erin.

"That's okay," he said. "Juice's fine." He stood there while she took the pitcher out

58

and poured him a glass. He smiled when she handed it to him. She smiled back.

I watched all this through narrowed eyes. He knew I was watching, and turned that charming smile my direction. Little scamp. I stuck with the narrowed eyes but allowed the corners of my mouth to turn up.

"We're gonna study for the spelling bee," Erin said, grabbing Jonathan's arm and pulling him into the living room.

"Right," I called after them. "I'll be down in my workroom. Yell if you need anything."

They fell to whispering. Despite my protestations to Meghan about the innocence of eleven-year-olds, I found myself curiously loathe to leave them alone.

I went back downstairs as my teen helpers arrived. They began filling oversized tea bags with the premixed herb and salt mixture. Then the Saltea Bags would be heat-sealed with an iron. While they worked, I finished packing the internet retail orders. By the end of two hours they had four piles of bath tea bags on the long table that ran down the middle of my workroom, and I had several boxes lined up along the wall, ready for UPS to pick up the next day.

Yet somehow I had managed to find an excuse to run back upstairs every ten minutes or so.

Man. Those teen years might be just as hard on me as they would be on Meghan.

"Is Barr going tonight?" Meghan asked.

"He said he was."

"Are we picking him up on the way over?"

I finished writing out a label for a jar of watermelon pickles and considered the pile of heavy canning jars we'd moved out of the pantry and stacked on the kitchen table. "I hadn't thought of that. It'd sure be nice if he'd come here first and help us carry all these preserves into the car."

Meghan smiled. "Good idea. You should get on that."

I rolled my eyes at her and went into the living room, snagging the phone off the table in the hall on my way. Barr answered his cell phone on the fifth ring as I was getting ready to leave him yet another voice-mail.

"Did I catch you in the middle of something? I have a quick question," I said after we said hello. He sounded harried, and I decided my exciting morning at Heaven House could wait until we were face to face.

"I can talk for a sec."

"Meghan and I decided we'd welcome the aid of a muscle-y guy this evening. How would you like to come over before the preserves exchange and help us load up?"

"I'm not sure I can make it tonight, Sophie Mae."

I sighed. More work. Crap. I was developing a real dislike for Andrew Maher, the new Chief of Police, despite the fact that I'd barely spoken to the man.

"Listen. I'll do my best to be there. I will. But I'll have to meet you at eight. Sorry I can't come help you and Meghan before."

"Yes. Well, you do sound pretty busy."

"Sophie Mae . . ."

"I'll see you tonight. If you can manage to tear yourself away."

"Oh, now, c'mon —"

I hung up.

Meghan looked up when I walked back into the kitchen. "He coming early?"

I shook my head. "He'll meet us there. He says. Maybe."

She set down the label she was holding. "What's wrong?"

"Nothing."

"Bull puckey."

"He works all the time."

"You knew that when you got involved with him."

"I guess I thought he'd make more time to spend with me."

"Oh, for heaven's sake. You know he's

61

completely infatuated with you, don't you?"

I bit my lower lip. Infatuated? Infatuation was short-lived, by definition. We'd been seeing each other for a little over three months. If it was just infatuation, then the end might very well be near. Had I mistaken our entire relationship? I felt a strange combination of panic and embarrassment at the thought.

"Oh, it's fine," I said, forcing myself to shrug. "But we're on our own with all those jars."

"Maybe I could call someone else to come help," she said, still watching me. "A guy I know."

I smiled. It felt like I was baring my teeth at her. "We've always managed before on our own. Did you bring out all the pickled asparagus?"

"What? Oh, no, I started labeling the applesauce first."

"I'll get them." I hurried into the pantry and started taking jars off the shelf.

And tried not to think about whether this was the beginning of the end of my new relationship.

"Can we stop by Beans R Us on the way?" I asked.

"Why didn't you grab a cup of coffee at

home?" Meghan sounded as tired and cranky as I did.

"Didn't have time to make any before we had to leave."

What a day. I'd worked in the morning, gone to see Philip in hopes of heading off a stalker, witnessed his collapse, covered the phones until Ruth could get there, worked my butt off when I got home, watched and worried about Erin and Jonathan, and then spent two hours getting our contributions ready for the preserves exchange. Meghan threw together a quick chicken quesadilla while I hauled the boxes out to the trunk of her old Volvo, and we rushed through dinner.

The food had helped, but I needed caffeine if I planned on getting through this evening without falling asleep on my feet.

"There'll be coffee there," Meghan said, and turned the opposite direction from Beans R Us.

Which was true; Heaven House always had a big pot of coffee going. Still, I felt a flash of irritation. Over-brewed and perpetually stale, the coffee at HH was egregious. I had to dress it up with cream *and* sugar, and I wouldn't normally mar any decent cup of coffee that way.

Meghan knew this. She just didn't want

to make the detour. And since she was driving, she got to make that call.

Definitely irritating.

Then she sighed, low so Erin couldn't hear her in the back seat. She'd had a long day, too. My irritation instantly morphed into guilt.

"How many people do you think will show up?" I asked.

She shook her head. "Hard to tell. When we all met to set it up everyone was excited. But now, with Philip in the hospital, some people might not come. I know I'd rather have put if off altogether."

"Couldn't. Not everyone knows what happened."

Her brief glance held exasperation. "Exactly."

Okay. So I'd stated the obvious. Sue me.

Six

Quiet murmurs and the smell of wet paint greeted us as we walked into Heaven House laden with boxes of asparagus and watermelon pickles. Erin staggered under the weight of hers, and once we were inside she immediately dropped it to the floor. The jars jostled together with a loud crystalline rattle. I put my box down on the first of three long tables arranged in the middle of the room and went back to make sure nothing had broken. Erin had made a beeline for the game room, where the sole attraction was a pinball machine. Erin had never seen one before her mom began spending time at HH, a fact that had initially surprised me.

Once Erin went back to pour a handful of quarters into Nardella's Treasures, I began unpacking our goodies. After tossing the third empty carton under the table and straightening the low-hanging cloth to hide it, I stood up and looked around for Meghan.

Instead, I saw Maryjake, which surprised me more than a little. I had been sure she'd pass on the evening's festivities. Huge dark circles underscored her pale eyes, and her hangdog demeanor was completely out of character. Her husband, James Dreggle, stood nearby but not too close, watching her every move as she arranged a precise pyramid of pint jars filled with bright yellow corn and attractive green beans. His thick, dark beard cloaked his expression. Maryjake finished stacking her veggies, then turned to the room and snapped her fingers, one of her standard attention getting maneuvers, but even that came across as desultory.

"Everyone, we're going to start the exchange soon, so please finish up your displays in the next few minutes."

Displays? I eyed the hodgepodge of jars I'd unloaded on the table and looked around again for my housemate.

Ruth Black, full of energy after her afternoon at Heaven House, assisted her Uncle Thaddeus with the dark jars of blueberry conserve I'd been hoping for. They were gorgeous next to the deep purple-maroon beets and brilliant orange pickled carrots.

Thaddeus Black, pushing ninety with good-natured verve, leaned on his gnarled cane and directed her efforts. Next to them stood tall, lean Bette, a potter and friend who lived down the block from us. She had a deep voice, didn't seem to own any clothing that had escaped the clay spatter of her trade, and made a mean batch of bread and butter pickles. Our neighbor across the alley, Mavis Gray, had brought brownie, cookie and biscuit mixes, the dry ingredients layered like geological strata visible through the clear jars; homemade convenience food, at your fingertips.

Jude shuffled from table to table and then seemed to settle in next to his own arrangement of red, orange, amber and green jellies lit from behind by a string of tiny white Christmas lights. They were quite beautiful, and I found myself smiling. His eyes flicked up to meet mine for a split second, and he smiled briefly in response before returning to an examination of the floor someplace in front of his shoes.

He was a rather good-looking guy, with thick blonde hair, green eyes and a round face. His light tan accented noticeably nice skin. Still, he always came across as painfully shy and awkward. He was supposed to be in charge of the preserves exchange, but it looked like Maryjake had steamrolled right over him. I resolved to spend some time coaxing him out of his shell this evening.

I was surprised to see Luke Chase walk out of one of the empty rooms at the rear of the building. Philip had made some noises about making it into a small daycare area, but like the meeting room it had no furniture and no real purpose as of yet. Evidently, from Luke's telltale paint-spattered T-shirt, it now had gray-blue paint on the walls. That was a start — though the start of what, I had no idea.

Luke walked over and spoke to Maryjake, who responded in a distracted manner. He seemed to repeat something, and this time she turned on him and pointed to the door. Seemed an odd thank you for painting well into the evening like that, especially as I knew he and Seth had been working on our chicken coop most of the day before coming over here. Of course, Maryjake was obviously still upset about what had happened that afternoon with Philip, so I needed to cut her a break. I considered going over and rescuing Luke from her mood, but then Seth came out, lugging a big plastic bucket of painting equipment in one hand and a can of paint in the other. He joined his brother, and together they pushed out of the swinging glass door to the sidewalk out front.

Ah — there was Meghan. Standing by the back door with a guy I'd never seen before. I waved in her direction, but she didn't notice. All her attention was focused on the man next to her. He was about seven inches taller than her five-foot frame, with longish black hair and an olive complexion. He looked older than Meghan, perhaps in his early forties.

I remembered her hesitant question about whether I'd seen someone this morning. And her offhand comment when she'd learned Barr couldn't — or wouldn't — help with loading up the jars of preserves. Something about calling someone else to come help. Was this the guy she'd had in mind?

Erin had forsaken Nardella and her Treasures for the time being and wandered around looking bored. I caught her eye and waved her over.

"Who's that? The guy your mom's talking to?"

"That's Kelly. They're going to the movies on Friday."

"They are?"

"I heard them talking. They've been getting around to it for a while."

I examined the child's pixie face, full of unspoken wry commentary on her mother's love life. But I believed her. How could I not have known about Meghan's burgeoning interest in this guy? I felt totally out of the loop.

But instead of asking Erin that question, I asked, "You okay with that?"

She shrugged. "Sure."

"Yeah." I nodded. "Why not?" Then why did I feel so uncomfortable about this stranger chatting up my best friend?

I thought of Meghan's ex-husband, Richard. He'd been good looking, too, but in a pretty-boy kind of way. This guy looked rugged and maybe a little worn and . . . solid. Richard was far out of the picture by now, living in California and more or less banished from Meghan and Erin's life. But he'd always been a problem, cheating on her and burdening their lives with a serious gambling problem. It wasn't until they'd split and she'd nearly lost the house we lived in now that I'd moved in with her and Erin. Newly widowed at the time, I'd needed their support as much as they needed mine.

But maybe this new guy she was interested in — finally interested in — would be good for her . . . ? There was no reason on earth I shouldn't like him.

Was there?

I shook myself. "Do me a favor. Try to arrange these jars a little better. Make them look nice. We're supposed to have some kind of display."

"Um. Okay." Erin started shoving jars around.

I hurried back out to the car for the carton of wine jelly still remaining in the trunk, keeping an eye on the fringes of the parking lot for shady-looking characters lurking behind bushes.

Instead, I got a brown-eyed handsome man parking next to the Volvo. Barr Ambrose got out, strode to my side, and pulled me to him. Long-legged, streaks of gray winding through his wavy chestnut hair, he wore jeans, a tan corduroy sports coat, and one of his signature string ties — this one a pewter steer's skull — with a white shirt. He smelled like wood shavings and leather.

"Mmmph," I said into his shoulder, which meant, "Damn, I love the way you wrap around me like we've fit together for years."

"What?"

"I'm glad you came," I said.

He smiled. "You hung up on me."

"Well . . ."

"All snitty-like."

I examined the toe of his cowboy boot. "Sorry."

He cocked his head. "I know I don't have a lot of time to spend with you. It won't be forever, though. I promise."

I licked my lips. "I know. There's no excuse for hanging up on you. All I can say is that it's been a pretty stressful day."

"Boy, I hear you." He exhaled loudly. "Now give me that." Hefting the heavy box, he preceded me back into Heaven House.

Erin had tidied things up quite a bit, and the three of us arranged wine jelly in record time. Meghan still stood with Kelly, laughing at whatever he was saying. Oh, brother: it was the complimentary laugh, the one that told a man how brilliant and funny he was. She had it bad.

"Okay, everyone. I think we're ready." Maryjake's voice was rough. Usually it filled the room with ease, but tonight I strained to hear her.

Barr stepped forward and cleared his throat. I frowned, unsure of what he was doing.

"Before we begin I need to make an announcement," he said. "This morning Philip Heaven became very ill and was rushed to the hospital."

No one looked surprised. Anyone who

hadn't known before coming to the exchange had become privy to this information by now.

"He went immediately into the ICU, but, I'm very sorry to say, they weren't able to save him."

What?

Barr continued. "Philip Heaven died at four p.m. today. I know this must be very distressing news to those of you who didn't know."

Jude's eyes flicked up again, and I knew he'd already been informed. For a moment I felt angry. He should have told us. Then I felt bad; Philip had been his cousin, after all.

Other faces were blank. Ruth Black's hand went to her mouth. Thaddeus looked stoic. Meghan's eye's filled with tears. Kelly put his arm around her and drew her close, his own expression speculative.

And then I wondered why the heck Barr hadn't told me Philip had died. What was I? Chopped liver? He must have known when I talked to him on the phone earlier. When he stepped back to my side I moved away from him. He shot me a look, but I was too upset to try to interpret it.

From the corner of my eye I saw Mary-jake teeter forward, and as I turned my head, she crumpled in front of Ruth Black's display. She hit the edge of the table with her shoulder as she went down, and one of the pint jars of beets teetered and fell onto the painted concrete floor, impacting with a loud crack! The glass broke and the pressurized contents burst out, painting the wall and floor — and my brand new white sneakers — with chunks and splatters of deep red goo that would stain forever.

The sound of the breaking glass grabbed the attention of everyone who'd missed Maryjake actually falling, and soon she was surrounded by bewildered participants of the Cadyville preserves exchange and whomever they'd dragged with them to the event. The beet juice surrounding her looked like blood.

"Maryjake? Maryjake!" James crouched beside her, shaking her shoulder. He leaned forward and pressed his ear against her considerable chest. It reminded me of what I had done to Philip only hours earlier. Surely she wasn't —

She sucked in a sudden, whooping breath, and her eyes popped open. When she saw her husband's face so close to hers, she recoiled and pushed him away. Hard.

"Leave me alone."

He fell back on his posterior, narrowly

missing a piece of broken glass on the floor. A flush infused his cheeks. Not the kind of response you expect from a loved one in distress whom you're trying to help.

Apparently emergencies brought some things to a head. Interesting.

Maryjake started wailing and shaking. Meghan stepped in and grabbed her.

"Stop it." Meghan's gaze rose to meet mine as I backed out of the crowd. She nodded, understanding what I was doing. "Not too cold." Her words cut through the babble of voices and Maryjake's high-volume hysteria.

I turned and ran to the bathroom, filling a couple of tiny Dixie cups with water. Then back to the gawker knot surrounding Maryjake. Her lips had taken on a blue tinge, and she was gasping for breath. Hyperventilating, big time. I held out both of the little cups of water to Meghan, who took them and promptly threw them in Maryjake's face.

Maryjake stopped gasping and stared at Meghan. We all did.

I smiled. So much for breathing into a paper bag.

We milled around, the awkward silence occasionally punctuated by a whispered comment. James had taken Maryjake home despite her weak protests. Erin stood with Meghan's arm lightly draped across her shoulder. Her gray eyes moved from face to face, watching the reactions of everyone in the group. Barr was in the restroom. Jude stood next to his table of jellies looking like he wanted to cry. Mrs. Gray and Bette silently cleaned up the beets and shards of glass.

No one seemed to want to take charge.

Standing with all those people, I felt very alone. Was there something more I should have done to help Philip earlier that afternoon? I had to wonder, but I genuinely couldn't think what it could be. I regretted giving him a hard time, even though he was so obviously ill. I regretted my complaining about his inefficiency and boorishness. So he wasn't a genius. So he lacked class. He'd just been a guy, a regular guy, who wanted to do some good and had a chance to try. Now he wasn't going to have a chance to try anything ever again.

A heavy curtain of depression settled over me. I wanted to go home and crawl in bed for several hundred years.

Instead, I spoke to the room. "I hate to say this." My voice sounded too loud in my skull. "But we should probably finish the exchange."

Meghan nodded. "Let's just get it over with." Her new beau stepped to her side — now where had he been? — and I saw her shoulders automatically shift toward him.

Murmurs throughout the room signaled general agreement, and people began moving to the tables, almost reluctantly picking up foodstuffs to take home. Missing was any banter among the volunteers. I was staring at a jar of sauerkraut with nary a thought of a Reuben sandwich in my head when Jude came to stand silently beside me.

"You knew," I said in a low voice.

"Yes. I'm sorry."

"You should have told us."

"I didn't want to ruin the exchange. It was supposed to be for morale among the volunteers."

I turned and stared at him, amazed. He looked away and blinked rapidly. Could it be that he hadn't known how to tell us? That was it, I realized. How very difficult to be Jude Carmichael on a daily basis.

Barr came out of the restroom and walked to my side.

"Are you okay?" I asked, concern over his appearance overriding my thoughts about Jude.

"I'm fine. Just a little off, I guess."

I eyed him, wondering what he wasn't telling me. He'd been in there a long time, I realized, from just after James had taken Maryjake outside until seconds before. His eyes looked red, and his skin pasty.

Kind of like Philip Heaven had looked that afternoon.

SEVEN

Neither Meghan nor I had considered the fact that we'd have to haul as many jars of preserves into the house as we'd loaded the car up with earlier. After the food exchange, Barr said he had to go back and finish up a few things at the cop shop, and we helped Ruth and Thaddeus take their gleanings out to their car. We made them promise they'd have a neighbor help them bring the heavy boxes inside the next morning, and they left with Ruth behind the wheel of their old Buick. Once we arrived home, Meghan tucked Erin into bed while I dragged in our own loot and began unpacking the cornucopia of goodies onto the kitchen table.

An hour later, with the pantry filled to the brim, I gave in and called Barr's cell phone. I couldn't stand the idea of waiting by the phone for his nightly phone call, all the while afraid that this was the night he wouldn't call. I'd realized I didn't know exactly where we stood or whether we were both looking for the same things from the relationship. It seemed silly in retrospect, but we'd never actually talked about our expectations.

He didn't answer. I looked at my watch. After ten. I didn't leave a message.

Five minutes later the phone rang, though, and I rushed to answer it. Meghan and I narrowly missed colliding in the hallway. Apparently I wasn't the only one expecting a phone call.

The caller ID said it was Barr. "I won't be long," I said, and snatched the phone off the charger. "Hello?"

It wasn't Barr. It was Sergeant Zahn, his direct supervisor at work, and he cut right to the chase. "Is this Ms. Reynolds? Detective Ambrose wanted me to tell you he's in the hospital."

"What happened? Is he okay?" My mind went immediately to the place I tried to keep under wraps, the scary ohmygod place that had to do with the fact that my boyfriend carried a gun to work and tangled with the dregs of society on a regular basis. In that place lived things like bullet wounds and knife fights and other disasters accompanied by the kind of special effects only found in bad action flicks. I wasn't a big worrier, and Cadyville wasn't Los Angeles, but the words "Ambrose" and "hospital" in the same sentence sent me right there.

"They're running some tests now. He asked me to call you. Thought you'd want to know he's here." His voice was gruff, but I tried to ignore that. It was no secret that the good Sergeant wasn't all that fond of yours truly.

"Can you tell me what happened?"

"He was at the station. His stomach was upset, and then he got light-headed and started having trouble breathing. Asked me to bring him into the emergency room."

Barr felt bad enough that he asked *Zahn* to take him to the emergency room? This was not good. I heard several voices in the background, and one of them was Barr's. He didn't sound happy, not at all.

Okay. No bullets. And dizziness trumped a knife wound every single time. But the word "hospital" still scared the bejesus out of me. Zahn was saying something, but all I could hear was a very loud, frightened voice in my mind clamoring to know that Barr was okay.

But Zahn couldn't enlighten me any further and made short work of getting off the phone. I dropped all notion of going to bed, laced up my boots with shaking hands, and grabbed my coat off the hall tree, calling out, "Meghan! Where are you? I have to go."

She appeared at the top of the stairs. "What's going on?"

"It's Barr. He's in the hospital."

"Hospital! What happened??"

"It's nothing to do with work. He's sick or something. I don't know. I have to get over there."

"Of course you do. I'd go with, but —" She gestured toward Erin's room.

"No, no, that's fine."

"I'll keep the phone with me. Call me when you know more. No matter what time."

"You sure?"

Her nod was emphatic. "Absolutely. Even if he just has a bad splinter. I want to know."

Her words brought a small smile to my face, because I knew her concern was as much for me as it was for Barr.

I ran out through a heavy downpour to my pickup. My hands had stopped shaking, and I jammed the key hard into the ignition and started the engine with a roar. Rain slashed down, pounding against the metal skin of the cab as I urged the Toyota through the dark, empty streets of Cadyville to the highway on-ramp. Our little town only had an emergency clinic. Fifteen minutes later I was in Everett, where Sergeant Zahn had taken Barr.

Philip had gone to the same hospital. I thought of his gasping breaths, how he clawed at the desk as if the slick surface might somehow yield oxygen to his starved lungs. Barr's symptoms mirrored a little too closely those I had witnessed that morning before Philip collapsed.

And then he'd *died.* What on earth was going on?

I couldn't seem to concentrate; I got lost downtown, not sure which street the hospital was on, and once I found it, I couldn't find the entrance to the parking garage.

"It's okay, he's going to be fine, just relax, it's okay, it's okay, it's okay," I whispered under my breath, cursing first at the red light and then at the blue-haired old lady who wouldn't move her huge lumbering PLYMOUTH out of my way. Deep breath. Okay, better. Found the entrance.

Parked.

And ran toward the emergency room.

The sliding door hissed open, too slowly, and I pushed through with my shoulder. The button on my jacket hooked on something, I don't know what, and my momentum spun me around in an awkward circle. I came to rest beside the reception desk, and the woman sitting behind it put her hand out to steady me.

"You okay, honey?"

"Fine. Good. Thanks. Barr Ambrose. Just brought in."

She nodded. Apparently staccato verbiage was par for the course in these situations. Which made sense. I couldn't be the only one who came in all a-dither looking for someone they loved.

Wait a minute. Love?

Did I just think that?

Uh oh.

Okay, maybe I'd thought around the idea a little. But not, you know, "I Love Barr."

Too soon. Too big. Too scary. Too . . .

"He's been admitted," the woman said, peering at her computer monitor. "Room 513."

"Can I go up and see him?"

"The elevators are right over there."

"Thanks." I turned and marched to the elevator. Forced myself to push the button. I hated hospitals. I'd spent too many long hours in them, helpless as they tried to save my husband from the cancer gnawing through his body. When the ding sounded and the doors slid open, I strode onto the

84

elevator like I was going into battle.

Not that I was, of course. Right? Dizziness, nausea. But still conscious. Not like Philip. Not like Mike. Surely something minor. I mean this was *Barr*. Mr. Tough Guy. Who happened to drink Earl Grey tea, but still. Upright Town Detective. All Around Good Guy. Mr. Call-Me-Every-Night-Just-To-Hear-My-Voice.

And he was sick. Seconds ago I'd been so scared and worried that I'd used the word "love," for the first time, if only to myself.

Inside the elevator, I pivoted. The woman behind the desk watched me with curiosity as the doors slid shut, cutting off her view and enclosing me in the tiny box. My control wavered then. The fear I'd so neatly dispatched returned with a roar. I didn't even know what else I felt, but I sure felt a lot of whatever it was. Especially around my solar plexus. And my throat. And the muscles along my jaw.

The elevator stopped, and I got off. Signs directed me to Barr's room. As I walked by the nurses' station the two RNs gave me a cursory glance, but must have decided I knew what I was doing.

Boy, I wished I did.

Room 513. The door was partly open.

What I saw inside made me want to cry.

There were two beds in the room. The one by the window was empty. In the bed by the door, the man I'd come to think of as strength itself lay stretched out, filling the bed from top to bottom with his long lanky frame. But that thing, that quiet strong presence, was absent. Even in sleep he had it, but lying there with his eyes closed, his long slender fingers limp on the hospital sheet, he looked abandoned and weak.

I'd watched the vitality fade like a receding light from my husband at the end, sat with him night and day in the hospice for those last two weeks, every second seeing him withdraw further and further from life. From me. Leaving me.

Stop it, Sophie Mae. Just stop it. That was then. That was Mike. This is Barr. And he's going to be fine.

I took a deep, whooping breath, and curled the edges of my lips into a smile. Barr opened his eyes.

Walking over, I put my hand on his cheek, and kissed him on the forehead. I could hear the subtle whoosh of the machines all around him, noted the tubes snaking into his nose, the IV dripping clear liquid into his arm. He looked up at me with a weak, but sardonic, grin.

"What?" I said.

He shook his head a fraction. "I'm glad you're here."

"Me, too. What happened?"

"Don't know."

"What do the doctors say?"

"Don't know."

"You don't know what they say?"

"No. They don't know what's wrong with me."

My anxiety ratcheted up another degree. I pulled a chair up to the edge of the bed and took hold of Barr's hand. "Sergeant Zahn said you were dizzy?"

He closed his eyes for a moment and nodded. "Wasn't feeling too hot at Heaven House tonight. Got worse."

A nurse walked in. "We should get some of the tests back within the hour," she said, but I put my finger to my lips and nodded toward Barr, whose eyes were still shut. As I stroked his arm some of the strain flowed out of his face and he slept.

"Visiting hours are long over," the nurse said in a low voice.

"I'm his girlfriend," I whispered. "I'd like to stay for a while."

"It really is best for him if you leave and come back in the morning."

Philip had been ill in the morning and dead in the afternoon.

"But —" I raised my voice, and Barr stirred in bed.

"Please."

Frowning, I stood up. "How can you not know what's wrong with him?" I whispered.

She hesitated, then gestured for me to follow her out to the hallway. At the nurses' station she turned, her eyes moving over my face as if she were trying to read something there. Finally she spoke.

"Most of the tests they're running right now are to exclude other diagnoses. If those come up negative, we think your man in there had contact with botulism toxin."

Botulism?

I knitted my fingers together. "That's serious, right? It could kill him."

"It can be very, very serious. But, if that's what it is, he seems to have had relatively minor exposure, and the antitoxin is already on its way from the CDC."

Stunned, I stammered out, "There was another man brought in this morning." I looked at my watch. "Yesterday morning, I guess. And then he died in the afternoon. Philip Heaven. He had many of the same symptoms. Was that botulism, too?"

Her eyebrows arched. "I don't know. But I'll certainly look into it. What was his name again?"

I repeated it, and she wrote it down. Then she smiled at me. "If you're worried Mr. Ambrose is going to die overnight, you can stop. If it's botulism poisoning, he'll make a full recovery eventually."

"And if it's not?"

She looked earnestly into my eyes. "Then you'll deal with that when we know more. But for tonight he needs his rest, and it looks like you do, too. If you stay, I'll have to insist you remain in the waiting room anyway. Go home. He won't even know you're gone."

No woman wants to hear those last words, but she was probably right. What else could I do but leave?

I wasn't proud of the tiny flicker of relief I felt as I exited the hospital into the fresh night air.

EIGHT

After a few false turns, I found my way out of the hospital parking garage and back to the highway to Cadyville. I suddenly understood what the phrase "sick at heart" felt like in real time.

It was late, but when I got home I found Meghan dozing on the couch, a copy of MFK Fisher's *How to Cook a Wolf* open on her lap.

I'd completely forgotten to call her.

A small fire crackled in the fireplace, and the room smelled of cedar and cloves. Light jazz played at low volume on the stereo. It was a wonderful atmosphere to walk into, welcoming and homey.

I struggled not to burst into tears.

Meghan started awake. "Oh! I didn't hear you come in." Alarm flooded her features as her eyes met mine. "Is Barr okay?"

I shucked out of my jacket. "I think so."

She seemed to relax a little. "What happened?"

I opened my mouth, but nothing came out.

"Honey, what's wrong?" She got up and came over to me, put her arms around my shoulders, and gave me a patented Meghan Bly hug.

That was all it took. I turned into a gooey, messy excuse for a woman, a puddle of angst and insecurity and fear. She led me back to the couch and made me sit. She brought me tea, strong and hot and heavily sugared. I spluttered and leaked tears and told her about Barr and the botulism and how Philip might have died from it and how Barr being in the hospital made me think about Mike. She took my half-drunk cup of tea away and brought me a glass of single malt Scotch.

Bless her heart.

I downed the Talisker. And she gave me some more.

And then she put me to bed.

Exhausted and a little tipsy, I drifted off to sleep surprisingly quickly. And I slept like a baby until nearly three a.m.

That's when I awoke and lay in bed, thinking. Someone had threatened Philip Heaven. He knew who it was. He hadn't taken them seriously at first, but when he'd whispered in my ear while we waited for the paramedics, he'd believed that was why he fell so terribly ill. And then he'd died.

Barr's symptom's matched his very closely.

Had someone intentionally given Philip botulism toxin? After an hour I managed to work myself into a real tizzy, wondering whether Barr had become worse during the night.

At six-thirty Erin found me sitting at the kitchen table with a big mug of coffee, on the phone quizzing the nurse I finally managed to track down on the fifth floor of the hospital. He wasn't any better, but he wasn't any worse, either. He was asleep. She also told me that the test for the presence of botulism toxin had come back positive and that Barr had already received the antitoxin. She didn't have any information about Philip, but she had passed on my suspicions to her superiors, and they had alerted the medical examiner.

I thanked her and hung up, wondering in a macabre way whether performing an autopsy on someone who had died from botulism would be dangerous. I suspected it might be, but I realized that, other than a vague notion that botulism could be found in poorly home-canned food, I knew very little about it. As I stared at the wood grain on a kitchen cabinet, I didn't even notice Erin had put together her own breakfast until she sat down across from me. Cereal and milk. And a bowl of peaches.

Home canned peaches.

"Don't eat those!"

She stopped with the liquid dripping from the spoon into her cereal bowl. Her mouth was half open and her eyes wide.

"What's wrong?" Meghan came in, and though her words were innocuous, I sensed she meant, "What's wrong *now?*"

I winced. "Botulism. It's confirmed. That's why Barr's sick. But somebody over there was on the ball, and he's going to be all right."

Meghan eyed the bowl of peaches.

"Am I gonna die?" Erin asked.

"Of course not," her mother said. "We've been eating out of that jar for a couple of days. They're fine." To prove her point she grabbed the spoon out of her daughter's hand and took a big bite of peach. "They're fine," she repeated after swallowing, and gave me a significant look.

I forced a smile on my face. "Sorry. Knee-jerk reaction."

"You want some?"

"Um, sure. But not right this instant. Maybe later." I had no doubt Meghan was right about the fruit, but I couldn't bring myself to eat any of it. "I'm going downstairs to look up botulism on the computer. Maybe I can get some idea of where it came from."

"Okay. But don't scare yourself. Bug, are you going to study for the bee this morning before school?"

Erin nodded and began shoving soggy cornflakes in her mouth at a record pace. She swallowed and stood up. "Can we leave at six-forty-five?"

Meghan smiled. "Sure. I'll be ready when you are."

The phone rang, and Meghan's eyes grew round. Phone calls before seven a.m. generally didn't bode well. She went to answer, and I sat with my eyes closed and my fingers pressed against my lips, afraid to move and selfishly praying the call had nothing to do with Barr.

But Meghan returned almost immediately. "It was a hang up." Her forehead creased. "Again."

"Again?"

"There were two of them last night when you were at the hospital. Reads 'private call' on the caller ID."

Crap. "I bet it's Allen, or whatever his name is."

"Probably. Next time it rings, you get it. Try to get him to stop, okay?"

Erin returned, laden with full backpack and clad in full winter weather garb. "C'mon, Mom." Her voice held no doubt as to what she thought of a mother who promised they could leave at six-forty-five and then couldn't get it together in time.

Meghan hustled into the hallway, scooping up a pair of boots on the way to the bench by the door. "Grab your lunch out of the fridge and we'll go," she called as she speed-laced her footwear.

Erin rolled her eyes at me, grabbed her lunch, said goodbye, and they were out the door.

Try to get Allen to stop? Sheesh. What a great idea, Megs. I took my coffee and went down to my workroom.

My desktop computer sat in the corner of my storeroom. Since I do a lot of my Winding Road business via the Internet, I spend a lot of time down there. There was one small window that didn't open but allowed in some natural light, and I loved the smell of the soaps curing on the shelves. It also made it easy to ascertain the availability of the different toiletries in my repertoire, so I wasn't popping up to check every time I

95

had to create a packing list or order supplies.

The morning was still pitch black outside. I switched on the little desk lamp and booted up the computer. Once it was online, I plugged the words "botulism symptoms causes" into the search engine and began to read.

Pretty nasty stuff. Slurred speech, nausea and vomiting, disturbed vision, and possible death due to paralysis, especially that of the respiratory system.

I thought of Philip Heaven, struggling for breath, his body refusing to cooperate. He'd basically suffocated to death. The thought made the coffee sour in my stomach. As a mild claustrophobe, I thought that would be a particularly awful way to go.

The most common way to get botulism was via home-canned food. It was fairly rare anymore and usually found in low-acid foods like beans or corn — things that anyone who does much home canning knows you have to put through a pressure canner.

I thought back to the offerings at the preserves exchange. Bette had brought some salmon from her annual trip to Alaska. Ruth had provided those beets, so beautiful in their jars or on the plate but not so attractive splattered all over the Heaven House floor, Maryjake Dreggle — and my shoes. Maryjake had brought jars of lovely golden corn which I happened to know came from a little roadside stand south of town and was the best I'd ever eaten, as well as green beans from her own garden. Had there been anything else that would need a pressure canner? I could only think of the pickles and jellies, fruits and chutneys, all of which were at relatively low risk.

Wait a minute. Philip had died before the preserves exchange. Maybe none of those items were even suspect. Maybe he'd eaten a can of grocery store soup from a damaged can. I'd always thought my grandmother was paranoid when she'd throw out any can that was the least bit dented. Now I had to admit she probably knew more about the possible dangers than I'd ever considered.

No one had eaten anything at the exchange that I knew of, including Barr. But thinking back, he hadn't looked so great when he'd shown up.

Philip and Barr hardly knew each other. How had they both . . . wait a minute. Slow down, Sophie Mae. No one had said Philip had died from botulism poisoning. Not yet.

But his symptoms were right on. And it wasn't like anyone would be calling me up once they found out, either. I needed more information. Official information, through unofficial channels. This time Barr was out of the loop, but I had an idea. Checking my watch I saw it was already eight a.m., an hour before Miss Manners said it was acceptable to telephone people.

However, Miss Manners didn't know Tootie Hanover was such an early riser, and I did.

NINE

Caladia Acres was a nursing home on the north edge of Cadyville where Tootie Hanover had lived for several years. I'd met her the previous fall when her son Walter died. He had been our neighbor. A facility that was intimate in a small-town way, Caladia Acres emphasized casual comfort in an attempt to overcome the sterile medical atmosphere found in most nursing homes. When I walked in, the air was thick with the scents of yeast and spices. Yum. The residents had been served cinnamon rolls for breakfast.

Ann Dunning, the nurse at the reception desk, nodded a hello and told me I'd find Tootie holding court in the library. I waved at a couple of the residents I'd grown fond of from my frequent visits, and they lifted their hands in greeting. Passing behind the three women and two men who sat with their eyes glued to a dramatic, tear-filled scene from some daytime soap opera on the big screen at the end of the room, I slipped into the tiny room they called the library at Caladia Acres.

The space was only large enough to hold a small settee and two chairs. All four walls held shelves of books, including on each side of and above the door, and around the single window in the north wall. A various hodgepodge of nonfiction and fiction, from literary masterpieces to light romances, how-to, history and biography, with a fair amount of religious works thrown in by some fervent benefactor, the books didn't seem to have any particular order or arrangement. I knew from experience, though, if a particular volume needed to be found in the collection, Tootie Hanover could put her hand on it within seconds. When she wasn't in her room or the dining hall, she gravitated to this room, with its spare light and the scent of old ink on yellowing pages.

When Ann told me Tootie was holding court, I'd expected to find her with a few people, but only one other woman sat in the small room with her. In contrast to Tootie's tall elegance and patrician features, her companion was short and solidly built, clad in mustard-colored polyester top and bottom, and sported short, unnaturally black curls above an attractive round face. Tootie's signature gray braid coiled on her head like a crown, and she wore a forest-green silk sweater over black slacks. That woman could show more style in a day than most people could muster in a year.

"Sophie Mae, come in. Have you met Betsy Maher?"

I closed the door behind me, glad it was solid wood and shut out most of the volume from the television down the hall.

I smiled at the woman sitting opposite Tootie in the leather-backed rocking chair. "I don't believe so. It's nice to meet you, Mrs. Maher."

"Please, call me Betsy."

"I'll be happy to. And I'm Sophie Mae. Reynolds," I added, since Tootie hadn't mentioned my last name. Which, come to think of it, was a little odd, since Tootie was a stickler for good manners.

Tootie's eyebrow raised just a fraction. "Betsy," she said, "is Andy Maher's mother."

It was the first time I'd ever heard Cadyville's Police Chief, Andrew Maher, called "Andy." I grinned, delighted at Tootie's resourcefulness. "Really. You must get to hear some fine tales from your son."

Betsy Maher's brown eyes twinkled. "He

101

does manage to provide me with a certain amount of entertainment. Sometimes it's hard to get him to tell me the really juicy stuff, though. If he had his way, I'd only get to hear about kittens being rescued from trees and commendations for bravery." She winked. "Luckily, he doesn't usually get his way, and I also get to hear about the woman who whacked her husband over the head with his own bowling ball."

This time I was the one raising my eyebrows. Betsy Maher was a pistol all right.

Tootie settled back in her chair and took a sip from the steaming cup of tea that had been sitting at her elbow. "In fact, Andy is going to be coming to visit this morning. He should be here any minute now."

"Is that so?" I asked. And we exchanged another look.

"Maybe you should tell me what it is you'd like to find out, before he gets here," Betsy said.

I blinked. "Um . . ."

"Oh, now, come on, dear. I know that's why you're here. And I'm willing to play my part, as long as I get to find out the good stuff, too."

Tootie laughed, and after a couple of seconds, so did I.

"Well," I said. "There was a death yester-

102

day. Philip Heaven. Did you know him?"

Betsy rolled her eyes. "I never had the pleasure personally, but I certainly did know *of* him — chock full of promises and not a leg to stand on when it came to following up on any of them. Put a few people around here in pretty bad straits as a result."

That reiterated what I'd heard from other quarters, but I felt kind of bad dissing poor Philip now that he was dead. Couldn't quite come to his defense, either. I satisfied myself by saying, "Yes, well, he had a good heart; it's just that some of his ideas were too big to implement as he imagined."

Tootie snorted. Betsy shook her head. I wondered if the taboo against talking ill of the dead became easier to break as more and more of the people you knew died. I got the feeling just being dead wasn't enough to get you off the hook with these two.

I continued. "Well, he got sick all of a sudden, and it's possible he was exposed to botulism. Someone else I know, and, um, care about is also ill, and it's because of botulism, although whatever amount he happened into was obviously a smaller dose than what I suspect killed Philip Heaven. Mrs. Maher — Betsy — I want to know what the heck is going on. Do the authorities know what happened to Philip? Was it botulism? If so, how was it introduced into his system? Did they find canned food that had gone bad in his apartment? And most importantly, I suppose, at least at this point: is there danger of someone else getting sick — or worse?"

Betsy pushed her palm against her chest, just above her abundant bosom. "My goodness! That's horrible. I knew the poor man had died, but had no idea someone else had fallen ill. Is it anyone I know?"

Her tone and posture reflected sympathy, but the glint in her eye betrayed her. Betsy Maher was a bit of a ghoul. I glanced up at Tootie, and her look conveyed wry agreement. It became instantly obvious that Betsy expected a bit of tit for tat in the information game.

"His name is Barr Ambrose," I said. "He works for your son — he's the detective for the Cadyville Police Department, and at this point not only is he in the hospital recovering from a comparatively mild case of botulism poisoning, but now the department is functioning without an investigator."

Betsy shook her head, another expression of sympathy, but the glint was still there. "Don't you worry, honey. We'll get to the bottom of it just as soon as Andy gets here."

"That would be great," I said, with a tentative smile.

While we waited for Betsy's son to show up for his weekly visit, unaware of the maternal snare that had been laid for him, she and Tootie chatted about the new activities director at Caladia Acres. She was introducing some unusual and interesting elements: art therapy, a series of games like indoor croquet that promoted a certain amount of physical activity and an atmosphere of mild competition.

Pretty soon Betsy steered the discussion to the personal lives of some of the people they lived with, and I tuned her out. I stood up and began perusing the titles arranged along the shelves. I had just moved to the opposite wall when I heard a male voice.

"Mother! How are you this fine morning!"

I turned to see Chief Maher. Before he'd taken over the Cadyville Police Department last year there had been rumors of dissatisfaction among the troops, but now everything seemed to be running smoothly. Or smoothly enough with only one detective in the budget. Whenever I'd been at the cop shop to see Barr, the Chief had been hunkered down behind an enormous steel desk in one of the few private offices in the

105

tiny building. Now I could see what a large man he was — at least six foot six inches tall and what you might call, uh, girthy. Despite his bulk, there seemed to be little fat on the man, and he moved with an easy grace that gave the impression of controlled power.

I liked what I saw, but his enthusiasm at seeing his mother seemed a tad exaggerated. His expression betrayed a certain amount of strain as he smiled at Betsy. He nodded at Tootie, who smiled and greeted him with a murmur, and then he turned to me.

"Hello . . . wait a minute. Aren't you Ambrose's . . . ?"

I nodded. "You've probably seen me at the police station a few times. I'm Sophie Mae Reynolds."

He blinked. For some reason the strain on his face became a little more pronounced. With what seemed like great care, he turned back to his mother, who so far hadn't uttered a word.

"How are you?" he asked again, with somewhat less enthusiasm.

"I'm fine, thank you, Andy. Peachy. Full of vinegar. And how have you been this week?"

He pressed his lips together. "I'm well."

"And how has Sophie Mae's dear detective been doing?"

Chief Maher sighed. "Not so well."

"That's what I heard. So? What the heck is going on? Is Cadyville suffering from a botulism epidemic these days? Do we need to alert the media?"

"Good Lord, no, Mother. Don't even joke about such a thing."

She narrowed her eyes.

He managed to withstand her glare for almost twenty seconds. Then he sighed again and rubbed his eyes with the heels of his palms. Sparing me a bleary glance, he pulled the small needle-point-covered ottoman away from Betsy's chair and sat down. His knees ended up by his ears, and if he hadn't looked so patently miserable, I might have laughed out loud.

"Are you the one who told the hospital staff Philip Heaven might have died from botulism?"

I nodded.

He looked unhappy. "Well, it turns out you were right, though how you knew I can't imagine. And I'm sure the doctors would have put it together on their own."

I made a noncommittal noise. "And? Where did he come into contact with it?"

He shifted and looked uncomfortable.

"Ms. Reynolds, I know you're concerned about Detective Ambrose, and that's the only reason I'm saying any of this in front of you. Please don't spread it around."

"I'll try to control myself," I said, not pointing out that he didn't appear to have many qualms about talking in front of his mother and her friend about things that weren't any of their business. After all, his indiscretion benefited me. If I'd been a betting woman, I'd have taken odds that he underestimated both his mother and her friends simply because they were old and female.

If only he knew.

The Chief continued to look unhappy. "I understand there was an event at Heaven House where the volunteers exchanged home canned food? Someone's preserves must have gone bad, and Heaven and Ambrose ate the spoiled food."

I shook my head. "I don't think so. For one thing, the exchange didn't happen until after Philip had collapsed. In fact, we were at the exchange when we learned that he'd died." I remembered the surprise on the volunteers' faces when Barr announced Philip's death the evening before.

The creases in his considerable forehead deepened as he listened. "That's odd timing," he admitted. "Perhaps Heaven got his hands on some of the goodies ahead of time."

Maybe. Especially if Maryjake's corn was the culprit. She obviously had had a bit of thing for her boss, and no doubt would have given him a little extra on the side, so to speak.

"In any case, the M.E. said it didn't help that Heaven was a heavy smoker," the Chief continued. "Botulism depresses the respiratory system, and his lungs were already compromised by his nicotine habit."

I thought of Philip's frequent forays into the alley, red and white pack in hand. Everyone who smokes is aware of the dangers, but I doubted anyone considered that it could make them more susceptible to botulism poisoning.

"Oh, my soul. What a terrible way to go," Betsy said.

Tootie smiled and examined the floor, and the Chief looked wry. Until that statement his mother had faded into the background as my own questions became more insistent. Now her face brightened again — at least until he said, "I only have time for a brief visit this time, Mother. I'm sorry."

"Oh, Andy. You just got here."

"I'll try to stay longer next time."

"All right. I understand."

I could tell she was hurt, that she wanted him to spend more time with her. Betsy Maher might have been a gossip and a tad morbid, but she was also smart and fun, and I hated to see her discounted by her own son.

He said goodbye to Tootie and me, kissed his mother on the cheek, and turned to leave.

"Chief?" I began.

He sighed and turned be to me, a look of tired warning on his face. "Yes?" Meaning, what now, and make it quick.

"With Barr, er, out of commission, who's investigating this whole thing? Are you handling it?"

"Of course not. I can't drop my duties as Chief of Police to investigate a case of botulism."

I cocked my head and frowned.

He continued. "The Health Department has jurisdiction, and I brought in someone from the state patrol to take over Barr's other cases while he's recovering. Anything the Health Department needs they can liaison with her. Don't worry, Ms. Reynolds. It's all being handled." He nodded toward the two older women. "Goodbye, Mother. Mrs. Hanover." Then he turned around and left without another word.

I grimaced at Betsy. "I'm sorry. He would have stayed longer if I hadn't quizzed him so much. I'm sure he fled to get away from me."

She shook her head. "No. He never stays long. He always promises to next time, but there's always something he needs to go do." She set her jaw and looked me full in the eye. "My boy has grown into an important man. I'm very proud of him. And I'm glad for any time that I get to spend with him."

I opened my mouth, but she continued, effectively cutting me off. "At least you had a chance to find out what happened to Philip and your boyfriend."

I knew more than I had before, but it only served to raise more questions. "It was very helpful, Betsy."

She smiled. "Knowledge is power. Or at least it is to me — power over my own mind. If I don't have enough facts, I tend to fill in the details myself, and sometimes my imagination can be a frightening thing."

I looked at her in surprise. "I know exactly what you mean."

On the way home, driving the sedate twenty-five miles an hour required within the city limits of Cadyville, I thought about what the Chief had said. Even if Philip had sampled some of the preserves before the actual exchange, I still didn't understand how Barr had happened into the botulism.

As for the state patrol investigator, I wondered what she was like, whether she was as smart as Barr, as able to deal with what sounded like a pretty complicated caseload. I couldn't imagine anyone doing Barr's job better than he did.

And I guessed he wouldn't like the idea of someone else doing his job at all.

Ten

The elevator doors opened, and I stepped out feeling guilty. I should have come to see Barr before going over to Caladia Acres. How would he feel about being bumped aside in my schedule by Chief Maher? Should I even tell him? It might be a bad idea to pile more stress on him right now. That man seemed to worry an inordinate amount about me.

As I walked down the hospital hallway, a stunningly gorgeous, auburn-haired woman exited room 513.

Room 513? Wait a minute. What the heck was she doing in Barr's room, with her peaches-and-cream skin and big brown eyes and cheekbones to die for? I tried to smile as she passed, but she looked right through me, and it slid off my face like warm butter. I found myself turning to watch her walk away. The view from that side wasn't very encouraging, either.

Barr sat propped up against a pillow and stabbed at the food on the tray in front of him. Tubes were still strapped to his face, but they were open-ended against his nostrils, providing a little extra boost of oxygen. Nothing to panic about. He shoveled a forkful of mashed potatoes into his mouth just as I walked in, necessitating a wave rather than a verbal greeting on his part.

"You look much better," I said.

He nodded and swallowed. "Feel better, too. Not a hundred percent, but not like hammered rat shit, either. Still don't have much wind. Did you see that red-haired woman leave just now?"

"Uh huh."

"That's my replacement. Detective Robin Lane, from Seattle. Not very happy to be here. It won't be for long though. I'll be back at work in a few days, and she can go back where she came from."

Right. Even though Barr had contracted a relatively mild case of botulism, it was still a wicked poison with long-lasting effects. It'd be at least a couple of weeks before he'd feel well enough to go back to work. Maybe more.

I smiled, suddenly quite cheerful after learning who the mystery woman was. "I'm sure you have enough sick and vacation time to take several weeks off, if you want to. Let someone else deal with your workload for a while."

He looked at me as if I'd suggested he eat a live frog. His pasty complexion and the slight tremor in the hand that held the fork belied the stoic face he seemed determined to wear. I wanted to take the fork and feed him the mashed potatoes and meatloaf myself. Except, frankly, it looked pretty gross.

And I didn't think Barr would appreciate being treated like a child. So I kept my hands to myself and sat down in the chair next to the bed. "You know about the botulism?" I asked.

"Yes." His voice was curiously quiet. His previous energy seemed to have leaked away.

"Do you know how you could have been exposed?"

"The Health Department was here asking me that earlier. They're really jumping on this."

"And?"

"Apparently that's what killed Heaven. They think I must have been exposed when I ate at his apartment the other day."

"His apartment? When were you there?"

"Day before yesterday. In the afternoon."

"What on earth for?"

"We had a meeting."

"About what?"

He pressed his lips together.

"Barr, he's dead."

After a few more moments hesitation, he capitulated. "He wanted to find out what he'd need to do to get a restraining order. Didn't want to make it official yet, so he asked me to stop by as a favor."

I felt my eyebrows rise. "He told me someone had threatened him. A few people, in fact, but one person in particular."

"That's what he told me, too," Barr said.

Threat. Meant it. Only a whisper.

"Did he tell you who it was?" I asked.

"He refused. Said he had to know more before he'd communicate anything officially. Wanted to make sure no one got in trouble if they didn't have to."

"It sounds like he was ambivalent about whomever he was afraid of. Like maybe he wasn't sure whether he should be or not."

Barr agreed.

I told him what Philip had said to me. As far as I knew, his last words.

We stared at each other for a few moments, wheels turning in perfect unison. Finally, I voiced what I'd been wondering all along.

"What if the botulism poisoning wasn't an

accident?"

Barr cocked his head to one side. "The Health Department is looking into it."

"The police aren't involved at all? Not even your Detective Lane?"

"She's not my Detective Lane. And no, she's not at all interested in following up on anything so mundane."

"But it's her job!"

"Treating botulism poisoning as murder? Try to convince her of that. Or Zahn. Or the Chief, for that matter."

I knew he was right. "Do *you* think it's suspicious?"

He blinked, suddenly looking as if he was having trouble keeping his eyes open. "Suspicious? Sure. Murder? Well, that's pretty wacky, but not impossible."

That was enough for me.

"What did you eat when you were at Philip's?"

"He'd made a big salad, you know with ham and turkey and cheese and a bunch of different vegetables."

"You're not much of a salad eater."

"I hadn't eaten since early in the day, and wanted to be polite. Didn't end up eating very much of it, so I guess that makes me lucky."

"I'll say."

He yawned.

"You seem to be winding down," I said.

"I am feeling kind of tired, now that you mention it."

"Okay. Let me move this." I swung the tray arm away from the bed. He hadn't eaten much. "Do you want me to stay until you fall asleep?"

"Nuh uh. Tha's okay . . ."

I stayed anyway, all of a minute and a half, until he was breathing regularly, and, I was happy to see, deeply.

On the way home I swung by HH to see if Maryjake was back at her desk. If anyone would know what the Health Department had found out, she would.

Rather than Maryjake, I found Ruth Black knitting furiously on something large and orange and very, very fluffy. She didn't look up when I walked in, and her fingers never stopped moving.

I sat down across from her. "What're you working on?"

The muscles in her jaw worked, and when she finally raised her head I saw she was crying.

She sniffed and held up the orange fluff. "It's an afghan, a wedding present for my niece."

"It's beautiful." I hoped her niece liked bright colors. Really bright colors. "Is everything all right?"

She shook her head and tears spilled onto her cheeks. "No. Philip is dead."

"I'm so sorry, Ruth. I had no idea you two were close."

Her hand disappeared into a desk drawer and returned with a tissue which she blew into with a wet honk. "We weren't. I hardly knew him, really. Maryjake was the one who organized the volunteers."

"Oh. Well, it's a real shame. Did you hear what they say he died of?"

The sudden fire in her eyes made me sit back in my chair. "I did not kill him. I don't care what those fools say," she said.

"Kill . . . ? What are you talking about?"

She slammed her knitting down on the desktop and leaned forward. "Those idiots over at the Health Department have decided my beets are what killed Philip. They found a pint jar of beets in his apartment, and it tested positive for botulism. So they find out I brought beets to the preserves exchange and make the assumption that the beets they found had to have come from my kitchen. *My* kitchen!" Her voice broke on the last word.

I frowned. It wasn't the craziest conclusion.

She waved her knitting needle at me. "I know what you're thinking. You're wrong. Not only did Philip die before I brought any of my canned goods to Heaven House, but I saw the jar they found up there in his apartment." She paused for effect, and I dutifully waited. "They were sliced." She nodded with satisfaction at this pronouncement.

I blinked. "Sliced?"

"Yes! I never slice my beets into rounds, and I don't can the standard round beets. I always use heirloom fingerling beets, about two or three inches long, from my own garden, and I leave them whole." She started knitting again, jabbing the needles into the yarn.

"And the jar of beets with the botulism were sliced. So they couldn't have been yours. Right?"

"Exactly. Plus, I don't use the brand of jar those nasty beets were in."

"What did the Health Department people say when you explained it all to them?"

"They . . . I couldn't make them . . . they just didn't listen to me. They acted like I was trying to get out of something. If he ate something I gave him and then died, my denying it wouldn't change anything, would it? I'd feel terrible, but it would still be an accident, right? Why would I make up such a story? And now they're taking all my lovely preserves away to be destroyed. It makes me sick."

I believed her. She didn't like the idea of people thinking she wasn't careful with her home canning, but if it had indeed been her fault, she wasn't the kind of person to try and blame someone else.

"So where did the bad beets come from?" I asked.

The needles slowed again, then stopped. "Oh, Sophie Mae. I was so upset about them thinking that I'd killed Philip I didn't even think about where those other beets could have come from."

Not good news at all. There was still a possible deadly risk out there, and the state Health Department thought they had the culprit.

"Do you think you could find out?" Ruth asked.

My attention snapped back to her. "What?"

"Can you find out where Philip got the beets? After all, someone needs to, and you were so clever last year when Walter died."

I sighed. Sometimes it seemed too many

people in Cadyville knew I'd investigated when Walter Hanover, our erstwhile neighborhood handyman, died after drinking a glass of lye. But this was the first time anyone had suggested I should try such a thing again.

"That was pretty personal. He died in my workroom," I said.

"Well, darn it, this is personal for me. I didn't poison Philip, and you know it. And there's someone out there canning beets who doesn't know what the heck they're doing. They must be stopped."

I almost laughed at her last statement, thinking it melodramatic. But was it, really?

The image of Barr lying in that hospital bed with tubes up his nose rose in my mind. The beets must have been in Philip's chef salad. Whether the botulism was an accident or murder, if there was any way I could keep someone else from getting sick, I needed to do it. And if I happened to salvage Ruth Black's kitchen reputation at the same time, so much the better.

As soon as I got home, I went into the pantry. Something about the neat rows of beautifully canned food calmed me. Perhaps it was related to the primitive safety of having a fully stocked larder. After rooting around, I found two jars of Ruth's beets from the exchange.

Not round. Not sliced.

Cylindrical and whole, just as she'd said.

I hesitated, then returned one jar to the shelf. The other one I took upstairs and hid in the back of my closet.

Then I began making phone calls. Bette took a break from working with her clay to talk with me, but didn't have any ideas about how Philip could have obtained any beets, Ruth's or anyone else's. As far as she knew, there would have been no reason for him to have any of the preserves ahead of time. Mavis Gray was next, and she said much the same thing.

I thanked her and called Maryjake's house, figuring she might be home since she was obviously not at Heaven House. James answered.

"Sorry, she can't come to the phone right now. She's in bed with a migraine."

"Okay," I said. "Would you mind if I asked you a couple of things?"

"About what?"

"About Heaven House."

"God. That place. All right, but I don't have much time. I have to get to the lab." James was a biologist who worked for a national environmental nonprofit doing field studies and research.

"Maryjake cans a lot of different things. Do you help her?" I asked.

"No. I contribute to the family table by hunting and fishing. Maryjake is in charge of preserving the garden produce."

Gosh, how manly. Still, I bet they managed to feed themselves decently, however arrogant James sounded about it.

I continued. "Do you know whether Maryjake uses a pressure canner?"

He hesitated. "I don't know. Is that the thing with the lid that screws down?"

"Sounds right."

"Well then, she uses one. I don't get it. How is this about Heaven House?"

"One more question. Does Maryjake can beets?" She hadn't brought any to the exchange, but she might not have brought samples of everything she canned, especially if she did as much of it as James implied.

"Hell, I don't know. What does this have to do with . . . is this about Heaven's death?"

"Well, sort of," I said. "He died of botulism, and they found some nasty beets in his kitchen."

"They think the beets were Maryjake's?" He practically barked the question.

"Nooo . . . they think they were Ruth Black's."

"Then what's with all these questions about Maryjake's canning? She didn't do anything wrong."

"I never said she did. There is some question as to where the beets came from, though, and I called to see if Maryjake could shed some light on where else Philip might have gotten hold of a jar."

"Not from us." The words were clipped. "I hate beets, always have, ever since I was a kid. We don't eat them."

Why hadn't he just told me that in the first place? Sheesh.

"I've got to go now," he said.

"Could you have Maryjake call me when she's feeling better?"

A pause. Then, "Sure." The phone went dead.

Nice.

I had some trouble tracking down Jude Carmichael, and eventually called Ruth at Heaven House to see if she had his number. She did. Apparently Philip's cousin, rather than living onsite as Philip did, rented a room from an elderly man whose wife had recently died. Mr. Oxford, Ruth said his name was, and he was a friend of her Uncle Thaddeus, who had introduced the two. Mr. Oxford made a little money by renting to Jude, and Jude provided a bit of companionship and some muscle around the house when needed, helping to maintain the yard, keeping the woodpile stocked, that kind of thing.

When I called, Mr. Oxford answered and assured me in his deep baritone that Jude would be home soon. He'd pass on the message to call me.

That left Thaddeus Black, though I was sure Ruth had already talked to him about the beets. I called anyway, and I was right. In fact, he'd been home when two people from the Health Department had come by to confiscate Ruth's beets, and the rest of her home-canned goods as well. Thaddeus could shed no light on the origin of the errant beets but was still very upset and spent considerable time reiterating Ruth's arguments about how it couldn't have been her preserves that caused Philip' death. I had to insist several times that I believed him, and that indeed I was trying to help Ruth find out what had really happened.

Finally, I managed to hang up. The phone rang immediately. Jude had received my message. I went through the whole diatribe about the wrong beets being blamed, or more accurately, the wrong beet canner being blamed for his cousin's death. Did he have any information at all about how Philip had obtained the tainted jar?

"I can't imagine. You say Ruth doesn't use that kind of jar?"

"She said she uses another brand."

"I bet she uses whatever she can find, like my mother used to. You're out at a garage sale, and someone is getting rid of a box of canning jars for a dollar. You take what you can get because the price is so right."

He could be right. Meghan and I had acquired most of our canning jars exactly that way. The lids and seals always had to be new, but the jars could be used over and over. People were always getting rid of them at garage sales. However, the type of canning jar wasn't the only argument for Ruth's innocence. In fact, it was the least important.

I could almost see Jude shrug on the other end of the line as I told him the type of beets the Health Department found were different from the kind Ruth grew in her garden.

"Besides, Philip died before the preserves exchange," I added.

"I don't know what to say. I wasn't even there when the Health Department came by, and by the time Ruth reached me on my cell and I got over to Heaven House, they were leaving. I mean, the jar was all packed up like hazardous waste or something, so I never saw it."

That meant Ruth was the only one who'd seen the beets in question, and she was the only one with a vested interest in them not being hers. Not a good position for her to argue from, I had to admit.

I still believed her.

And the more I learned from talking to the other volunteers, the more I realized just how darn odd the circumstances of Philip's death were.

ELEVEN

I'd been neglecting business errands for days. I needed more beeswax for lip balm — it was amazing how fast the stuff ran out — and the printer had left a message that a fresh order of Winding Road labels and letterhead were ready. I also had to meet with the home economics teacher at the high school to talk about a class she wanted me to give on traditional recipes for homemade cleaning products.

By the time I got home there was no hope of being in time to help with dinner.

Meghan, of course, had things well in hand. An intoxicating scent welcomed me as I opened the front door. Chicken in the oven, something with onions, and something else . . . Parmesan? Nothing like that smell — sometimes a bit too much like old gym socks, but absolutely lovely in concert with all the other goodness wafting on the air.

The phone rang as I was hanging my

jacket on the coat tree in the front hall.

"I'll get it," I called and snagged the cordless off the hall table. "Hello?"

"Hello, Sophie Mae Mae Mae." The singsong voice was instantly familiar.

Great.

"Oh, gosh, lemme guess. Is this by any chance *Allen?* This wouldn't be *Allen,* would it? Because I was so hoping you'd call."

"Really?"

I sighed, loud enough to be heard on the other end of the line. "No. Not really."

"Oh. Well you don't have to be so mean about it."

Honey, you have no idea. "What do you want?" I asked.

"I told you. I want to talk."

"Sorry, don't have time for a nice little convo about death right now. And you have to stop calling here and hanging up."

"I don't want to talk to them. I want to talk to you."

Hmm. If he was calling when I wasn't home in hopes of reaching me, then he wasn't following me around. At least not all time. It wasn't much, but it made me feel a little better.

"You have to stop calling me here," I said, trying to keep my voice gentle but firm. Was this guy mentally unbalanced or merely . . .

inappropriately smitten with me? "It's bothering my housemates."

There was a long silence. "Well, when would be a good time to call back?"

I almost laughed out loud, but stopped myself just in time. So polite. At least he wasn't your run-of-the-mill stalker. "There isn't a good time, Allen, not for that." I took a deep breath. "I'd still like to help you. Are you still having thoughts about harming yourself?"

"I'm not calling the Helpline! I'm calling you!" His tone went from zero to sixty in one-point-five seconds. "Don't talk down to me, don't you dare. What do you know, anyway? You're just some stupid woman in a dorky little town with nothing better to do than hang out at some community center."

"Allen, I need you to settle down."

"Don't talk to me like that! I thought you understood!" He hung up.

Any thought of laughter had completely disappeared. I made my hands into fists and willed them to stop trembling. Had I done the wrong thing? The right thing? Was he dangerous after all? I had a sudden thought and grabbed the phone back off its cradle. Punching in *69, I licked my lips and waited.

The number was unavailable.

Well, of course it was. A ten-year-old could cover their telephonic tracks these days. Unless I went to the police I'd probably never find out who Allen really was. And for some reason I wasn't quite ready to do that.

In the kitchen, the scent of dinner was even stronger. The oven did indeed contain chicken; boneless breasts soaked in buttermilk and Worchestershire sauce all day, then rolled in a combination of bread crumbs and grated parmesan, sprayed with olive oil and baked to crispy perfection. Meghan stood by the counter, mixing together melted butter, heavy cream and more parmesan for capellini alfredo, and Erin gave the room-temperature, marinated vegetable salad a stir at the kitchen table.

I closed the oven after inspecting the contents. "That was my stalker."

"What?" Meghan sounded distracted.

I sank onto a kitchen chair and snagged a black olive from Erin's salad. She tried to slap my hand, but missed. I stuck my tongue out at her, and she grinned.

"Allen again. I told him to stop calling and hanging up when you answered because it was bugging you."

Meghan turned toward me, still stirring her Alfredo sauce. She shot a quick glance at her daughter, now eyeing me with real interest. "You didn't."

"I did. And he asked when it might be more convenient for him to call."

"He didn't."

"He did."

"You have a stalker?" Erin asked. "Does he talk dirty?"

I tried not to smile at the look this question engendered on Meghan's face. "No. He's just lonely, I think."

Erin rolled her eyes. "Figures. You can't even get a spooky stalker."

"Nice," I said. "Real nice."

They laughed, and I joined in. But as we bustled around, I felt a little hollow inside. Could Allen really be dangerous? Surely not, I told myself.

In fact, I told myself that several times.

The doorbell rang just as the water for the pasta was beginning to boil. I answered it and was delighted to find Tootie Hanover leaning on her silver-headed cane. An newer model sedan was pulling away from the curb, and she half-turned to wave at the driver.

"What a wonderful surprise!" I said. "Who brought you over?" Usually either Meghan or I picked Tootie up from Caladia Acres when she came over.

"Andy Maher, actually. He's taking his mother out to dinner."

I was glad to hear that. "Betsy bully him into giving you a ride?"

"He's a nice man. I like him. And you have to understand Betsy is not the least demanding mother a Chief of Police could have."

"No kidding. Anyway, I'm glad he could drop you for a visit. You're in time for dinner."

"I should hope so. Meghan did invite me, after all."

Oh. "I guess we've been talking about other things since I got home. She forgot to mention it. I'm just glad you're here."

I took her coat, hung it on the hall tree and led her into the fragrant kitchen. Everyone exchanged greetings. Tootie eased into one of the wooden ladder-backed chairs at the table. She sat and listened to Erin chatter on about the spelling bee and Jonathan for a bit, back straight and head held high despite the arthritis pain she battled on a daily basis. The white coil of braid atop her head gleamed in the overhead light. She still wore the long silk forest-green sweater over black slacks, and the elegant effect was ruined only slightly by the swath of white hair Brodie had deposited on her pant leg as he trotted from cook to cook, casting yearning looks with those big brown eyes so perfectly suited for begging. A smile warmed her face as Erin wound down, and we all took our places at the dinner table.

"How is your young man?" Tootie asked me.

"He seems to be doing better." Barr, who was in his forties, would have loved to hear her call him my young man.

"Botulism is terrible. I knew twin brothers who died from it when I was a young girl. Of course, a woman whose daughter they had —" she glanced at Erin "— hurt gave it to them on purpose, so that's a little different. Do you know where it came from?"

I stared at her. "You know someone who used botulism as a murder weapon?"

"Well, she was never caught." Tootie put a ladylike portion of chicken in her mouth.

"Then how exactly do you know about it?"

She looked sideways at Erin, who studied her with an attentive gaze, and swallowed. "It was my second cousin, actually. And they wouldn't have been able to prove it, not then. But I heard her talking to my older sister, so I knew what happened."

135

"Did they deserve it?" Erin asked.

Again the sidelong look. "I don't think anyone deserves to have someone else take their life. Not even the state. But in that case, even I have to admit, there might have been a certain amount of . . . justice in what happened. Of course, I didn't find out about it until well after the fact. It gradually became common knowledge in town, but it was still only a rumor as far as the law was concerned." She left Erin to think about that a while and turned to me. "So do they know where the botulism originated?"

"Apparently the people at the Health Department think Ruth Black's beets were contaminated. They found some beets in Philip's kitchen, and she brought beets to the preserves exchange. The problem is that Philip got sick before the preserves exchange, and the beets they found are different than the beets Ruth cans."

Meghan jumped in. "The Health Department came by this afternoon. They took away everything we got from Ruth at the exchange."

Wow. They moved fast. I thought about the beets in my closet with a twinge. Should I have done that? With a sinking feeling, I asked, "Did they take everything else?"

She shook her head. "No. But they gave

136

me a heck of a lecture about home canning."

"I bet they did."

Erin laid her fork down on the table. "Isn't botulism the same thing as food poisoning? Zoe got food poisoning last year. She felt really bad, but she didn't end up in the hospital or anything. Could she have died?"

"Your friend probably had ptomaine, honey," Tootie said. "That's another kind of food poisoning, and it's a lot more common."

"Then botulism is worse?"

"It certainly can be," I said. "It's a toxin released by an active bacteria. Thing is, there are a lot of inactive spores of that bacteria around all the time, and most of the time they don't hurt anyone. They need a warm, wet environment without any oxygen in order to activate. That's when the toxin is released."

Meghan wrinkled her nose. "This is lovely dinnertime conversation."

"Sorry."

But she was the one who continued. "Doesn't acid kill the bacteria, too?"

I nodded. "And high heat. That's why the food needs to contain a certain amount of acid naturally, or you have to add an acid like vinegar or lemon — pickles, for example

137

— or use a pressure cooker."

"What's a pressure cooker do?" Erin asked around a bite of salad.

"Don't talk with your mouth full," I said. "It uses pressure to raise the temperature of the jars without letting them explode."

Meghan grimaced. She felt pressure canners and pressure cookers were dangerous.

"I can't believe they use the botulism poison to erase wrinkles." Tootie snorted. "Idiots."

I shrugged. "I don't care if someone else wants to inject a toxic substance into their face, but I sure don't want to." Botox was all about muscular paralysis to preserve beauty. Not high on my list of priorities right now.

"Did you know the paralyzing agent in botulism can benefit people with Parkinson's disease or muscular dystrophy?" I asked. Like digitalis, botulism was both poison and savior.

Meghan changed the subject then, but as we continued plowing through the mountain of food on the table, I kept coming back to what Tootie had said earlier about the mother who'd poisoned the brothers in retribution for hurting her daughter.

What had Philip done to make someone want to kill him?

■ ■ ■ ■

Meghan returned from taking Tootie back to Caladia Acres after dinner and went into her office to check her schedule for the weekend. Erin was up in her room doing homework. I tried watching a little television, but nothing caught my attention. I really needed to talk to someone about what had been weighing on my mind. Meghan, as my best friend, won the honor.

"Got a minute?" I asked, setting a steaming cup of strong black tea on the desk in front of her. "There's something I didn't want to talk about in front of Erin."

She closed her laptop and sat back in her chair, lacing her fingers across her abdomen. "The stalker truly is dangerous, isn't he? What else has he done?" Her narrowed eyes said she'd been expecting this.

"What? No, no. This has nothing to do with that guy. I swear to God, Meghan, earlier he actually asked when it would be convenient for him to call back. What kind of nut does that? I'm sure he's harmless."

The expression on her face didn't change an iota. "We'll see. So something else is going on?"

I paused. A huge philodendron wound its

139

way up a trellis in the corner of her office. The tiny fountain in the massage room behind her gurgled softly but failed to sooth me.

"Well? What?"

I sighed and plunged in. "I think someone may have deliberately poisoned Philip."

The look on her face could have stopped an oncoming truck. It didn't stop me, mind you, but it did warn me of the reception my theory would receive. I laid it out in a systematic manner, citing Ruth's insistence that the offending beets had not come from her kitchen, Philip telling me someone had threatened him and asking Barr about how to get a restraining order, and finally, Philip's cryptic words to me before the paramedics had hauled him off to the hospital to die.

By the time I finished, she'd leaned back in her chair and was examining the ceiling. Now she rubbed both hands over her face and sighed.

"You're not kidding, are you? You know, just because you thought Walter didn't kill himself, and lo and behold it turned out you were right, it doesn't mean Philip's death has nefarious roots. For Pete's sake, the poor man died from botulism, not arsenic."

"Barr thinks it's suspicious, too."

"Great. So he can do something about it. You don't have to."

"He's sick."

"There are other people in the Cadyville Police Department."

I tried to explain that Chief Maher and Detective Lane didn't have the most receptive attitudes in this situation.

"This is not your problem," Meghan insisted in a dangerous voice.

I held up my hands. "Okay, okay." But of course I didn't agree, not at all. Philip had grabbed my arm and as much as told me someone had poisoned him; Ruth had specifically asked me to find out where the offending beets had come from; and, last but not least, my boyfriend was in the hospital, possibly due to some twisted killer's plan.

"You promise?"

I smiled. "Stop worrying." I stood up. "I'm getting more tea and going downstairs to get a few things done before I go to bed. Do you want any?"

She looked vaguely dissatisfied. "No, thanks."

"Okay. See you in the morning."

She said something, but by then I was already out in the front hallway, and I pretended not to hear her. Sue me. At least I didn't make any promises I couldn't keep.

TWELVE

Okay, so I had to admit I was a little spooked when I got to Heaven House that night. I'd worked for a couple of hours, then called and talked to Barr at the hospital for another. Finally, Meghan went to bed. Now it was late and dark, and the ugly hulk of the building squatted in the murky light filtering through the fog from the street-light. It was even darker in the alley where I parked, but the only way I could get in was to "borrow" Meghan's key, and the only key she had happened to be for the back door. I was lucky she still had that; she didn't spend as much time at HH as she used to.

Barr would've had a fit if he'd seen me wandering around town alone in the dark, using a key I wasn't even supposed to have to get into a building that could very well be a crime scene. Sneaking. And very, very carefully ignoring the fact that there seemed to be someone interested in noting my whereabouts and activities. My stomach clenched at the thought of my friendly stalker lurking in the fog-ridden shadows.

I shoved the door open, stepped inside and shut it behind me. Locked it.

Inside, it was pitch black, the kind of frightening absolute darkness that makes you entertain the idea, if only for a few moments, that maybe you've really, actually gone blind and will never see light again in your life. Smothering dark. Darkness so thick it coats your lungs, clogs your arteries . . .

My fumbling hand found the light switch and the overheads came on. It suddenly became easy to breathe again.

Okay. So far, so good.

The main room looked as boring and uninspired as ever. No chalk outlines on the floor. No police tape. No suspicion from anyone in authority that Philip's death wasn't completely accidental. How do you poison someone with botulism? Did someone simply hand the beets to him and hope?

Was it possible his death really was an accident?

Anything was possible. Some things were just unlikely. I don't know what it said about me that I found the idea of murder far more likely than an accident.

Flipping on light switch after light switch, I made my way to the stairs that led to Philip's office and apartment on the second floor.

On the first step I hesitated. There was no light in the stairwell. For some reason I was more inclined to abandon my little investigation now that I was faced with going up to Philip's office in the dark.

Great, Sophie Mae. Way to act like a girl.

Shaking my head at myself, I clomped up the steps, taking a certain amount of comfort in the noise my waffle-soled boots made on the worn wood. On the landing, I could just make out the outline of the doorway to Philip's office, a rectangle of light leaking out around the door.

Wait a minute. Light? Inside Philip's office? The carpeted hallway silenced my footsteps as I crept to the office door and ever so slowly pushed it open.

There was no one in the room.

I let out a whoosh of breath, allowing the muscles along my shoulders to unclench a little. Someone had left the light on, that was all. The desk was still askew from when the paramedics had removed Philip to the ambulance, and a dark stain streaked the wall behind it.

The place smelled terrible. I maneuvered

my way to the window, opened the blinds and twisted the paint-encrusted handle of the double-hung sash and pulled up. Outside, the fog put the street scene into soft-focus, giving it an almost romantic quality. The damp winter air drifted in, and I bent to take a deep breath of it before getting down to business.

Two black metal file cabinets hunched in the corner. I pulled out the top drawer of the first and flipped through the paperwork, then moved on to the next. Grant applications here. Foundation-related information there. Correspondence . . . here. I quickly worked my way through the official Heaven House files and found nary a threat. Closing the last drawer, I considered my options. Eyed the desk for a moment.

In the second drawer I discovered still more files. None of them contained threatening letters. But hang on — there were other places to keep files. I switched on Philip's computer. It was new and fast and the operating system loaded in no time.

Unfortunately, his computer was password protected.

Crap.

I got up and paced a few times in the narrow aisle between desk and file cabinets.

Stopped and looked out the window, thinking.

I had no clue what Philip might choose as a password. I just didn't know the guy well enough.

Movement down the block caught my attention. Someone crossed to the other side of the street, deep in the shadows. The figure jogged down to the vehicles parked across from Heaven House. It was a man, and he wore what looked like an old army pea coat and a funky knit hat with long tasseled earflaps. He stopped behind a truck. Didn't come back out. Then a pale face slowly edged around the cab of the pickup.

The guy was looking straight at me.

My head jerked back from the window. Was that Allen? I peeked around the sash again, only to see his retreating back. I seemed to have scared him as much as he scared me. Still, fresh air had lost its charm. Down came the window, quickly followed by the blinds.

It was just some guy who couldn't sleep, out for a walk. Right?

Back at Philip's desk, I parked my posterior in his fancy ergonomic chair. Leaned back. Considered whether I could sleep here all night instead of trundling out to my truck in the alley in the dark.

The chair was comfy, but not that comfy.

Absently, I glanced at the post-its Philip had stuck around the perimeter of his monitor. Call Gloria. Dry cleaning. Marlboros. Paycheck to Maryjake. Snickerdoodle.

Snickerdoodle?

Looked like a password to me. I entered it and waited expectantly.

Nada.

Wait a minute. One post-it was wrinkled and smudged, like it had been there a long time. And how many smokers needed to remind themselves to pick up more cigarettes?

None, that's how many. I squinted. That wasn't an ess at the end of Marlboro. It was a five.

I typed in Marlboro5.

Bingo.

Feeling pretty darned pleased with myself, I clicked around and found more of the same information I'd discovered in the hard copy files: grants, foundations business, etc. I felt kind of bad as I opened his email. There were bound to be some secrets in there I didn't want to know.

At least I didn't want to admit I wanted to know. And, I argued with myself, whatever I stumbled into might help to find his murderer. Even Philip would have agreed that was worth a little invasion of privacy, right?

But I didn't have a chance to invade much. Right there in his email program was a "folder" he'd named Mean People.

It would have been cute if someone hadn't killed him.

Only two emails occupied the folder. A quick scan revealed each contained a certain amount of vitriol. I clicked the print button in the email program.

Headlights illuminated the other side of the window, and I glanced at the clock on the computer. Almost one o'clock. I sighed and began a more careful reading of the first email in the Mean People folder.

The sender's address was ad@caladiaacres.com. I couldn't tell who it was from exactly, but Tootie's favorite nurse, Ann Dunning, fit the initials. If she wasn't the one who'd sent it, it wouldn't be hard to find out who did.

Once again, I couldn't help but shake my head at Philip's tendency to make promises and not follow through. He'd agreed to put together a visitation program for some of the nursing home residents who didn't have family or many local friends. The idea was to tap into the Cadyville High School's requirement that seniors perform a certain number of hours of community service before being allowed to graduate. It was a great idea, and should have worked. But once again, he'd dropped the ball; the Caladia Acres participants had been disappointed, and several students at the high school had to scramble in order to graduate on time.

The program had been salvaged at the last moment, from what I could tell, but only because whoever had sent the email to Philip had stepped in and taken over. And boy, was she, at least I thought it was a she, peeved at having to do so. Her anger snapped and snarled throughout the email as she outlined Philip's various failings. She ended by saying she planned to pass on details about his ineptitude to the Heaven Foundation Board.

"They should know how ineffective the head of their community center in Cadyville is, even if he is a member of the precious Heaven family." *Especially* since Philip was a Heaven, I thought.

I frowned. The printer hadn't made a peep. I checked to make sure it was on and had paper. Tried again. It wasn't doing a dang thing. Fine. I went back and forwarded the email from Caladia Acres to my Winding Road email address and opened the second threat.

This one was less businesslike than the first and had a shrill tone to it. Apparently Philip had been answering the Helpline just after starting it, and a runaway teenaged girl had called. Instead of giving her the 800 number that would enable her to talk to someone who specialized in runaways and would help her find a place to stay, contact her parents for free, or help her get back home, Philip had taken it upon himself to advise her personally. She had apparently told him how much she hated living at home.

He'd had the audacity to tell her he thought she'd be better on her own.

Well, this girl, Lisa Koller, was seventeen and headstrong. The email was from Lisa's mother, Mandy Koller, infuriated that Philip would say such a thing. Lisa's father had recently died, and Lisa had a mad-on at the world. She'd gone back home the next day. Again. She'd actually been staying with friends, as she always did when she wanted to punish her mom, only to throw Philip's "advice" in Mandy's face for weeks.

I wondered how bad Mom really was. The email was well-written, no spelling or grammar mistakes, and simply, if vehemently, accused Philip of overstepping his bounds.

151

She sarcastically thanked him for giving Lisa more ammunition to use against her. And finally, she informed him that she was going to report his abuse of the Heaven House Helpline to the Heaven Foundation.

Sounded familiar.

It didn't look like Philip had responded to either of these emails. I forwarded the second one to my Winding Road address, wondering whether both senders had indeed contacted the foundation. Then I erased my tracks in the "sent mail" folder.

Car headlights washed the drawn blinds once again as I shut down Philip's computer. A few people must be moving around Cadyville at this late hour, keeping odd work or social hours, but the bars and restaurants had been closed since midnight. I chided myself for being paranoid, for having the ego to think the sporadic traffic in my sleepy little town could have anything at all to do with me personally, and shut off the overhead light.

Got pretty dark again after that.

Out in the hallway, I felt my way toward the stairwell. There was Philip's apartment, right there, at the other end of the hallway. It would be locked, right? I couldn't help it, though. I tried the door.

The knob turned easily in my hand. Uh,

oh. Ethical dilemma.

But when would I get another chance to look around where Philip lived? When might I be able to check out where he — and Barr — must have been poisoned? My bone-crushing weariness evaporated. In the dark, my shoulders straightened a fraction. Not much of a dilemma after all.

I walked in and flipped the light switch by the door. Sconces along the walls illuminated the ceiling, painted the same sage tone as the walls. A huge-screen TV dominated one corner, and a bank of dark brown leather furniture curved in front of it. Thick Turkish rugs punctuated and softened the beautifully grained cherry wood floor. Recessed lighting accentuated the modern paintings on the walls. I ventured closer and peered at them. The artists were just names to me. Still, I bet they were quite expensive; everything in the place had that feel.

The kitchen must have been completely redone before Philip moved in: slab granite counters, saltillo tile floors, maple cabinets, and a sink you could take a bath in. I continued, almost against my will, into his bedroom and bathroom. Expensive fittings, marble and fine linens. Philip had generally opted for casual clothes.

Lots of cotton and wool. Jeans. Now that

I thought about it, though, he'd dressed more Town and Country than LL Bean.

This was the abode of a man with a ton of money. What the heck was he doing in Cadyville, running community programs?

Maryjake had an obvious crush on Philip. Why? He may have had money, but he didn't have much in the way of class. Had he returned the interest?

Back to basics. Not a lot of food left in the kitchen — either he didn't eat at home much or else the Health Department had stripped out the remaining food for testing.

A thought struck me — could there still be a danger of botulism poisoning in here?

That did it. I'd looked enough. Trotting back toward the door, though, I saw a beautiful roll-top desk, and paused. I mean, he was dead, right? What did he care?

The articulated top rose, smooth as silk, exposing a series of cubby holes and drawers. God, I'd always wanted a desk like that one. Rummaging through the neatly organized paper, I discovered a notice from Cadyville Electric. The bar of red ink along the top grabbed my attention, as it was intended to do. They were getting ready to shut off the electricity at Heaven House. Last notice.

Under it was a shut-off notice from the

gas company. And a first notice of non-payment from the phone company. What the heck? Why wasn't Heaven House paying its bills? And why were the notices in Philip's apartment instead of his office? Or in Maryjake's desk downstairs? I knew she wrote out some of the Heaven House checks, and then gave them to Philip to sign. I'd seen her do it. Maybe the utility bills were handled differently. Sent to the main foundation office, for example.

Only, they hadn't been.

Then I found a bank statement. Heaven House had only four hundred dollars in the checking account. There should have been more. I squinched my forehead. Maybe the foundation sent a monthly stipend. Maybe . . . I shook my head. I didn't know what to think.

And why were the Heaven House bank statements in his apartment as well?

Chewing on what I'd learned so far, I shut off the lights and locked the apartment door behind me. Unsure of what I'd expected to find, or what to do with what I had discovered, I had an odd sense of making progress.

Hopelessly lost, but making good time, as the bumper sticker says.

Thirteen

I believed Ruth hadn't canned the beets that killed Philip. I believed Philip had been threatened in a way that made him afraid, something beyond a threat to report him to the foundation. A physical threat. Something dire enough that he actually inquired about how to take out a restraining order. A threat from someone he didn't want to name. Because he didn't want to get them in trouble? Because he was so afraid of them? Because he wasn't sure who they were? No, not the last one. He knew who his killer was, and would have told me, or someone else, if he hadn't died from the botulism poisoning so quickly.

Seemed a risky proposition for his murderer, but the gamble had obviously paid off.

The late notices and unusually low bank balance at Heaven House were odd, but not that surprising. Philip's inefficiency was mind-blowing. I could easily see him grabbing the mail on the way in, taking it up to his apartment so he could drop his coat or change his shoes or use the bathroom, and leaving it there instead of taking it over to his office. He wasn't a man used to consequences, and a few late payment notices would likely leave him not only unfazed, but oblivious. As for the bank balance, if he were the one in charge of the banking then the same thing applied. On the other hand, if Maryjake was involved with the banking, it made very little sense.

Early Friday morning, I dragged my tired carcass out of bed and padded downstairs. Stumbling into the kitchen, I found Meghan eating a muffin that looked like it was made out of wet sawdust. At least she'd slathered it with some of Jude's tasty-looking apricot jelly.

I shook my head at the notion of joining the fiber fest, opened the refrigerator and reached for the bacon. It was a bacon and eggs kind of day. And fried potatoes. A woman needs her sustenance, if not her sleep.

Meghan said something as I clattered pans in the cupboard.

"What?" I came up for air holding the old cast-iron frying pan that had belonged to my grandmother.

"I've got a date tonight. You can watch Erin this evening, can't you?" she repeated, turning to the editorial section of the Seattle Times and feigning what I knew wasn't really nonchalance. Meghan Bly, cute and lithe and intelligent Meghan, hadn't gone on a date for at least two years.

"That guy you were with at the preserves exchange?"

"Mmm hmmm." She licked her finger, and as she turned the page I saw the headline *Cadyville Creep Continues Attacks*. Was that the same jerk who assaulted the woman in the alley, the one Barr had told me about on the phone? I thought about the lurker in the pea coat and tasseled earflappy hat from the night before. He'd looked pretty creepy in my opinion, all sneaking around in the fog.

"Kelly O'Connell," Meghan said, still not looking at me.

I refocused on our conversation. Crap. Erin had told me at the preserves exchange that Meghan and Kelly were finally going out on Friday, and I'd completely forgotten.

"Oh, no. I'm so sorry," I said.

She looked up. "What? You can take Erin

to the hospital, can't you? She'd love to see Barr."

"I'll go see him this afternoon," I said. "They're letting him go home tomorrow."

Her face lost all animation, and she examined the floor, radiating disappointment.

"It's okay, Megs. We'll work it out. Tonight is my night to volunteer for the Helpline at HH, is all. Can't Erin go over there with me? She can hang out and do her homework, and then dink around with that silly pinball game until I'm done. It'll only be nine-thirty when we leave. And tomorrow's Saturday."

Her expression alternated between relief and hesitation. "I . . . I don't think so, Sophie Mae. Maybe she could stay with Tootie tonight."

"What? Why?"

She bit her lip. "That guy. The one who's been bugging you. He knows you were at Heaven House on Tuesday. He might look for you there again. And what about this whole theory you have about someone deliberately killing Philip?"

"I thought you said I was nuts to think that."

"I didn't say that. Not exactly. And the more I think about it — and I've been thinking about it all night — the more pos-

159

sible it sounds. Tell me again what he said when he got so sick."

"Philip?"

"Yes, Philip." She sounded exasperated.

I repeated his whispered words to me. "Threat. Meant it."

"That's all?"

"He passed out then."

"Sounds like he was really afraid."

"He was terrified. He knew something was wrong, and seemed to know who did it."

"Well, even if you are completely wrong —"

"Thanks a lot."

"— I know you. I don't want Erin dragged into some crazy investigation."

I was stunned. And hurt. "You think I'd put her in danger?"

"Not on purpose. Besides, it'd be a pain for you to have to watch her while you're answering the phone."

"The Helpline doesn't ring that much, and you know it. I'm happy to bring her with me, and you know Caladia Acres isn't set up for overnight guests. But you do what you feel is right. You're her mother, after all."

Her smile was tentative. "Don't be mad."

"I'm not."

"Of course she can go with you. Just, you

know, be careful. Okay?"

"I promise. So, what are you doing on your date with this Kelly character?"

She tried to hide the grin that came to her face at the mention of his name, but couldn't. Oh, Lord. But I knew that giddiness myself lately, and found myself grinning back at her.

"We're going out for Thai food and then over to Monroe for a movie."

"What are you going to see?"

"I have no idea." There was that grin again.

"Gotcha. I'll be here by five to take over Erin."

"Thanks. But we're not leaving until six."

"Bet you wouldn't mind the time to do a little primping, eh?"

"Um, no, I guess not."

"What's he do?" I asked.

"He's a financial consultant."

"That sounds . . . interesting."

She laughed. "More like really boring. But he doesn't talk much about his work, so I haven't nodded off yet."

"What's his association with Heaven House?"

"He's a volunteer there, just like us. I met him when we were both working on the free legal aid project. It took a lot of research."

"Whatever happened with that?"

She shook her head and stood up. "I don't know. We gave our report to Philip and never heard another word. Anyway, Kelly wanted to get away from the rat race in Seattle, and he conducts a lot of his business online. So he moved up here about three months ago. When he heard about Heaven House, he saw it as a chance to give something to his new community, and thought it might be a good way to meet people."

I smiled. "Turns out it was a good way to meet someone."

She blushed, swear to God, and ducked her head. It was pretty cute, seeing her all flustered. She stepped out of the kitchen, then turned around and met my eyes. "Thanks, Sophie Mae."

"No problem," I said. "I hope you guys have a great time."

She turned back and headed toward the stairs. "We will," she called over her shoulder.

Sighing, I put the egg carton back in the fridge. Breakfast seemed like too much work now. I'd muddle through on coffee until lunch.

I was happy for my friend. Heck, my best friend. But I couldn't help but wonder about this Kelly guy. Meghan's past taste in men wasn't much of a recommendation for him. And he was so new to town; how much did anyone here know about him?

Down in my workroom, I packed another dozen boxes with retail orders off the Winding Road website. Then I went back upstairs to put out the sign I used to alert Joe Allingham, our trusty UPS driver, that I needed him to stop. It was so nice to have that service that I tried at least weekly to have a treat for him, even if he was only doing his job. I wrapped up some of the lemon cookies that Meghan, Erin, and I had made the past weekend so Joe could have them for an afternoon snack.

Cookies encased in foil, I opened the front door to put my makeshift sign out by the sidewalk and found Luke unloading a bale of chicken wire from the back of their work truck. Luke hefted it onto his shoulder and came up the sidewalk toward me. Seth met my eyes through the window of the pickup, blinked rapidly a couple of times, then turned his attention to the street as he pulled away from the curb.

"Wouldn't it be easier to go around to the alley with that stuff?" I asked Luke as he veered toward the side of the house.

"Hey, Sophie Mae. Yeah, probably, but it's

pretty light. 'Sides, Seth has to run back to the hardware store to get more fence staples."

This was going to be the best-built chicken coop for miles around, I thought as I went back inside and headed for the phone. I'd made enough inroads on my workload for the morning. Now I could take a break and find out more about the people Philip Heaven had angered with his ineptitude.

Fourteen

I leaned against the reception desk at Caladia Acres and watched two snow-haired men play a hot game of checkers, waiting for the young volunteer to track down Ann Dunning. After I'd confirmed that she was ad@caladiaacres.com, she'd agreed to talk with me over a cup of coffee. Her puzzlement at my request had filtered through the phone line. Maybe she thought I wanted to talk about Nana Tootie, as Erin called Petunia Hanover, or perhaps something concerning the massage-related work Meghan did at the retirement home. My roommate offered gentle rubdowns to the residents as well as training the nursing staff in therapeutic massage techniques. I'd managed to verbally duck and weave my way through the conversation with Ann, and I was pretty sure she had no idea I wanted to talk to her about the nasty email she'd sent to Philip Heaven.

"King me!" crowed the taller player, waving a red checker in his companion's face.

"Yeah, yeah, here ya go," his friend said, handing over a previously captured piece.

The clatter of dishes anticipated the early lunch soon to be served in the dining room, and the scent of something warm and savory rode the air. None of the residents paid any mind to me, though I saw a few I knew in passing, having spent many hours on the premises with Tootie and her friends. Then I remembered this was when Tootie et al had their weekly mah jong tournament in the activities room toward the back of the building. No wonder none of her particular cronies were wandering about.

The muscles in the back of my neck and shoulders relaxed an iota. I'd been afraid I'd have to explain my presence to Betsy Maher. I didn't want her to know I was investigating Philip's death. It's a well known fact among my friends that I'm a terrible liar. I fidget and fuss and flush and stutter. If we exchanged more than five words, the Chief's mother would be on me like a cat leaps on a particularly enticing, wiggly bug.

The mah jong would keep them busy through the first seating in the dining room. I crossed my fingers anyway.

A woman with a pair of silver barrettes holding her long brown hair away from her face lugged a karaoke machine through the front door. In her other hand, she juggled a large notebook and microphone. I smiled at her and she smiled back. Must be the new activities director Tootie and Betsy had been talking about. I wanted to be there when they started in on the singing. Knowing the folks who lived at Caladia Acres, Frank Sinatra and Lena Horne would have some serious competition.

My thoughts returned to Ann. Her email had been angry, very angry, yet well thought out and to the point. Furthermore, it seemed to me that she was right to be upset about how Philip had effectively scrapped the senior visitation project, leaving so many people high and dry and Ann scrambling to see it through on her own. I could see drafting such a missive under the same circumstances, but certainly didn't consider myself capable of killing anyone over such a thing.

But I was me, and Ann was Ann. I didn't know her well enough to judge whether she had a temper or tended to hold a grudge. For now she was a viable suspect.

As I pondered her ability to commit murder, Ann emerged from the hallway that led to the residents' rooms. "Sophie Mae —

hi! Want to go in the dining room?"

I shook her cool, plump hand and said, "I've been standing here smelling something wonderful cooking for the last few minutes, and my mouth is positively watering." My stomach growled right then, punctuating my words.

Ann flashed a smile, showing off two cherubic dimples in her pink cheeks. "We're not serving the early lunch for another half an hour, but there might be some pastries left over from breakfast. I'll see what I can dig up." She nodded toward the source of the clattering dishes, and her glossy dark hair swung forward and back in one smooth motion.

"I won't say no," I said, following behind her ample backside, unfortunately clad in classic nurse-white. This cheerful woman had written that vitriolic email. It was a stretch, but from our past interactions I knew she was intelligent, capable, and brooked no B.S. from anyone.

Ann led me to a table in the corner, well away from two women lingering over cups of tea on the other side of the room. I was happy for the privacy. At least I wouldn't have to be coy; according to Meghan, subtlety wasn't exactly my strong point.

"Have a seat," she said. "I'll be right back.

Do you want coffee? Or tea? We have a nice herbal blend."

"Coffee would be great. Black."

She walked away, and I belatedly covered a gigantic yawn with my hand. I was too darn old to handle two nights with next to no sleep with any kind of grace.

Ann returned with a small tray holding two steaming cups and a plate of fruit Danish. She watched with amusement as I dug in, suddenly starving. Yum.

"These are fabulous Danish," I mumbled.

"We get them fresh from Cadyville Loaf and Latte," she said, referring to a recently opened bakery and coffee shop. "You're lucky any are left today. Usually they're gone by ten." She took a bite of her own Danish, and we chewed contentedly for a few moments as I mused on how to start.

"You know Philip Heaven died a couple of days ago?" I asked, and took a big swig of the strong, hot coffee.

Ann looked startled. "Um, I heard something about it."

"It was botulism." I licked cherry goo from my fork.

She grimaced and put her cup down. "That's a terrible way to die."

"I guess you know how that would work, being a nurse and all."

She narrowed her eyes. "Very painful. And extremely frightening. The mental faculties remain, but the botulism toxin progressively paralyzes the muscles."

"Mm hmm. He got sick really fast."

"Have they found the source?" she asked

Watching her carefully, I nodded once. "Presumably. The Health Department discovered a jar of unsavory beets in his kitchen."

She leaned back in her chair, ignoring her half-eaten pastry. I took another bite of mine.

"Is that why you wanted to talk to me?" she asked. "To find out more about botulism?"

I swallowed. "I found an email on Philip's computer, and it made me curious. You must have really hated the guy."

If I'd been expecting a big reaction, I didn't get it. Ann just looked confused. "What?"

"The email you wrote him was very angry. You even threatened to inform the board of the Heaven Foundation about his ineptitude."

She grimaced and waved her hand in the air as if dispersing a foul odor. "That man had horrible delusions of adequacy, and fell far short of even that. I know he's dead, but that doesn't change what he was when he was alive, so I'm not going to sugar-coat it. And I did more than threaten to report him to the board; I did it."

"What happened?" I asked.

"You read my email? You know about the senior-to-senior project?"

"I pieced together an understanding of it, I believe."

She ignored me. "Seniors over at the high school were paired with residents here who wanted to take part in the program. They had to spend a requisite number of hours with 'their resident,' talking, reading to them, etc., but we also encouraged the high school kids to get the seniors here to talk about their lives. I ended up adding another incentive to the program, a kind of extra credit that would look good on college applications even if it wasn't a graduation requirement.

"Several of the students participated. They brought tape recorders and took notes, interviewing some of the men and women here about how things were a half century or more ago. Then they wrote down the stories, or at least transcribed the tapes. It was terrific for the kids to hear some of the stories about World War I and Korea, and to learn about how much things have changed in recent decades. These are kids who have never heard a record, have always had cell phones and microwaves and computers. A few of the residents . . . well, I'm going on and on. You can tell how excited I was about the project."

I smiled. Her palpable enthusiasm had chased away much of my own weariness. "From what you say it doesn't sound like the program fell through."

Her empty coffee cup clinked loudly against the saucer as she put it down with just a tad too much force. "It did, though. Philip completely dropped the ball, didn't call any of the people he needed to, never followed up on any of his promises, never actually *did* anything except talk about how great it would be. There were hoops to jump through with the school board to get it approved as an official program, paperwork to fill out, and then the coordination and supervision of the kids themselves. I expected to be involved peripherally with the latter, but I ended up having to step in and take care of the whole shebang."

Her voice had begun to rise. I kept my mouth shut, willing to let her own momentum carry her forward.

"If I'd wanted to do it on my own, I wouldn't have submitted the idea to Philip.

He'd sent a letter out — do you know this?"

I shook my head.

"When he first opened Heaven House he sent a letter out to businesses, volunteer agencies, the library, medical institutions, all over Cadyville, announcing that the foundation was looking for ways to invest in the community and asking for program ideas. There was a formal submission process, and then he supposedly went through and chose. I don't know how many people or organizations responded, or how many possible programs were voted on by the foundation's board of directors, but my senior-to-senior project was finally given the go ahead."

"Did the Heaven Foundation provide you with any money?" I asked.

Ann looked sour. "I asked for resources to coordinate and handle the application to the school board, all that stuff I ended up doing myself. The foundation approved funds for someone to help with all that, but no one involved with the program at either Caladia Acres or Cadyville High saw any money — or any help."

I felt bad, getting her upset all over again. She had good reason for the email she'd sent to Philip, and good reason to report him to the foundation. They needed to know if he was that incompetent.

And what had happened to the money the foundation had provided for the program?

I took one last bite of Danish, stuffed to the gills now. "What was the foundation's response when you told them what happened?"

"They apologized. In writing. Which was nice, but didn't help in any practical way."

I stared unseeing at the innocuous watercolor decorating the wall next to our table. Why hadn't the board of directors done something about Philip?

"I have to say," Ann interrupted my internal musings. "I still don't understand why you're here. Are they trying to decide whether or not to keep Heaven House open? I didn't realize you were involved with them to that degree."

"Er, no. Not really. Those beets I mentioned? There's some question as to where they came from. Whether it could have been intentional."

The incredulous look on her face made me regret stating it so blatantly. Meghan was right about my lack of tact.

"You think I actually killed that man by giving him botulism?" she asked.

"Of course not." Even I could hear how weak my voice was.

"Well, that's just stupid, Sophie Mae. I'm surprised at you."

"I'm sorry. Please don't be angry. I'm just trying to find out why so many people were mad at Philip."

"Because he was a jerk. And you know what?" She stood up, and I rose to my feet with alacrity. "If I *had* decided to kill him, I'd have used a damn shotgun."

FIFTEEN

"Meghan called me," Barr said. He was wearing the rust-colored cotton pajamas I'd brought him. They'd been tucked into the bottom drawer of his dresser, and my bet was they were a gift. Barr was not a pajamas kind of guy. They looked good on him, though.

I paused in tidying his bedside table. "That's nice. She wanted to visit you, but she's had a hard time finding the time." I'd told her not to worry, as he'd had a regular stream of co-workers and friends stopping by to see him.

"So she said. But she also told me about your stalker. Allen."

"Oh, now why did she go and do that?" I sank into the chair set against the wall.

"Because she's worried about you. And because she knew you wouldn't want to bother me with it right now."

"Well, maybe she's right. But is that the

craziest thing, to worry about you? Besides, this guy is probably harmless. I'll wait him out, and he'll get bored."

Barr gazed at the ceiling as if begging someone up there to give him patience. Then he looked back at me. "I need to tell you something. And when I'm done, you have to go tell Detective Lane about Allen."

I snorted.

"I mean it," he said. "She's pretty good, from what I can tell, and she's handling most of my caseload while I'm out of commission. Including finding the man who's been attacking women in Cadyville over the past few weeks."

"The 'Cadyville Creep'?" I couldn't keep the sarcasm out of my voice. Why journalists gave cute nicknames to criminals was beyond me.

"He raped one woman, and beat another so badly she ended up in the hospital."

I blinked.

"And while that's bad enough, it's not the worst part. Sophie Mae, his attacks aren't random. All of his victims report getting odd phone calls for a few days before the attack. The next edition of the *Eye* will include that information, and it was in the Seattle papers today, in hopes of convincing anyone who has been getting strange phone calls to be on high alert."

Meghan had been reading that story over her morning coffee, but she hadn't said a word to me. Instead, she'd called Barr. She couldn't talk to me? She had to call my boyfriend instead?

"High alert," I repeated.

"Yes. Like you need to be on right now." His voice was stronger when he was talking about work, but a distinct note of frustration had crept into it as well.

"I'll be careful. Very, very careful. I promise."

"And you'll tell Lane about your phone calls?"

"I'll stop by the station on my way home."

He relaxed back against the pillow. "One more thing. They're letting me out of this place at noon tomorrow. If you can pick me up, we can stop by my place to pick up a few things before going home."

My puzzlement must have shown on my face because his eyebrows lifted, and he said, "You didn't know?"

"Know what?"

He licked his lips. "Meghan acted like you two had talked about it."

"About what?"

"My coming to stay at your place for a few days. She said it would make her feel better to have me there, and frankly, with all the strange things going on, I'd feel better, too."

"Well, of course you should stay with us. It's the perfect solution. You're not a hundred percent yet, so we can take care of you while you scare off any bad guys."

He allowed a small smile to cross his face, but still looked concerned. "This is all news to you?"

I sighed. "Meghan and I are a little off-kilter lately. I told her someone threatened Philip, and she's not very happy about it. Plus, that guy, Allen, keeps calling the house and hanging up. And she's pretty distracted with her new boyfriend."

"Boyfriend? The one she was with at the preserves exchange?"

I was surprised he'd noticed. "Yeah. Kelly something. O'Connell."

"But you guys are okay, right?"

"Me and Meghan? Oh, sure. We're good."

At least I hoped so.

Detective Lane paced the tiny conference room at the Cadyville police station while I told her about the phone calls I'd been getting from Allen. She wore black jeans and a white button-down shirt. Her auburn hair cascaded across the shoulders of a black leather jacket which looked old and worn but was no doubt brand new from Nordstrom and had cost a gazillion bucks. The jacket matched her black leather boots. She looked like she should be on a runway, not chasing nefarious characters.

When I'd finished, she paused and leaned her back against the wall. "What kinds of things has he described doing to you?"

"What? Nothing. He seems to want to talk, is all."

"About death."

I nodded.

"When he calls, does he give you a rundown of what you've done all day, so you know he's been following you, watching you?"

"God, no. He's really quite polite."

She frowned at that. Handing me a sheet of paper, she said, "Fill this out. I'll be back in a minute."

Kind of curt, I thought as I bent to my task. Soon, Detective Lane returned and took the form back, running her gaze quickly over it. She gave the distinct impression I'd provided the wrong answers.

Her tone was speculative, her forehead furrowed. "So you're Sophie Mae Reynolds."

"Yes."

Her eyes looked into a distance that wasn't there, like she was trying to remember something. "What kind of work do you do?"

"I'm a soap maker."

She removed a small black notebook from her jacket pocket, flipped through it. Stopped and scanned the page.

She looked up at me. "Ah."

"Ah?"

"Sergeant Zahn gave me a heads up about you."

"What's that supposed to mean?"

"Seems you like to stick your nose into situations. Why are you really here?"

Stick my nose . . . ? I felt myself flush.

"I'm here because Barr Ambrose insisted that I tell you about this nut job that's been calling and leaving me notes."

"Ah. Detective Ambrose. I see. He's your boyfriend, right?"

I nodded reluctantly. She made it sound like we were in the eighth grade.

"Well, better safe than sorry. Thanks for coming in."

"Can I ask you something?"

She smirked. "Go ahead."

"Are you investigating Philip Heaven's death at all?"

"He's the guy who died from botulism the

other day? Hardly. The Health Department has that well in hand. I have bigger fish to fry, looking for the Cadyville Creep. I'm going to get him. And I'm going to get him fast."

"You don't think Philip's death was at all suspicious," I said in a flat voice. "And you think you're going to breeze in here and solve our cute little crime spree right away, even though Detective Ambrose has been working on it for weeks."

Her features turned hard, and she folded her arms over her chest. Neither of us said a word for several seconds, and I found myself growing increasingly uncomfortable. The seconds grew into what had to be minutes, even if they probably weren't. But by then there was no way I was going to be the one to break the silence. If she wanted to play games then she could very well just —

"Sergeant Zahn was right. You like to stir up trouble. Problem is, people who like to stir up trouble often find themselves smack dab in the middle of it."

I held up my palm. "I was only —"

"No, seriously. I can't have it. I assure you that I'm more than capable. They brought me in to handle things because I'm good. I'm good, and I'm fast. You'll have to trust me on that, and stay out of my way."

"Out of your way."

"Yes. Out of my way."

I thought of Barr lying in the hospital bed. There because someone had poisoned Philip Heaven and gotten sloppy. It was enough to want to find Philip's killer — murder was wrong, plus I felt a strong desire to solve the puzzle. But I really wanted to find out who'd hurt Barr, who'd turned him from the strong confident man I knew into the faded husk currently inhabiting a hospital bed. Again, the possibility that he could have died crossed my mind.

I pushed it away.

What if this woman standing in front of me was as good as she said? She had a certain something, as the French say, only, you know, they say it in French. The way she carried herself. Proud, even a little arrogant, but quietlike, exuding confidence.

"Listen," I said. "There are a lot of suspicious circumstances surrounding Philip Heaven's death. It simply makes sense for the police to look into it further."

She smiled. "Just leave the investigating to me, and stop the small-town busybody thing, okay? Stick with making your little soaps."

Oh. She really shouldn't have said that.

Small-town busybody, indeed. And the condescension in her tone when she referred to my "little soaps." I swear, I could feel the skin tighten across my cheeks, and I had to stop myself before my lips drew back to show my teeth. Her own expression became wary.

"Are you kidding?" I put on my best poker face, which, granted, wasn't much of one. "I can't even tell you how delighted I am that Chief Andy brought in someone from the big city to help the rubes figure out who did what to who out here in the sticks." My tone had taken on a slow western twang to accentuate my sarcasm, though in the back of my mind I cringed at the notion that Chief Maher might learn I'd called him something that sounded like we lived Mayberry. "I'm sure you'll manage to do a right nice job of it, too."

Her face flushed and her eyes flashed anger, but by then I couldn't have cared less. Thoughts of Philip and Barr, and the general good of society being served by a murderer being caught had fled my brain. I wouldn't be proud of it later, but all I could think of was how unbelievably rude this uppity woman from, excuse me, Seattle — not New York or Chicago or flippin' Paris — but Seattle, had managed to be in a matter

184

of a few minutes.

She pointed a finger at me. "I'm not asking. I'm telling you. Keep out of it. All of it. And I'm not going to tell you again."

I smiled as sweetly as I could manage. "I understand."

I'd show her small town. I'd show her busybody.

My foot tapped as the coffeepot hissed and gurgled on the counter. I desperately needed an afternoon caffeine fix. Not much sleep the night before, and plenty yet to do this afternoon, including clearing out the guest room so Barr would have a place to stay.

Meghan came in and ran tap water into a glass, drinking it all down before turning to me with a sigh. "Four clients in a row." She reached her arms, sinewy from the regular workouts of performing deep tissue massage, up to the ceiling and arched her back like a cat. "I feel like I've been digging ditches."

"Why did you call Barr and tell him about Allen? And why did you invite him to stay here without even mentioning the idea to me?"

She looked surprised, and then sheepish. "I'm sorry. I called to see how he was and how he was planning on getting by alone at home, and as we talked I sort of spilled the beans about that Allen character. Then I got the bright idea that he ought to come stay with us and went ahead and asked him right then. I really didn't think you'd mind having him around."

"Of course I don't mind! It's a great idea, and I wish I'd thought of it, I really do. But it seemed like maybe you went around me on purpose, and I couldn't figure out why."

"I wouldn't do that!" Chagrin pinched her features. "I told you, it just kind of came up."

The conversation was taking a defensive turn. I put my hand on her arm. "Meghan, thanks for offering Barr a place here to recover. It's awfully nice of you."

Her face relaxed a little. Why was she wound so tightly lately? I mean, that was my frequent M.O., but she was usually zen personified.

I continued. "I'll clear out the guest bedroom." I knew Meghan wasn't comfortable with Barr staying in my bedroom, not with Erin around. But readying the fourth bedroom upstairs, which we primarily used for storage and junk, would be a challenge.

"Oh, don't bother," Meghan said. "The bed in there is terrible. Erin can move into my bedroom with me, and Barr can have her room."

"I like it," I said, reaching for the full cof-feepot, "but won't she —"

The front door slammed. Her head jerked up in alarm, and I completely forgot about my coffee.

"Erin?" Meghan called.

Something heavy hit the floor. Brodie yelped. We both were out of the kitchen and in the foyer in an instant.

Erin knelt over the little corgi, petting him. His little butt wiggled, which is how he wagged the tail he didn't have, and he strained to lick her face.

"I'm sorry," she murmured. "I didn't mean to scare you."

"What happened?" Meghan asked.

But she didn't get an answer. Erin wouldn't look up. She bent over her dog and buried her face in his fur. I walked over and knelt beside her.

"Bug? Are you crying?"

Sniffle.

"You're going to get Brodie all wet. And then we'll have to blow-dry him like when he gets a bath. He hates that blow dryer, you know."

She sighed and leaned back and gave me a look designed to let me know just how stupid she thought that ploy was. She had,

187

however, stopped crying.

"C'mon," I said, and got to my feet.

"Where." She sounded angry as much as sad.

"Kitchen."

"Spiced pears," Meghan said. "And you can tell us what's going on."

Erin sighed.

"And ice cream," I said.

She cocked her head and stood up. Out of the corner of my eye I saw Meghan shake her head. We trooped into the kitchen, Brodie's toenails clicking on the hardwood behind us.

We settled around the butcher block table and dug in. I stuck to ice cream, somehow not in the mood for pears right then. So, of course, I had an extra dose of ice cream while listening to Erin.

"Jonathan's dropping out of the bee," she said.

"He is? Why?" Meghan asked.

"His dumb friends think it's dumb. They started teasing him about hanging out with me and studying, called him a brainiac. And some other stuff."

"And he didn't like that."

" 'Course not. But he just, like, totally gave in and dropped out. I mean, he didn't stand up for himself at all."

188

"And he didn't stand up for you, either," I said, taking a stab at why she might be so upset.

She shook her head. "He acted like he didn't even know me, all day," she whispered. "Wouldn't talk to me, or even look at me. Then when I asked if he wanted to come over after school, he told me to leave him alone."

"That wasn't nice." I said. Meghan gave me a look. "It wasn't," I insisted. "And I bet it made you feel pretty crappy, too."

Erin nodded, and her throat worked."

"It's not your fault if he's a jerk," Meghan said.

"Maybe he'll change his mind," Erin said, a glimmer of hope crossing her features.

"Maybe he will. Maybe he won't. Either way, you can go ahead and win that spelling bee yourself," I said.

"Oh, no. I'm not gonna do the bee without Jonathan."

"Well, I won't make you," her mother said. "Of course I wouldn't do that, but I think you should still do it. The bee wasn't all about Jonathan, was it?"

"Well . . ."

"You were only doing it because of him?"

"No . . . well . . ."

"Oh. Gosh, Erin." Meghan couldn't keep

the disappointment out of her voice.

I jumped in. "It sure would be cool if you went ahead and did it by yourself. Especially if you do well. That'd kind of show him it's not dumb after all, wouldn't it?"

She bit her lower lip and glanced up at me. "Maybe."

"Well, think about it, okay?" Meghan knew when to back off, and I followed her lead. "How do sloppy Joes sound for dinner?"

Erin brightened. "With macaroni and cheese?"

Meghan smiled. "Maybe."

Sixteen

Kyla and Cyan worked hard that afternoon, helping me wrap cocoa butter and jojoba soap with bands fashioned from torn banana paper and labels printed with the Winding Road logo. Kyla was a senior at Cadyville High, and spent most of the time we worked talking about the colleges she'd applied to. As she enthusiastically rambled on about moving out and living in a dorm, her sister rolled her eyes and made noises of disgust from the other side of the table. I imagined she'd heard it all before, and perhaps felt left out of things. In another two years she'd be going through the same thing, though.

In the meantime, maybe she'd have a friend who'd be interested in taking over Kyla's after-school job with Winding Road; I could already tell I'd be losing the older girl's help come summer.

That made me think about the second email Philip had received, the one from the mother whose daughter had called the Help-line.

"Hey, do you guys know a girl named Lisa Koller?" I asked.

Cyan snorted.

Kyla paused in wrapping a bar of soap, glanced up at me, then resumed her work. "Sure. She's in some of my classes."

"So she's graduating this year?"

"Yeah."

"Tell me a little bit about her. What's she like?"

Cyan looked horrified. "You're not thinking about hiring her, are you?"

"I take it that wouldn't be a very good idea," I said.

The older girl shook her head, apparently in agreement with her sister. "Cyan's right. She's bad news."

"How come? Trouble?"

She made a face. "Sort of. Not bad. But she's a royal pain in the you-know-what. Tries to boss everyone around, thinks she's hot stuff, acts like the whole world owes her."

"Does she have a lot of friends?"

"She used to. But after her dad died she started being mean to all of them, and after a while no one wanted to deal with her anymore. I mean, we all knew she was, like, traumatized, and it was real sad and all, but it got so it was like she didn't want anyone to be her friend, even when we tried."

"That must have been kind of hard, trying to help and having her push you away."

Kyla nodded. "It was. I felt pretty guilty for not trying, but what were we supposed to do?"

"It's hard to help someone who doesn't want it. I bet if she needed you now, you'd be there," I said.

"I guess."

Cyan snorted again. Kyla ignored her.

"How long ago did her dad die?"

"Couple of years. We were sophomores. He was in a car accident on Highway 2."

I seemed to remember that. Drunk driver swerved into his lane and ran him off the road, from what I could recall.

"And her mother? What's she do?" I asked.

"She's a bookkeeper or something. My mom knows her pretty well. She's — Hey, who's that?" Kyla interrupted herself, pointing out the back window.

I glanced over my shoulder before turning back to the label in my hand. "Luke Chase. He and his brother are building a chicken coop for us."

"What for?"

I lifted one eyebrow. "So we'll have a place

to put the pullets once they're old enough this spring." Meghan and I had done our research and decided having fresh eggs from our own hens would be worth a little extra work. I was already dreaming of those gorgeous orange yolks you get when they eat fresh greens, of homemade mayonnaise and real angel food cake . . .

"They sound like a stinky pain," Kyla said, sealing her opinion with a curled lip.

"Is that his brother?" Cyan asked.

Another glance up from me. "Yeah, that's Seth."

"How old is he?" Cyan seemed much more interested in the boys than in chickens. Who could blame her?

I put down the bar of soap and walked over to the window. "I'm not sure. Seth is a couple years younger than Luke, I'm guessing. Maybe twenty-one?"

The girls joined me at the window.

"Hmm. Maybe a little younger," Kyla said, her voice sure. Well, she'd be able to tell. I'd steadily lost my ability to estimate the age of others as my own age increased.

"Does Luke have a girlfriend?" she asked. "He's cute."

"I have no idea," I said, smiling. "But I thought you had a boyfriend."

"She does." Disapproval weighed Cyan's

tone. "And he's applying to the same colleges she is, so he can be with her."

Kyla shrugged. "Hard to tell what's going to happen with us. Besides, I was just asking."

Luke looked up then and saw the three of us standing at the window watching them. I waved, and he raised a hesitant hand in response. I turned back to the job at hand, feeling like a dirty old woman. Kyla joined me, her fair complexion reddening.

Cyan boldly studied the boys for a few more moments, unabashed that they were aware of her gaze. "I wouldn't mind a boyfriend of my own right now," I heard her say under her breath before she also came back and got to work.

I frowned. She was only sixteen, and even Seth was way too old for her. It was probably adolescent fantasy, as so many quick crushes like that are. I hoped so; her mom would kill me if she found out I had anything to do with Cyan getting involved with either of the Chase boys.

The brothers finished up their work on the coop for the day, and shortly after that the girls finished up their work for me and left for home. I took a break and went out to check Luke and Seth's progress.

Situated at the end of our large backyard, their new home was bound to make our future hens happy. We'd only planned on getting four of them to start with, purchased as day-old chicks in a few more weeks and then raised under lamps in the old mudroom off the kitchen. Hopefully the "guarantee" of getting pullets as opposed to cockerels from the local feed store was a good one, since we weren't allowed to have any roosters within the city limits.

The boys had finished the A-framed roosting house where the chickens would sleep, as well as the adjacent nesting house. The latter structure was a rectangular box on legs that contained two removable frames where the hens would lay eggs, and sported an angled roof that lifted up so we'd have easy access. Two-by-fours protruded from the ends so the girls would have a place to perch and preen off the ground when they weren't in the roosting house. Both the roosting and nesting houses had their first coats of red barn paint. I was also pleased to see that they'd nearly finished stapling the heavy two-by-four-inch wire to the exterior frame. Now they had to put the chicken wire over the top — more to keep predators out than to keep the chickens in — and add several inches of round gravel to the floor for easy cleanup with a hose. It made me want to go buy those cute little baby chicks right away.

Back inside, I took a quick inventory in my storeroom to see what I needed to mix up next, and discovered the gel room fresheners I'd recently added to my product list were more popular than I'd anticipated. Time to make more. I'd gather the ingredients tonight and be ready to manufacture the next day. Kyla and Cyan and I could work as a kind of assembly line.

The sound of the phone ringing upstairs registered somewhere in my consciousness as I dug out my recipe and double-checked the various adjustments and improvements I'd made to it over time. Erin opened the door at the top of the stairs and shouted down to me.

"Sophie Mae! It's for you."

She held the phone out to me with a bored look as I came up the stairs. Would it have killed her to bring it downstairs? Heck, it was probably just Allen anyway, all revved up for a chat about the Grim Reaper.

I braced to hear his voice. "Hello?"

"Sophie Mae. It's Rhea Waters." Kyla and Cyan's mother.

"Hi, Rhea. How have you been?"

We chatted for a few minutes, catching up

in a superficial way as acquaintances who never quite got around to being good friends do. Then she said, "Kyla said you were asking about Mandy Koller. Are you looking for an accountant?"

My ears perked up double at that. I wanted to know more about Mandy Koller, *and* I was looking for an accountant.

"As it happens, I have been thinking about offloading some of my Winding Road bookwork," I answered truthfully.

"Well, I can't recommend Mandy enough. She's bright, savvy about taxes, efficient, and her rates are quite reasonable."

"She sounds terrific. Do you and your husband use her?"

"Oh, heavens no. We don't have very complicated taxes, and she specializes in small businesses." Rhea's husband, a nondescript man whose name I could never seem to remember, was an electrician. "But I've known her for years. I know I'm recommending her as a friend, but I assure you everything I've told you is true. If you're wondering, check out her website. She offers a free consultation so potential clients get a chance to interview her."

"You've known her a long time?"

"Oh, yes. For well over a decade. We used to be neighbors. When her husband died, it was so tragic. But she pulled herself together and got her degree, and now she's working her tail off getting her CPA business off the ground."

Hmmm. "So she doesn't have a great deal of experience," said the side of me who never wanted to add debit and credit columns ever again.

"I wouldn't steer you wrong. Just give her a try."

"Thanks for the referral, Rhea. I'll check her out."

"You won't regret it."

If I ended up with an accountant, great, I thought as I hung up. But at the very least I had an excuse to go talk to Mandy Koller, and I could guarantee the subject of Philip Heaven and his penchant for dispensing advice willy nilly would come up in the conversation.

Mandy's website looked like it had been professionally designed, and as Rhea had said, she offered a preliminary consultation. I called, got her voicemail, and left a message asking to set up an appointment as soon as possible. I was pushing it, since it was already late February, smack dab in the middle of tax season.

I packed up four retail orders from my website before the tantalizing fragrance of

Meghan's cooking wafted down from the kitchen. It was early, only five o'clock, but I followed it up the stairs like some cartoon character snagged by the curlingly visible scent of pie cooling on a window sill.

Not that we were having pie, mind you. Sloppy Joes, made with Meghan's mother's homemade tomato sauce and a boatload of spices, and a casserole of macaroni and cheese laced with sharp cheddar, parmesan, and cream cheeses and sprinkled with bacon sat in the middle of the butcher block kitchen table. Erin was setting the table with plates and silverware, while Meghan tossed a simple salad of greens with balsamic vinaigrette.

She spoke to me over her shoulder. "Mary-jake called. She wanted to know if we had an extra jar of pickled asparagus. She didn't get any at the exchange, and it's one of her favorites."

"It's one of my favorites, too," I grumped.

"Which is why we took so few jars to give away. Take some over to her tonight, okay?"

"Oh, all right."

We ate, and Erin helped me with the dishes while Meghan ran up to change and primp. I packed a tote bag with Erin's homework and a book to read in case she finished early and tired of Nardella's Trea-

200

sures. Then I put in a hardback novel for me and the pickled asparagus for Maryjake. I was thinking about adding a snack when the doorbell rang. I glanced at my watch and muttered something under my breath.

"What?" Erin asked, all wide-eyed.

"Never mind. It's six, we're already behind, so grab your shoes and let's go go go." I knew Maryjake would be waiting for me, no doubt tapping her toe and thinking bad thoughts about volunteers who showed up for their shifts late.

"Geez. Okay."

I went to answer the door, but Meghan already had it open. I stopped dead in my tracks when I saw her practically fall into the arms of the man on the doorstep.

He was handsome, I had to admit that. When she pulled back from their hello kiss I saw how well their looks complemented each other. But there was no way this was their first date, was it? Because I could feel the fire between them from where I stood thirty feet away.

Then I saw he wore an old pea coat. A funky hat peeked out of the pocket, a tassel hanging down from the earflap.

My breath caught in my throat. I recognized both the coat and the hat — and now the man.

Why had Kelly O'Connell been watching Heaven House last night?

I coughed.

Meghan turned. "Oh, Kelly, this is my housemate and best friend, Sophie Mae Reynolds. Sophie Mae, Kelly O'Connell."

I pasted a smile on my face. "Hi, Kelly."

"Hey. Saw you at the preserves exchange, but with all the excitement I didn't get a chance to introduce myself." He didn't seem to recognize me from the night before. Of course, I'd had the light behind me, and he probably couldn't see me very well. Or, maybe he was simply a better actor than I was.

"Erin!" I called. "Come on."

"I'm *coming*." She clattered down the stairs and snagged her coat off the hall tree. She greeted Kelly and wished her mother a fun evening as I got my own coat, and we practically ran out the door. I really wanted to find out more about Kelly; maybe Mary-jake could enlighten me, if she wasn't too mad at me for showing up after my shift had officially started.

Seventeen

Maryjake was indeed waiting, but she didn't seem at all upset that I was late. In fact, I was pretty sure she hadn't even noticed, she was so involved in conversation with Jude when Erin and I walked in.

"I'm going to set up Erin in the game room to do some homework, okay?"

Jude, crouched over a pile of papers at a nearby table, paused in leafing through them to give me a brilliant smile. "There's a new table and chairs in there, but it's kind of loud and crowded now. Might be hard to concentrate. We've got people working, putting up some shelves."

It was the first time I'd seen him genuinely happy.

"The Chase brothers?" I asked.

He nodded.

Maryjake jumped in. "Shelves for games and books, and a dartboard on the back wall. The pool-slash-ping pong table and a big television will be here next week."

"Wow."

"I know. Jude is making it a real game room, where teenagers can come after school and hang out. It'll be great."

He looked away, modest, but the smile remained on his face. That room had been slated to be a game room for teens from the beginning. Philip had only been gone for four days, and Jude was already more efficient.

"So are you taking over Heaven House?" I asked him.

His gaze met mine for an instant before flicking away. He had very nice eyes, a light, clear green under that thick shock of blonde hair. Philip had had mostly red eyes, and mostly no hair. It was hard to believe they'd been related.

"It looks that way," he said. "The board hasn't voted to confirm it yet, so nothing's written in stone."

Maryjake said, "But they told him to go ahead and move into Philip's apartment upstairs, so that sounds like they want him to keep HH going, don't you think?"

As they spoke, I'd been looking around, seeing the place as if for the first time. There was real potential there. "From what I can see, they couldn't choose anyone better," I said.

Blushing a little, Jude looked down at the floor. "Thanks."

"Let me know if you need any help packing up or moving. My little pickup is at your disposal," I said.

He turned a little redder. "I might need to take you up on that. I don't have much to move, but I can't fit anything very big in my little compact."

"Anytime," I said.

Erin tugged at my arm. I looked down. "Sorry. Let's find you a good place to do your homework."

"I don't have very much. And it's Friday. Can't I go play pinball?"

I waffled. She had a point, but I didn't want to get on her mother's bad side. "Tell you what — you do half your homework first, and then you can go play Nardella."

She made a little groaning noise in the back of her throat.

"I thought you said you didn't have much homework. If that's true then it won't take you very long to do half of it, now will it?"

"Oh, fine. But can't I do it in the game room? Please?"

I was pretty sure Erin had a bit of a crush on Luke Chase. Harmless enough.

"Sure," I said.

To her disappointment, the boys were almost finished. She marched over to the long table that now ran along the wall opposite the windows and began wrestling with a metal folding chair.

"Let me help you," I said.

"I've got it."

I smiled and left her to it. From the main room I heard Luke offer to help her. This time I didn't hear such a quick refusal.

The front door opened. I turned to see Ruth Black stride in. She wore a bright red wool coat with a wild multi-colored scarf and cowboy boots. Her knitting bag hung from one hand.

Maryjake called out a greeting, and Jude murmured something I couldn't hear. I said hello and walked over to where she'd plopped into the worn wooden chair next to Maryjake's desk.

"Hi, everyone. Gosh, it's a busy evening here, isn't it?" Ruth said, looking at the pile of papers in front of Jude and cocking her head at the pounding that had commenced in the game room.

"The Chase boys are putting up some shelves in the game room," I explained.

"And a dartboard," Maryjake added, again. She seemed awfully excited about the dartboard.

"Well, that's lovely," Ruth said. She shrugged out of her coat and retrieved a pair of circular knitting needles with something tweedy hanging off them.

"Ruth? Did I get my scheduling mixed up?" I asked.

"Hmmm? No, I don't think so." She went back to her knitting.

I tried again. "Are you answering the Helpline tonight?"

"Oh, no. I just stopped by to see how things were going here. And because I knew you'd be here."

"Well, I'd sure appreciate the company," I said, thinking rather wistfully about that hardcover novel I'd brought with me. I hadn't had time to read for ages, and a nice slow evening answering the occasional Helpline call had seemed like time with excellent reading potential.

"Oh, that's sweet, honey. But I'm not staying long. I just wanted to see what you found out about those beets. Did I tell you those people from the Health Department came and took *all* of my canned goods? Jalepeno jelly and pickled cauliflower, even. Every last jar."

Pickled cauliflower? Yuck.

"You did mention it, Ruth. I'm so sorry. I

know you must have had quite a store," I said.

"A whole pantry full, plus everything we got from the preserves exchange the other night. I mean, Uncle Thad and I had made some inroads on last fall's canning over the winter, but there was an awful lot left. I think they ought to have to pay you when they take your food away like that."

"But didn't they do it because of the botulism?" Jude asked.

I glared at him, and his eyes widened.

Ruth stopped knitting and stared at the wool on her lap, her still hands clutching the knitting needles. "Those weren't my beets that killed Philip," she said through clenched teeth. "Those beets came from someplace else." She looked up at me. "Did you find out anything?"

I shook my head. "I'm sorry. No one I talked to, and I talked to everyone that was at the exchange — except Maryjake here, come to think of it. No one I talked to knew anything about canned beets. Apparently you're the only one who makes them."

Ruth started knitting again. "Well, that's stupid. I can't be the only one who cans beets. And I keep telling you" — her voice rose now — "I keep telling you that I don't can beets like that. Sliced. Round. So someone else has to. My dear friend Hannah used to can them that way before she died, and I know it's how most people do it."

"Yes, I'm sure someone else in Cadyville cans beets like —" I began.

"What about you? Do you know anyone who cans beets?" Ruth asked Maryjake. Jude had returned to sifting through the pile of paperwork.

"Did James tell you I called?" I added.

Maryjake nodded, then lifted her shoulders in a shrug. "I don't know what to tell you. I don't like the things, and neither does James. Are you sure those beets weren't yours, Ruth?" Her voice sounded a little rough, and something else rode in it. Anger? I wouldn't be surprised. Did she actually blame Ruth for Philip's death? "Did you drop them by early, before the exchange?"

The older woman stood up. "You know I didn't, Maryjake Dreggle." She stuffed her knitting back in the bag and slipped her arms back into her long vermillion coat. "I did not bring anything here before the exchange. I did not can the beets they found in Philip's apartment. And I did not kill him."

And with that she turned and stalked out.

"Ruth, wait," I called, but she ignored me.

I started to go after her, but the phone rang. I looked at Maryjake, and she looked at me, then pointedly at the phone. With a grimace I grabbed the phone off the hook.

"Heaven House Helpline," I answered.

"Um. Hi. I was wondering if you could give me some information about women's shelters in the area." The woman sounded like she was on the verge of tears but still managing to keep it together. Staying as matter of fact as possible, despite imagining all sorts of horrible things that could have happened to her, I gave her all the referral numbers I had and encouraged her to call back if she needed any more help. With great dignity she thanked me and hung up. I silently wished her well and cradled the phone.

Ruth was long gone by then. Jude was talking in an undertone to the Chase boys in the corner, waving his arms as he described who-knew-what. Erin had finished half of her homework, or at least what she told me was half her homework, and had retired to the game room to indulge in Nardella's Treasures. Maryjake was nowhere to be seen.

Grabbing the phone off the hook, I accessed an outside line and prayed no one would decide to call the Helpline for a few minutes.

Barr was awake and itching to be out of the hospital. He sounded both tired and bored.

Well, good, because I had a job for him. I told him about Kelly, and how I'd seen him outside Heaven House after midnight the previous night. Of course, that necessitated revealing what I'd been doing there then, so I went ahead and filled him in. He took it well, all in all, and promised to make a couple of calls to friends of his at the station to find out more about Mr. O'Connell. I thanked him profusely, so relieved to have him on my side. All evening I'd been thinking about Meghan, out on the town with this character we knew virtually nothing about, and the more I thought about it the more the sick feeling in my stomach grew. That poor woman was beset with the worst taste in men.

I settled back and cracked open my book, feeling almost wicked for taking the time to read when I should have been doing bookwork. But I was going to see an accountant, right? So maybe I could slack on the bookwork a little. Plus, I'd had a pretty crappy week, overall. I not only deserved to read my book, but to do it in a bubble bath.

I'd take what I could get.

At least for five minutes, until Maryjake came back downstairs from where she'd presumably been in the office. She slid onto the chair where Ruth had been sitting earlier and let out a big whoosh of breath.

"It's been a week, hasn't it?" I said by way of commentary.

She gave me a look. "It's completely and totally sucked, Sophie Mae. Utterly and awfully sucked. Sometimes I feel like I'm going insane."

"James said you had a migraine the other day."

She nodded. "I get them when I'm stressed. It's like someone stuck knives in my eyes."

"Sounds painful," I said. And a little too graphic.

"You can't imagine."

"Are you afraid you'll lose your job?" I asked.

She looked horrified. "If Jude keeps HH going? I do good work, I really do. Why would they fire me?"

"They wouldn't, of course. I didn't mean to worry you. Obviously Jude has things under control." There you go, Sophie Mae, as tactless as ever. "And I'm sure you're a great help to him."

She snorted. "You could say that. He

doesn't know much about the day-to-day business stuff."

"Stuff like banking and paying bills and things?"

"Philip preferred to do most of that without my help, and Jude's the same way. So I guess he's figuring all that out for himself."

I hoped he did a better job than Philip did, or else the lights at Heaven House would be shut off within a week.

She continued. "I mean that he needs to know about how to put together proposals for foundation funding, or how to deal with the city council and the mayor."

"Really? I didn't know you had much contact with them."

She fidgeted with a hangnail. "We did at first. Then the HH projects kind of slowed down, and they lost interest in what we had to say. But I think Jude can change that. He needs to understand the past interactions, though."

No doubt. I added the city council and the mayor to the increasing list of people whom Philip had managed to alienate.

Changing the subject, I asked. "Maryjake, what do you know about Kelly O'Connell?"

"He's pretty good-looking, isn't he?"

"I guess so. I was wondering more about

his personality."

She gave me a yeah-sure look. "He's nice. Asks a lot of questions, and he's interested in the answers, you know? Not like most guys. He and Philip spent a lot of time dinking around, talking about all kinds of stuff. Blah blah blah. I mean, I thought it was booooring, but Philip really liked him."

Huh. I glanced around. "What about Jude?"

"What about him?"

"They were cousins, right? Were they close?"

Maryjake looked skeptical. "I think Philip wanted to be close. I mean, he brought Jude out here to work with him, brought him into the foundation, actually. Jude's mother was Philip's father's sister. But the old man, Nathaniel Heaven?"

I nodded. Philip and Jude's grandfather.

"He was an old-school kind of guy, and he didn't like the man Jude's mother married. So he pretty much disowned her. Philip felt bad about that, and he's the one who insisted Jude should come live in Cadyville and help with HH. He's got a degree in sociology, after all, totally qualified to work in a community center like Heaven House."

214

Sounded to me like he was way overqualified.

"Anyway, he came here, from someplace out east, I don't know where, New York or New Jersey or New something-or-other. But he and Philip never got very close. It's a shame, really." She looked at her watch. "Oh, gosh, I've gotta go. Hubby's waiting."

That surprised me. I could see James waiting for Maryjake, but I had a harder time imagining her giving a darn whether he did or not.

She threw her things together and hurried out. As the door swung closed behind her, I sat back and looked around the room. Jude had returned from inspecting the Chase boys' work. Now he stood in the corner, staring at me. I met his gaze until he looked away. The phone sat there like a lump on the desk. Clangs and dings issuing from the game room indicated Erin was still playing pinball. Luke and Seth moved in and out, packing up their tools.

I motioned Jude over. He shambled across the room to me. "Do you know much about Kelly O'Connell?" I asked.

His eyebrows drew together. "He seems like a good enough guy."

"Meghan mentioned that he's a financial consultant, up here to get away from the rat race in Seattle," I prompted.

"Sounds right."

"You don't know anything else?"

"Not really. He showed up one day and offered to help out however he could. I suggested to Philip that he help with the books, but Philip wasn't really interested." He sighed. "And believe me, Philip could have used some help with the books."

No kidding.

"So what did he end up doing? Volunteer-wise, I mean," I asked.

"Um . . . now that you mention it, I'm not really sure. He was here a lot for a few weeks, and then showed up less and less frequently. He spent a bunch of time with Philip, I know that."

Curious. Especially, since I thought Jude knew everything that went on at Heaven House.

EIGHTEEN

I eyed the jar of asparagus pickles that sat smack dab in the middle of Maryjake's desk. I'd forgotten to give them to her before she left. I hadn't had time to put together a snack before we had to leave to come over to the HH, and now I was feeling a little peckish.

No. I could wait until we got home. Otherwise, I'd just have to bring Maryjake another jar.

I repacked my book, of which I'd read a grand total of four pages, with Erin's things and began bundling her into her winter garb in order to venture back out into the brisk evening. The temperature had dropped, and there was a bite in the air that reminded me a bit of my childhood in Colorado. We might see some snow flurries before morning. Though it snowed only a few times a year in western Washington, when it did everybody went nuts. Schools closed, people avoided going to work, traffic was impossibly snarled, trees fell, and frequent power outages brought out the generators and firewood.

This wouldn't be one of those storms, or at least I didn't guess so. We'd have heard about it on the television and radio for days, as weather was big news in the Northwest. After all, we had to know when to stock up on water and batteries and otherwise panic unnecessarily, and the good folks on the local news were more than happy to keep us informed of any possibility of danger.

Boy, was I ever in a bad mood, thinking mean thoughts about anchor people who were probably nice as pie. It didn't help that I was a very tired camper after all my late nights.

Erin snugged her hat down over her ears. Jude had agreed, at my request, to stick around and walk us out to the Toyota after my Helpline shift was over. I wasn't sure if he'd be any great deterrent for a stalker — or a killer — but I figured it'd make Meghan happy.

The phone rang.

"I've got it," I called. "Heaven House Helpline."

"Hi, Sophie Mae. Are you getting ready to go home now?"

"Allen."

"I like it that you call me that."

"What else am I supposed to call you? You wouldn't tell me your real name."

"But you're the only one who calls me that. It's like a thing between us."

Sudden fear stabbed through me. "Stop it. There is no thing between us. Leave me alone."

"But I like you."

"Please. Leave me alone," I whispered.

"Oh. Gosh. You're really scared, huh. Don't be scared. I'm not trying to scare you."

"Then go away and don't call me anymore."

Erin watched me with round eyes. She scratched her nose with one mittened hand and waited. I could hear Allen's breathing through the phone line.

"But —" he said.

"Please." I hung up.

Had I made things worse? I might have sent someone with suicidal tendencies over the edge. But I didn't care, not anymore. There was only so much I could handle.

Jude looked at me kind of funny, but didn't comment at the grip I had on his arm as we went out to my truck.

"Will you watch me drive away, see if

anyone follows? Look for their license plate number?" I asked.

His eyebrows knit together. "What's going on?"

I glanced down at Erin, who said, "Tell him."

"I seem to have picked up a stalker. He called right before we left. He knows where I am and that my shift is over."

Jude opened my truck door and boosted Erin in. "Get in and lock the doors. I'll stay behind you all the way home, see if anyone follows."

Relief eased the muscles in my neck. I slid into the driver's seat. "Thank you. That makes me feel a lot better."

"No problem. Just wait until you see my headlights come on before you go. It's that little Civic over there." He pointed.

"Okay. Hey, what about the Helpline?"

He patted his pocket. "Already forwarded to my cell phone. And I keep the referral numbers with me all the time. It'll be fine."

"You okay, Bug?" I asked as we waited for Jude's headlights to flare. I regretted talking Meghan into letting her come with me. She'd been right: Erin would have been better off staying with Tootie.

Beside me, she nodded.

"Not scared?"

She shook her head, but I could see her jaw was clenched. "I thought you said this guy wasn't scary."

"I'm just being careful."

"Right." That one word overflowed with a combination of fear and anger.

The ride home was uneventful. The only headlights I saw behind me were Jude's, and he hung way back, giving anyone else who might want to follow me a chance. Allen either wasn't waiting on my route home, or else had seen Jude was following me and decided not to play. Either way, Erin and I hustled from my truck into the house. I waved to Jude to let him know we were fine, then shut and locked the door behind me.

The house had an empty feel. Meghan and Kelly were still out.

"Want a snack?" I asked Erin.

"No," she said, hanging her coat on the hall tree. "I'm going to bed."

"Hey, I'm sorry, okay?"

"Whatever. Goodnight."

For the first time, I got really good and angry at Just-Call-Me-Allen.

Mandy Koller had left a message on my voicemail. A client had canceled, and she had an appointment available at 9:40 the next morning. I called back, reached her voicemail, and left her a message saying I'd be there.

Ah, the electronic age.

I sat on the sofa and tried to read my book but couldn't concentrate worth a darn. Meghan wasn't exactly late, since she hadn't told me when she'd be home. I'd decided to go downstairs and use some of my nervous energy to get some work done when she and Kelly walked in.

"You guys have a good time?" I asked.

They looked at each other, all starry-eyed. This time it didn't strike me as all that cute.

"We had a great time," Kelly said. "We're going for a picnic with Erin tomorrow."

"Um, in case you hadn't noticed, it's winter. And raining. And possibly going to snow."

"I've reserved a yurt up in the mountains. The Forest Service lets you use them. It's covered, and there's a woodstove. Even if it's pouring down rain, we'll be snug as a bug. Or as three bugs."

Good Lord. A *yurt*? Ack.

But more importantly, Meghan and Erin off for a secluded picnic with someone who could very well be a wacko? No way.

Meghan smiled.

I tried not to scowl. "Sounds grand."

Then I made sure to infringe on their

romantic goodnights like a nosy mother, until finally Kelly gave Meghan a big smacker of a kiss and opened the front door.

"See you later, Kelly," I called.

"See you," he said, and left.

Meghan turned on me with a glare. "What was *that* all about?"

"Don't go on that picnic tomorrow. Please."

Her head jerked back a fraction in surprise. "Why not?"

"I don't trust him."

"I don't get it. You don't even know him."

"Do you?"

"Know him? More than you do, that's for darn sure, and I plan on learning a lot more."

It didn't matter. Serial killers were known by their neighbors — and their wives, for that matter — as nice guys. This tack wasn't going to work.

Taking a deep breath, I said, "I saw him outside Heaven House last night."

She looked at me like I was nuts.

"Late. Like, one a.m. He was on the street, hiding behind a truck and watching me in the window."

"The window. Of Heaven House."

"Uh, yeah. Upstairs." I held up my hand to stop her before she got started. "I was

223

there to check out the threats Philip told me he'd received. I had to find out more, I just had to. You understand that, right?"

Her eyes narrowed. "How did you get in?"

"I kind of borrowed your key," I said in a small voice.

"You stole my key to break into Heaven House and snoop through, what, Philip's office? And while you were there saw Kelly, or at least *think* you saw Kelly, on the street? It might not have even been him, right? But if it was, he lives very close to there. Did I mention that? Maybe he couldn't sleep. Maybe he was taking a walk. One of the reasons he moved here in the first place was so he could walk around at night without worrying about getting mugged."

I chose not to mention the Cadyville Creep right then.

She continued. "Because of that you don't want — what is it exactly that you don't want? For me to see him anymore? Is that it? Are you jealous? That I've finally met someone I get along with as well as you get along with Barr?"

"Of course not! Meghan, I —"

"You know what? I don't want to hear it. I'm going on that picnic with Kelly tomorrow, and Erin is coming with us. End of story."

She turned and stormed upstairs. Meghan had been mad at me before, but never like this. I'd only been trying to protect her, get her to slow down a little until we could find out more about this O'Connell character, but instead I ended up with a sick tremor in my stomach and no hope of going to sleep anytime soon.

I worked until almost four a.m. before finally tumbling into bed and sleeping like the dead. When I stumbled down to the kitchen at eight, showered and dressed but feeling more than a little gritty and light-headed, Meghan stood staring out the window at the wet yard, coffee cup in hand. It hadn't snowed after all.

I hesitated. "Where's Erin?"

"Out watching them string wire on the chicken coop."

The Chase brothers had apparently begun work already. No doubt they'd be done by the end of the day — unless, of course, they had to leave for one of Jude's many projects at HH.

"When do you go pick up Barr?" Meghan asked. Her tone was strained, but she was obviously trying to act like things were back to normal between us.

I was game. "Noon."

"Before we go, I'll make sure Erin's room is cleared out enough for you to move him right in."

"Okay. Thanks."

"No problem."

I poured a cup of coffee, and we sipped in silence for a few minutes.

"Did you get any sleep?" Meghan asked.

"Some."

"Here. At least eat this."

"Oh, Meghan, I don't need —"

"Eat it."

I took the proffered slab of banana bread, slathered with cream cheese. "Thanks. Um, Meghan?"

She put her coffee cup in the sink. "Yeah?"

"Just be careful, okay?"

A pause, then she looked at me and nodded. "I know you have my best interests at heart. I just wish you knew Kelly. He's one of the good ones."

"But, still."

"I'll be careful. I promise."

NINETEEN

The sun tried to break through the crumpled clouds above, mere hints of yellow light touching a patch of wet grass here, a moss-covered tree limb there. Anywhere else in the country they'd laugh, but in the Northwest in February we counted that as a partly sunny day. I was just happy to have a brief reprieve from the rain, despite the bite that remained in the air.

I drove past Caladia Acres, following Pine Street as it narrowed and veered north, soon turning into County Road 18. Five minutes later I was well out of Cadyville and winding among small acreages. Llamas and alpacas peered over fences, dogs lay on front porches surveying their territories, and red barns reached gray slate roofs toward the brightening sky. Watching the numbers painted on mailboxes at the end of the driveways, I found 18223 and turned onto the bladed gravel road.

Ahead, the Kollers' putty-colored manufactured home was surrounded by a neat, well-maintained fence made from recycled plastic the same dull beige of the house. Nearer the structure, the encouraging green spikes of bulbs in the precise flower beds promised spring was indeed on the way, despite Puxatawny Phil's usual failure to spy his shadow. A tiny two-stall horse barn sat diagonally back from the house four hundred yards or so, with one end open to a small paddock where a huge white horse with shaggy feet the size of hubcaps watched my pickup approach with laconic disinterest.

I stopped the vehicle and turned off the engine, got out, and slammed the door. Stood there for at least a minute, facing the house with my hands on my hips, telling myself I was giving Mandy a chance to notice I was there, but in reality gathering enough moxie to interview a stranger about her daughter.

Then I thought of Barr the first time I'd seen him in the hospital bed, and of Philip, gray and struggling for breath and now very, very dead.

Across the road, crows began to gather on the bare branches of a lone alder tree. Their harsh calls raked the clear air like claws on a blackboard.

Following up on the emails Philip had received had to be done, and no one else seemed willing to do it. Galvanized, I crunched across the driveway, but before I reached the front step the door opened, and a dark-haired woman wearing jeans and an orange fleece zipper-front warm-up jacket stepped out to meet me. Freckles sprinkled her upturned nose, and her lips turned up in a grin that revealed perfect white teeth.

"Hi," she said.

"Hi." I stood looking up at her, and at that moment it seemed that the lack of sleep over the last three days would crush me into the gravel beneath. Taking a deep breath, I said, "I'm Sophie Mae Reynolds. I have a nine-forty appointment to talk about my business accounting needs."

She beckoned me in. "Of course you are. Coffee's on. Let's see what I can do to help you out."

The living room was overstuffed and comfortable, the kitchen floor worn, the décor overall unimaginative and far more about function than aesthetic. But the coffee was hot and strong enough to strip tar off a roof, just the way I needed it, and the air smelled of bacon and onions and other good things. We settled into the breakfast nook tucked into the end of the kitchen, steaming cups between us, and with a view of the muddy paddock. It was so bucolic and soothing I didn't know if I'd be able to haul my sorry carcass out of there when my hour was up.

"Tell me about your business."

I did, explaining that I'd designed, manufactured, and marketed handmade toiletry items for a little over two years, and that my wholesale and internet business had picked up to the point where I really needed some help with the bookkeeping. "Taxes are such a pain that I've been farming them out from the beginning, but I'd really prefer someone with a better understanding of my business do them."

She nodded her understanding. "You make soap? Like from lye?"

"That, and melt-and-pour."

"I've done some of that, too. It's so much fun — and fascinating how you mix a bunch of oils and butters and beeswax and stuff together with a little lye from the cleaning aisle at the grocery store, and you end up with something that gets you clean in the shower."

Her enthusiasm made me smile. I knew other people who made soap, had in fact taught several classes, but it was always nice to meet someone who was interested. We talked about soap making for a bit, and she asked several pertinent questions about the particulars of how I did business.

"Well, I can help you take care of the accounting side of things. We'd work out just how much or how little help you want," she said and quoted me her rates. They weren't too cheap, which would have been a red flag, but they seemed manageable. I asked for and got the names of three clients and permission to call them for references.

"Rhea Waters gave you a huge thumbs-up," I said. "Couldn't say enough nice things about you."

"Oh, Rhea's a sweetie, she really is. I don't think I've had a bigger cheerleader since I decided to start my own business."

"Her daughters help me out," I said. "They said they go to school with your daughter. Lisa, isn't it?"

A shadow crossed her face, and she looked down at her cup. "That's right. She's a senior at Cadyville High."

"I also volunteer at Heaven House."

"Really." Now she looked wary.

"I heard about someone named Lisa who'd called in on the Helpline, and the guy who ran the place got in some kind of trouble for the advice he gave her. Then when Kyla and Cyan were talking about your Lisa the other day it sounded like they might be one and the same girl."

"Philip Heaven overstepped his bounds," she said, getting up and grabbing the coffeepot. She brought it back to the built-in table and topped off my cup. "She ran away. Well, what she called running away, which was to go stay at her boyfriend's house for a few days without telling me where she was. I don't even remember what her reason was that time. We've had a lot of problems ever since her dad died a couple years ago." She slid back into the seat across from me and took a sip from her cup. "Drunk driver."

I nodded. "I remember that. I'm so sorry. I lost my husband several years ago, but it was to cancer."

"I'm sorry, too, and for you. I had to try and keep things together for Lisa and her little brother and me, and it was . . . hard. I missed Steve so much — still do. Things are better now; I went back to school and got my CPA license and I'm finally getting my feet under me, at least financially." She took another sip of coffee and looked out the window at her massive white horse. "Lisa had a hard time, though. And I didn't know what to do to help. She seemed to hate me. Still does, most of the time." Mandy sighed and closed her eyes for a moment. "I don't know. Maybe he was right. Maybe she is better off away from me."

That darn near broke my heart. I hardened my resolve and plunged on. "Did you report Philip Heaven at the time?"

"Sort of. Not that I heard anything back, but I did write a letter to the muckety-mucks at the foundation that funded that place. Don't think it did any good. I imagine he still answers the Helpline himself and tells anyone who calls whatever he pleases."

"Not exactly."

Something in my tone made her sit back. "What do you mean?"

"He's dead."

Her hand flew to her mouth. "What happened?"

"Botulism poisoning. A few days ago."

She grimaced. "Oh, man. That sucks. I don't care what a jerk he was, no one deserves that."

As I drove down Mandy Koller's driveway to the county road, I considered our conversation. Not only did she genuinely seem to be unaware that Philip had died, but it apparently never occurred to her that I was sitting in her home more because of his death than because I needed help with my accounting. I'd never met anyone so non-defensive in my life.

It was my good luck she could be a real help to Winding Road Bath Products. That was the upside. The downside was that I was still no closer to discovering Philip Heaven's murderer than I had been a couple days ago.

Or was that really true? Finding out more about the email threats from Ann and Mandy had led me to discount them as real suspects. They hadn't threatened him physically, after all, only threatened to report him to the foundation. And both of them had done exactly that.

It didn't sound like the foundation cared much about what Philip did with his little community center brainchild. Their apathy was no doubt due in large part to his last name being Heaven, and the favorite grandchild of the foundation's founder. It was such a shame, because Heaven House had a lot of potential. Now, with Jude in charge, I hoped it would finally live up to it and become an institution that provided real help to the citizens of Cadyville.

Anyway, I was pretty sure Ann hadn't killed Philip, and after talking with Mandy, I was pretty sure she hadn't either. And no, the latter opinion was not influenced in the least by the fact that I was looking forward to having her take over a big chunk of my accounting. Honest.

So who was left?

I took a deep breath. I could go home and take a quick nap before I picked Barr up, or I could drop by HH yet again and see what I could dig up.

Oh, but a *nap*. The thought held magical appeal. I veered toward home.

TWENTY

"I can't figure out how the killer did it," I said.

Brodie cocked his corgi head at me and made a noise low in his throat. Meghan and Erin were gone by the time I got home, presumably out in the wilds of yurtdom in the Cascade Mountains.

That left me and Brodie. I was going to take a nap, really, I was, but my nerves were kind of jangled from all the coffee, and I was a little afraid if I fell asleep I'd be down for the count. I had to pick up Barr in half an hour, after all.

Now that it was right there in my face, I kept thinking about what it would be like to have my boyfriend around the house on a constant basis.

Good. Right? Sure. Besides, it would only be for a little while.

I sat in a rocking chair on the covered front porch, wrapped up in a big down coat.

The rain spattered down onto the pavement of the street, causing minute movements of the grass blades in the front yard. I'd pulled a black wool watch cap down over my ears and no doubt presented a very pretty picture.

And I talked to the dog. He was a very good listener.

"So whoever killed Philip had to get the botulism laden beets to him in the first place. How, exactly, do you do that? Do you have access to his apartment? Do you give them to him personally and take the risk he'll tell someone where he got them? How could you be sure he'd eat them? Did he really like beets? A lot of people don't."

Brodie did that gruff throat thing again.

"Trust me, they can be scrumptious, steamed and tossed with butter and a little fresh tarragon," I said. "But I don't think I'll be able to bring myself to eat any for quite a while."

But Brodie couldn't have cared less about my culinary preferences. He was looking toward the side yard. Seeing the fur along his spine ruffled up all stiff made my own adrenaline pump, and I scrambled to my feet. He started barking, sharp, alarmed barks.

Luke and Seth walked around the corner.

"Hey, dog. How's it goin'?" Luke said easily.

Brodie shut up and wiggled his butt.

My own hand was shaking a bit as I waved. "You boys must be nearly finished."

"Just spread the last of the gravel. You're all set."

"That's great!" My enthusiasm for getting the chicks had been weighed down by the events of the past few days, but now it surfaced again. "How much do we owe you?"

Luke held up a finger and walked over to his brother. They conferred for a few moments, then Luke called out a figure to me. "You don't have to give it to us right now," he added. "Sometime next week'll be fine."

Relieved, I bobbed my head. "We'll track you down."

"Sounds good," Luke said and walked out to the street. Now I saw their truck parked down the block, in front of their house. Seth followed and paused as he shut the front gate. He lifted a hand and a shy smile lit his face.

I waved back. "We sure appreciate all your hard work. Those chickens are going to be the happiest in town, thanks to you two."

His head ducked in embarrassed acknowledgment, and he followed Luke home.

I should go look at how it all turned out, I thought, pulling the down coat tighter around me and sitting back down in the rocker. In just a minute or two . . .

I was freezing when I woke up. Old, arthritic Brodie didn't seem very happy either, having been stuck out on the porch with me. My back was stiff, my eyes puffy, and my hands felt like ice cubes. I reached up to feel a cool streak on my face and found a little trail of drool.

Nice. What must the neighbors think?

The rocker was tucked far back under the porch overhang, so maybe no one had noticed me slumbering all slumped over it. At least I hoped so. I liked to think that at least one or two of them might have been interested enough to come check on me. I wondered whether Allen had come to stalk me and found me slobbering on my front porch. That would be a turnoff, no doubt.

I could only hope.

Oh, God. What time was it?

Inside, the phone was ringing. I staggered in to pick it up.

"Sophie Mae? Are you all right?" Worry infused Barr's voice.

"I'm so sorry. I had a fight with Meghan last night, and I didn't sleep very well and

239

had an appointment this morning and came home all exhausted and fell asleep on the front porch — can you believe that, the front porch? And I just woke up, and I'm on my way. You're still at the hospital, aren't you?"

A brief silence as he absorbed all that.

"I'm still here."

"Be there in a jiffy, I promise. Leaving right now."

"Hey, slow down," he said. "I'm not going anywhere. But for the record, you scared me, not showing up when you said you would."

"Sorry, really, really I am."

"I'm just glad you're okay. See you soon."

I hung up, loaded with guilt. Brodie waddled over to his bed by the door, directing a baleful look in my direction before curling up and putting his head on his cold paws.

I didn't blame him.

When I got to the hospital, Barr was dressed and impatient to leave. I grabbed his stuff and followed behind as the nurse wheeled him to the entrance, much to his muttering chagrin.

Outside, it had finally begun to snow.

Big, fat, fluffy flakes drifted down from

240

the heavy clouds above. Already a scant layer of white covered everything except the pavement, dark and wet-slick against the dazzling alabaster blanket. Barr had stopped his grumbling as soon as we went outside, and I looked down to see an expression of pure delight on his face. I realized it was reflected on my own. We were both from a part of the country — Wyoming for him, Colorado for me — where it seriously snowed in the winter. While I might have complained about it when I lived there, at heart I missed the white stuff after all.

I retrieved my Toyota from the parking garage. Once Barr was ensconced in the passenger seat, I flipped the heater switch on high and maneuvered through the panicked drivers toward the highway that led to Cadyville. It would take us a while to get to his little house on the edge of town, what with the crazies on the road who thought snowflakes in the air meant they had to drive as erratically as possible. I concentrated on avoiding them. Barr watched out the window for several minutes.

Out of the blue, he turned to me and said, "Kelly O'Connell doesn't seem to exist."

A minivan cut in front of me. I braked and switched lanes, forming my response: "What the hell is that supposed to mean?"

"Owens was on last night. I called him and had him do a preliminary check. He got back to me almost right away — no record of any males named Kelly O'Connell in Washington state."

"When you say 'record,' do you mean he hasn't done anything illegal?"

Barr took a deep breath. "I mean he doesn't have a phone number, an address, a car registration, or a driver's license."

My heart bucked, and I had to remind myself to pay attention to the traffic. "Are you saying he's using a fake name?"

"Maybe. Or he's not really from Seattle. Owens will try to do a more in-depth check when he comes in for his shift today. As a favor to me, I might add."

"And a favor to me. I understand. But, Barr, Meghan's dating this guy, whoever he is. In fact, she's out in a freakin' yurt with Erin and him *right now*."

"I'll find out more when I can," he assured me. "Do you know where they are?"

I shook my head. "Someplace in the Cascades." My hands were white on the wheel, only unlike the other drivers around me, it wasn't because of the weather.

At Barr's house I helped him find a suitcase and a big duffel bag, and we filled them with everything we thought he might need during his sojourn at the Bly-Reynolds homestead. Traffic was bumper to bumper by then, and it took half an hour to get across town. He was gray with exhaustion when I helped him inside and up the stairs to Erin's bedroom. I went back down to unload his things from the car.

When I hauled them up to his new, if temporary home, he was reclining on the bed, propped up by the big purple hippo. He looked upset to see me carrying the heavy bags, but I waved off any apology before he could speak.

"Don't start. That's why you're here, after all. So we can take care of you. Do you want help getting into your pajamas so you can get some sleep?"

His answering look told me just what he thought of that idea. "I'm fine in my sweats. Just going to take a quick nap."

"Okay." I walked over to the window and opened the curtains so he could see the snow still coming down outside. When I turned back, he had begun to snore lightly.

Downstairs, I let Brodie out to do his business. Then I found some leftover split pea soup with ham in the freezer and heated it up. A thick slice of homemade bread with butter and a glass of cold milk to wash it all down. I felt like a little kid eating that meal, and figured Barr would welcome some of the same when he woke up. I put the rest of the soup in a bowl, ready to heat, and went into the living room.

I couldn't sit down, restless energy prompting me to pace while I waited for Meghan and Erin to get home. I was worried, and not only because she was out there with some guy that didn't exist on paper. The snow would be much worse in the mountains, and I didn't even know where to send help if they needed it. Getting back would be difficult at best. They had shelter, and would probably be okay if they had to stay out there all night, but the very thought made me more anxious than ever.

I'd built a fire, swept and mopped the floor in the kitchen and entryway, dusted the living room and scrubbed the toilets in both the upstairs and the downstairs bathrooms when the phone finally rang. I was tidying the books on the shelves in the living room by then, and ran to pick it up before it woke Barr.

The caller ID said it was a wireless call, but no name or number. Figured. I may have had a bit of an attitude in my voice when I answered.

Not Allen. Meghan. Thank God.

"Be there soon," she said. "We only now

got to where there's some cell phone reception, and I knew you'd be worried."

"Talk about understatements. Where are you?"

"Coming south on Highway 9. The traffic's bad, but we got off the mountain before it really started to storm."

"Everything okay?"

She sighed. "Yes. It's fine. And we had a wonderful time, thanks for asking. Is Barr there?"

"He's upstairs, asleep. Getting packed up and over here took it out of him."

"Tell him he can stay as long as he needs to. See you soon."

We rang off, and I realized I hadn't asked for the number of the cell phone she'd obviously been calling from.

Still, I felt a lot better.

TWENTY-ONE

Meghan didn't get home for almost another two hours. I knew the traffic would hold them up — the roads turned into parking lots when it snowed, and everyone desperately tried to get home, but I was getting worried all over again by the time they finally came in a bit after nine.

Barr sat at the kitchen table, insisting he didn't want to be treated like an invalid. "I only need a little more rest than usual."

"Okay," I said, and pointed to the bowl of hearty soup. I reached for a chunk of bread and the butter.

"A guy could get used to this," he said, spooning up a bite.

The front door banged open, and I left him to his dinner. The sharp scent of winter cold greeted me in the foyer. Erin came in first, blinking sleep out of her eyes and rubbing at the imprint of rough upholstery on her left cheek. Meghan came in next, ruddy-cheeked and glowing even after hours spent in traffic. Kelly entered behind them, carrying our big picnic basket and an empty wine bottle. Brodie toddled over and gave him a big, brown-eyed doggie grin.

Traitor.

"You made it," I said, taking the basket and bottle from Kelly.

He shucked out of his coat and laid it on the bench by the door. "What an experience! I've never seen people react to snow like that in my life. I have to say, I'm in fairly desperate need of your facilities."

Huh. If he were from Seattle he would have known what to expect from a Northwest snowstorm. I waved him toward the downstairs bathroom.

Erin trudged to the stairs. "Remember that you're sleeping in my room," Meghan said. Her daughter mumbled something in response, still half asleep.

Once they were both out of earshot, I grabbed Meghan's arm and said, "I have to talk to you."

She raised her eyebrows and waited.

"There is no Kelly O'Connell."

Now she just looked puzzled. "Of course there is. He's using our bathroom right now."

"He doesn't exist. No driver's license, no

247

address, no car registration, no phone number."

"Well what do you expect? He just moved here. Jeez, will you leave the poor guy alone?"

"But he moved from Seattle, right? There's no record of him anywhere in Washington State. He isn't who he says he is."

She blinked, then rallied. "Exactly how is it that you know this?"

"I asked Barr to find out some more about him. He called one of his friends at work."

"You . . . you asked . . . how *dare* you?"

"Hey. He was acting suspicious the other night, at HH."

"So were you!"

"And we don't know anything about him. So go ahead and get mad at me. And at Barr, if you want. I don't care. But pay attention. Your boyfriend isn't who he says he is. Don't you want to know why that is? Doesn't it make you wonder what else he might be lying about?"

Her eyes shifted over my shoulder and widened. My stomach dropped. Slowly, I turned to find the individual in question standing in the doorway behind me. Barr appeared behind him, looming a good five inches over his head.

Kelly stiffened, but didn't turn around.

"Maybe we should find a place to sit down," he said.

"Living room." Meghan's words were clipped.

The three of us trooped in behind her. Kelly joined Meghan on the sofa, but she scooted away to put a little distance between them. Barr sank into my favorite big cushy chair, and I stood by the fireplace. Kelly looked around at each of us, finishing with Meghan. She looked resigned and sad. I felt awful for her. It wasn't her fault she had such terrible luck with men.

"I'm not from Seattle," he said.

"No kidding," I said.

Meghan glared at me. "Let him explain."

I shrugged. Barr watched the drama without comment.

Kelly took a deep breath. "I'm actually from New Jersey. I'm an investigator, brought in by the Heaven Foundation to find out what Philip Heaven was doing with the money he was siphoning from Heaven House."

Oh. Wow.

Barr asked, "Is your name really Kelly O'Connell?"

"It is. And before you ask, no, I'm not licensed to officially investigate anything here. You could probably do something with that if you wanted. I know that. But I think the board would be happy to agree that I'm simply doing them a favor."

So they were paying him under the table and hoping to keep it quiet.

I thought about the bank statements and the utility shut-off notices I'd found in Philip's apartment. "I don't understand why Philip would need to steal from Heaven House. It was supposed to be his baby. And he had a trust fund, didn't he? Not exactly hurting for money."

"It wasn't enough. The trust fund gave him an allowance, but not a huge one. His grandfather didn't want him to be dependent on it, wanted to give him an appreciation of money, not take it for granted. You know, I spent some time with him, and I believe he genuinely wanted Heaven House to be a success at first. He didn't have a clue how to make that happen, though. Once he saw it failing, I think he gave up and began treating the money the foundation provided as his own."

"I take it this had been going on for a while," Barr said.

Meghan sat slumped in the corner of the sofa, and Kelly kept shuttling his gaze toward her. But he answered. "The foundation thought everything was fine. Then they started getting complaints. Finally Heaven's cousin, Jude Carmichael, contacted the board two months ago, and they learned many of the programs Philip had delineated in his reports to them were either failing or never got off the ground in the first place."

"Did Jude know you were investigating Philip?" I asked.

He shook his head. "No one did. I was just another volunteer. One that happened to get pretty close to the boss."

"Did you find the money?" Barr asked.

Kelly sighed. "No. It seems he spent most of it."

"Did you kill him?" I asked.

"What?"

"Sophie Mae!" Meghan, however upset she was with her new beau, was aghast that I'd ask such a thing. Even Barr looked surprised, and a little amused.

I held up my palms. "Well, you came out here as a kind of fixer, right? To save face for the foundation, take care of a family problem for them, and find the money Philip had squirreled away if any was left."

Kelly let out a big, easy laugh. "I think you've seen a few too many episodes of *The Sopranos*. Just because I'm from New Jersey doesn't mean I'm a hit man." He snorted out another laugh. "Murder by botulism poisoning. I love it."

His amusement faded when he saw none of us were smiling. "Really?" Narrowing his eyes at Barr, he asked, "The botulism wasn't an accident?"

"There's no official investigation at this point," Barr said. "But there are some suspicious circumstances that warrant looking into. Philip received a threat. More than one, I understand, but one in particular that worried him enough to consult me on a semi-official basis. He mentioned it to some other people, as well, but didn't say who it was from."

Kelly looked thoughtful. "Huh."

"You wouldn't happen to know anything about that, would you?" I asked.

"I might. I just might."

We all waited. After a several seconds of silence he seemed to make a decision. "Philip was having an affair."

I grimaced. "With Maryjake Dreggle?"

Meghan's jaw dropped.

He nodded. "So that's not news to you."

She said, "Well, it's sure news to me. Barr?"

He shot me a questioning look. "I had no idea."

I paced back and forth in front of the fire. "I saw her react to Philip's illness the day he died. It wasn't exactly the reaction of an employee. But I couldn't be sure."

"Well, I'm sure," Kelly said. "I saw them together. And then after he died I went up to his office and found a letter in Philip's desk from James Dreggle. He knew about the affair, and he warned Philip off in no uncertain terms."

"Were you there on Thursday night?"

He blinked. Realization dawned on his face. "That was you in the window? What were you doing there in the middle of the night?"

I gave a little shrug. Meghan looked vaguely satisfied.

"Do you have the letter?" Barr asked. I could see his energy was fading.

"I'll bring it to you tomorrow." Kelly turned to Meghan. "When I came out to see what was going on with Heaven House, I met you and found myself in the difficult position of having to lie to you about why I was here and where I came from. But I never lied to you about anything else, I promise you that. Especially about how I feel. I can't expect you to trust me when I say that, but I really like you. And Erin is a gem. I can't even tell you how much I enjoyed today, even with the snow and the crazy traffic." He glanced at me. "And being outed by your housemate."

She still looked skeptical, for which I was glad, but I couldn't help hoping Barr would ask another favor from his co-workers, and Kelly O'Connell would come out clean.

"But you live in New Jersey," she said.

"For now. I've always moved around a lot. Who knows where I'll end up?" The corners of his mouth turned up.

Her return smile was tentative, but it was there.

Kelly left after a few more words alone with Meghan. Words which, by the way, she chose not to share with Barr and me. By then we were all tired for various reasons and elected to delay further discussion of Kelly's revelations until morning. I helped Barr get settled in Erin's room again, and he fell asleep immediately. Meghan joined Erin in her bed, and I went to mine.

Alone. Just as well, I thought. I was so exhausted I'd probably snore. Or worse, drool. Bleah.

Some time later I heard the phone ring, but couldn't claw my way to consciousness in time to answer it. The sound stopped, and I allowed myself to drift again.

"Sophie Mae." The whisper beside my bed startled me, and I sat straight up.

"Meghan?"

"Thaddeus Black is on the phone for you. It's about Ruth."

What on earth? Heart thudding, I took the phone Meghan proffered. "Hello? Thaddeus?" I shivered in the chill night air and reached for my big fluffy robe laid across the end of the bed. The snow outside reflected any meager light it could find a million times, making the other side of the curtains glow.

"I'm so sorry to call you this late."

"That's okay. Is something wrong?"

"Ruth is in the hospital. She wanted me to phone and ask you to come."

"Oh, no. Is she okay? What happened?"

"She was attacked. He beat her quite badly."

"Who did?" I breathed.

"Well, the lady from the police keeps talking about a creeper. Do you think she means a peeping Tom?"

"The Cadyville Creep?" I swung my legs over the side of the bed and slipped my feet into the yellow ducky slippers waiting on the floor.

"That sounds right. Do you know what she's talking about?"

"I'm afraid I might. Was she . . . ?"

"Was she what?" Thaddeus asked.

"Raped?" The word lashed against my sensibilities as I tried to connect such a horrible act with spunky Ruth.

The question flustered her uncle. "Oh, no, nothing like that," he said. There was a pause, and then he asked, "Can you come?"

I picked at the leg of my blue-striped flannel jammies and mentally sighed. "Sure. I'll be there as soon as I can."

"Thank you. I wouldn't ask you myself, but she so wants to talk to you."

"As soon as I can," I repeated, and we rang off.

Out of the flannel jammies and into a pair of jeans and a long-sleeved T-shirt with a thick wool sweater over the top. As I dressed by the light of my bedside lamp, I got angrier by the second.

Meghan came in, all bleary-eyed and worried looking. "What's going on?"

I told her about the Cadyville Creep attacking Ruth. "And she wants me to come to the hospital."

After she railed for a few minutes against anyone who would stoop to attacking a seventy-year-old woman, Meghan fell silent.

I was lacing up my boots when she asked. "Why?"

"Why, what?"

"Why you?"

That gave me pause. Why me indeed? Ruth and I were friendly acquaintances, but not really anything more than that. At least, we hadn't been until she started counting on me to prove her beets weren't the ones that killed Philip.

"Sophie Mae?"

"I really don't know. But I'll let you know once I do."

"Be careful, and give Ruth my love," Meghan said. "Tell her we'll come help with anything she needs, okay?"

"Of course." If Ruth were going to choose someone at random to call, I'd have thought it would be Meghan. She was a much nicer person than I was.

I slipped into Erin's room on my way downstairs to check in on Barr. His breathing was heavy but not too labored. I thought about waking him, but just couldn't bring myself to do it. At the top of the stairs I stooped to pat Brodie on the head and told him to take care of everyone. He rolled over on his back and looked at me upside down. Maybe he didn't look like much of a watchdog, but I knew he'd raise holy hell if anything happened.

I bundled up, and then spent a downright silly amount of time and energy on furtive glances around the eerily silent yard and street before hurrying out, jumping in my truck and quickly locking the doors.

It was almost midnight. Again, I thought. I was getting a little tired of being tired. Everyone else seemed to have found their way home except for a few snowplows on the highway. The orange streetlights above turned the stark white blanket a bright amber. The air was electric with cold. With no one in my way, I made good time to the hospital.

By now I'd become an expert at locating the entrance to the parking garage.

TWENTY-TWO

Thaddeus Black leaned on his cane outside the room where the nice lady at the information desk downstairs had told me I could find Ruth. Relief replaced the worry and weariness on his lined face. He met me halfway down the hall and grabbed my arm.

"I'm glad you're here. She's so upset."

"How is she physically? Did he hurt her badly?"

Sadness crossed his face. "Bad enough, poor girl. Black and blue, and the bastard knocked her down, cracked a rib."

I winced. As we neared the room, moving slowly to accommodate Thaddeus' shambling arthritic gait, he hesitated. "The lady detective is still in there with her. Asking her questions about that creep fellow."

Hmm. "I think I'll join them."

"I don't know," he said. "She seems kind of . . . tightly wound, if you know what I mean."

"Yeah. I know what you mean. But from everything I've heard she's very good at her job."

He scowled. "She'd better be."

I gently pulled away from his grip and went into Ruth's room. He didn't follow me in, electing to stay in the hallway. I wondered what Detective Lane had said to intimidate him so.

Ruth appeared frightened half out of her wits. Lane loomed over the older woman with a massive notebook in her hand and a severe expression on her face. She greeted my entrance with a moue of exasperation.

"What are you doing here?"

Ruth turned her head on the pillow, exposing the bruises on her face and one side of her neck. A lump rose to my throat. How could this strong and kind woman have elicited such violence? Her eyes met mine with a surprising intensity, as if she were trying to communicate something directly to me through pure willpower.

"How are you feeling?" I asked her, ignoring the question.

"Awful," she croaked. "Detective, could you leave us alone for a few minutes? I need to talk to Sophie Mae."

Lane's expression was flatly unemotional. "There will be plenty of time for you to visit with your friends, Ms. Black. Right now I need you to answer my questions so I can find out who did this to you. You do want me to find the bad man who hurt you, don't you?"

Ruth and I both stared at her. Good at her job Lane might be, but good with people she definitely was not. She seemed to think anyone who lived in a small town must possess less than an average IQ.

"Of course I want that, Detective," Ruth said. "I'm just not sure I can tell you anything more. I was in my carport, unloading a few supplies from the grocery store from the car when he came at me from behind. He was wearing a mask, so I didn't see his face. He didn't say anything. He punched me, knocked me down, and left. That's all. I told you again and again. I didn't see anything else."

Detective Lane scowled. "He didn't say anything?"

Ruth darted a glance my direction. I raised my eyebrows. "No," she said. "Not a thing."

"Can you tell me what he was wearing? How tall he was? Build? Any smells you noticed? His breath, maybe?"

"No. Nothing. I don't remember any of that."

I moved a visitor's chair closer to the bed and sat down as Lane continued to hammer away with her questions. Something was off, but I couldn't figure out what. Ruth was vehement as she denied knowing anything more about the attack or the attacker. Could she be blocking out part of the event and feel embarrassed that she couldn't remember? Or was she holding something back?

"Okay, one last question." Detective Lane's tone held frustration. "Have you been getting any funny phone calls lately?"

Ruth looked puzzled. "What do you mean, funny?"

"Peculiar. Obscene. A strange man wanting to talk to you, but he won't tell you who he is. Even hang ups."

I ignored the shiver that skittered down my spine.

"No. Nothing like that."

Detective Lane flipped the notebook closed and gathered her coat from the chair by the window. "Thank you Ms. Black. I hope you feel better soon. If you think of anything that might be helpful, please give me a call. Ms. Reynolds, may I speak with you a moment outside?"

I stood. "Sure."

Ruth tried to sit up, gasped, and fell back.

"I'll be right back," I said. "I promise."

She nodded, but didn't say anything.

Outside, Detective Lane led me toward the elevators, away from a curious Thaddeus Black.

"I don't know why she'd fight me on this. She must know more."

I bristled.

"Now, settle down," she said. "I'm only trying to help. She may just be scared. And sometimes I'm not very good at putting people at ease."

I gave her a look, which she at least had the good grace to take with a sheepish grin.

"So when you're talking with her, see if you can't find out more about what happened. You're her friend. She'll talk to you. I especially want to know more about any phone calls."

"Like I've been getting."

"Well, sort of. More menacing, frankly. Why, are you still getting calls?"

"Why, yes, thank you for asking, Detective. I got one last night while I was at Heaven House."

Displeasure settled on her face, and she tossed that gorgeous mane of hair. "You need to be careful. You're on someone's radar. Whether it's the Creep's or not, I don't know."

"At the police station you made it sound like my little stalker was a joke," I said, my voice rising.

She pressed her lips together. "It didn't sound like the same guy. But neither does this, and the attack was quite violent. You shouldn't go anywhere alone. So far he hasn't attacked anyone who wasn't alone."

"I can't alter my whole life."

"You can. Or it might just be altered for you."

Her authoritarian tone raised my hackles, but that last statement resonated in my gut.

"What if Ruth really didn't get any phone calls?" I asked.

"Then your Cadyville Creep is stepping things up. And that makes him even more dangerous than before."

With a certain amount of trepidation, I returned to my friend's room.

Thaddeus had returned to his niece's bedside, but as soon as I walked in she shooed him away. He left with the attitude of someone who was content to do what he was told.

"Shut the door," Ruth said.

I reached behind me and swung the door closed.

"All the way."

The latch snicked into place. I waited, half

afraid to hear she wanted to tell me. Had her attacker done more to hurt her than was evident? No. She would have told Detective Lane and the hospital staff. Ruth was no shrinking violet, no way, no how.

She took a deep breath, which made her wince again, which made me wince in sympathy. "That man? The one the *Eye* is calling the Cadyville Creep?"

"Did you remember something else about him?" I asked.

She shook her head. "No. I didn't have to. He's not the one who did this to me."

I sank into the visitor's chair. "Ruth? Who hurt you? Do you know?"

"Yes. No. I know who didn't attack me. That Creep man."

I spoke carefully. "And how do you know that?"

Silence. I waited it out. She'd wanted to talk to me. If she had to summon her resources first, I'd let her.

When the pause had grown to fill the room, she finally said in a low voice, "You can't tell anyone. Promise me."

I shook my head. "I can't promise that without knowing what you're going to tell me."

"You have to."

"Just tell me whatever it is."

265

"No. Promise or leave."

"Oh, come on."

"I mean it."

Her eyes told me she did mean it. Knowing I'd regret it, and feeling completely bamboozled, I said. "Fine. I promise not to tell anyone. Now, spill."

Her eyes held mine for a few moments, gauging whether I'd merely told a convenient lie. "Whoever it was knew about my beets. And about the other beets, the ones that killed Philip."

"What!"

"Shhhh. Not so loud. I don't want Thad to hear."

"Good Lord, Ruth, why not? What really happened in your carport this evening? Did it even happen in your carport?"

"Of course it did. I didn't lie about anything." Fear infused her features. "I'm sorry, Sophie Mae. I shouldn't have insisted you come out here, especially in the snow and all. I was just frightened by the whole experience, and my daughter lives in Arizona, and —"

"Ruth, please, I'm glad you had Thaddeus call. You must have been terrified. Please tell me what I can do."

She took a shaky breath and closed her eyes. "Maybe you could check on Uncle

Thad over the next couple of days? They want to keep me in here for observation after what happened." She opened her eyes, staring up at the ceiling. "I'm kind of an old fart to get beaten up, and since I take a blood thinner, they're afraid of complications."

Dread settled in my solar plexus, but I tried not to show it on my face. "I'm sure you'll be fine, and Meghan and I will be happy to check in on Thaddeus."

"Thank you."

"Now. Are you going to tell me more about what happened?" The bit about her attacker mentioning beets was chafing at my brain like sandpaper.

"I'm not saying anything more."

"But, Ruth . . ."

"He said he'd hurt Uncle Thad if I told anyone, Sophie Mae. I've already placed too much temptation in your way. I know you promised not to tell, but if, after all, you decide you know best, I swear on everything I hold dear I'll deny everything except what I already told Detective Lane."

Try though I might, I couldn't get her to change her mind.

TWENTY-THREE

The clatter of dishes woke me Sunday morning, and I rolled over to look at the clock. Seven thirty. Not bad. I'd managed to get a few good hours of sleep and felt almost refreshed. Sucking in a deep breath, I threw back the covers and slipped into my poofy robe.

I needed coffee, and I needed it now. Then a shower, and down to my workroom to put together six dozen air fresheners. Kyla and Cyan, who were coming in for a couple of hours in the afternoon, could label and wrap them for packing, and I'd have UPS Joe pick them up the next morning.

Plus, I wanted to tell Meghan and Barr what had happened to Ruth, and the more I thought about what Kelly had told us about James Dreggle's letter, the more I wanted to talk to Maryjake and get a feeling for what she knew.

Erin's bed was empty, the covers pulled

up to the pillows. Down the hall, the door to the spare bedroom was open. Barr stood by the window, dressed in a clean pair of sweatpants and a navy, waffle-weave V-neck. I missed the bolo ties he always wore to work. His usual cowboy boots had been replaced by a pair of sheepskin slippers.

"I'll get dressed later," he said in an apologetic tone as I ran my gaze up and down his lanky figure.

I smiled. "Don't bother. You're allowed to take it easy."

"Maybe." His eyes crinkled at the corners, and he glanced around the room. "You store some interesting things in here." He had a framed photograph in his hand, and now he held it out to me.

Oh, no. Not that.

Bundles of lavender hung from the ceiling, gathered from our garden last summer and suspended to dry. The scent inundated the room, and I took a deep lungful, curiously uncomfortable to see that particular picture in the hands of the man I seemed to be falling in love with.

He grinned. "You're beautiful."

My hand flew to my frizzed braid despite the fact that he was talking about the picture, not my current state of morning dishevelment.

"Here, I'll take that," I said.

He narrowed his eyes. I shouldn't have shown my eagerness to take the photo away from him.

The wedding photo.

Mike and Sophie Mae Reynolds. Getting hitched. Until death did we part. It seemed like we'd been married for a long time, until he got sick. Now, in my middle thirties, I knew the mere six years we'd had together had been only a drop in the bucket of time.

If Barr wanted to snoop around and look at my old pictures, fine. But I didn't want to look at that one. I hadn't, not since Mike had died over five years ago.

"Sophie Mae," Barr breathed.

"What?" I sounded cranky.

"You were so . . . you were a lovely bride."

"Um. Thanks." Did that mean I wasn't so lovely now, eleven years later? Well, what do you expect, Sophie Mae? Eleven years is eleven years. You're a widow, for heaven's sake.

"Come here."

I walked slowly toward him, then strode the last few steps, faking a confidence I didn't feel. Might as well get it over with. He held the picture out, and I took it.

Mike looked so young. That fresh face. That expression of amused intelligence. I missed his wicked sense of humor.

Then I looked at myself. Well, I don't know about lovely, I thought, but not bad. Not bad at all.

My green eyes sparkled with happiness, and my skin glowed smooth and tan. My hair, even longer then, fell in snaky curls down to my waist. I didn't wear a veil, only a single lavender orchid tucked in among the loose blonde waves.

"You ever think about getting married again?" he asked.

"I . . . no, not . . . I don't know." What was I supposed to say? Ack! "Have you eaten yet?" I blurted.

He looked surprised, but answered without protest. "No."

"How about some huevos rancheros?"

Carefully replacing the photo in the box from which he'd taken it, he nodded. "Sounds excellent."

"Get back in bed. I'll bring it to you."

"You don't need to do that . . ." But he was moving slowly toward Erin's room.

"Trust me — don't get used to it," I warned over my shoulder. "This is aberrant behavior for me."

I scrambled eggs and constructed a plate of food while I filled Meghan in on Ruth's attack. I know, I know — I promised not to tell anyone. If Ruth had spilled everything she knew about the man who attacked her, I would've felt a lot guiltier, but she'd practically given me permission by saying she'd deny it anyway. Never mind that that rationalization might not make sense to anyone but me.

Keeping the story short, I pointed out that my theory about Philip being murdered was supported by what Ruth had told me. Meghan reluctantly agreed. She also said she'd stop by and check on Thaddeus Black that afternoon on her way to Caladia Acres for a massage therapy session.

I took a tray up to Barr, who was obediently propped against an assortment of pillows and stuffed animals. He peered at what I held: new potatoes roasted brown in a hot oven, covered with chili con carne, then a layer of eggs scrambled with green onion, topped with grated cheddar cheese, guacamole and sour cream. A little bowl of salsa perched on the side in case he wanted some heat first thing in the morning.

Setting the tray on his lap, he took a swig of orange juice and dumped all the salsa on his rancheros. I took that as a good sign.

While he worked his way through breakfast, I snagged the occasional bite from his plate and repeated what I'd told Meghan about Ruth. I assured him that I believed her about denying everything. Ruth had a better poker face than I did, and I bet she could lie a lot better, too. Of the two of us, she'd be the most convincing.

I was lucky that both Meghan and Barr believed me. Unlike Meghan, however, he wanted to try and convince Ruth to talk to Detective Lane.

"She won't do it. You're more than welcome to try, but she's dug her heels in. Plus," I added, "it would prove I'm not trustworthy."

"You're not."

"Hey —"

"And you shouldn't be, not for this. She should know that."

"She does. That's why she stopped herself from telling me, even though what happened obviously terrifies her."

"Do you think she knows who the killer is?"

I shook my head. "She's frightened, not stupid. If she could pinpoint Philip's murderer, she'd broadcast it far and wide." Chewing on a bite of chili beans and egg, I considered. "When will you check out Kelly's story?"

"I've already called."

I looked at him in surprise.

"What, you think I'm not going to get my butt out of bed just because you slept in this morning? I've been up for hours."

"Hours — right," I said. "Did I mention I was at the hospital in the middle of the night?"

He grinned at me. I wrinkled my nose at him. "So what did you find out?"

"Nothing yet," he said. "I should know more this afternoon."

"When is he supposed to bring over the letter James wrote?"

"Sometime today."

"If we take him at his word, James is our primary suspect, right?"

"Sophie Mae . . ."

"I'm just going to drop by Heaven House and have a chat with Maryjake. You'd think she'd know whether her husband killed her lover."

"No, you can't —"

"Gosh, should we wait for Detective Lane to do it?"

He glared at me.

"Or maybe you'd like to put your badge in your pocket and go talk to her yourself."

Anger flashed across his face. "Maybe I will." He put the half-eaten plate of huevos rancheros on the bed and swung his legs over. Standing quickly, he strode to where

I'd hung his clothes in the closet.

"Oh, now, stop that."

He ignored me.

"I'm not driving you."

He ignored that, too.

But when he reached down for his shoes, he stumbled and nearly fell. I managed to catch him and get him to the bed.

"Dizzy?"

He was breathing as if he'd been running around the block.

"Criminy, I can't believe they let you out of the hospital. Now stop being so macho and get back in bed. Eat the rest of your breakfast." I marched to the door. "I'm sorry I made you mad, but I was just making a point: if I don't talk to Maryjake, no one will."

A steady rain melted the snow. It filled the ditches with freezing water and made everything gray again. The flood plain south of town would be a glistening sheet of wetness, punctuated by the spears of spent corn stalks. If we were lucky, the rivers wouldn't climb over their banks.

I had to assume Maryjake herself wasn't the killer. Even in the dark, Ruth wouldn't have mistaken her for a man, nor could I see Maryjake beating the older woman black and blue. Still, I'd keep my mouth shut about the attack on Ruth; I may have broken my promise by telling Meghan and Barr what I knew, but I wasn't going to endanger Ruth — or Thaddeus — any more by blabbing it far and wide.

Maryjake was ensconced behind her desk at HH as I had hoped, looking rumpled and sleepy. Her eyes turned wary when she saw me walk in the door.

"Hey," she said.

"Hey." I glanced around. No one else was in the big room, and the burgeoning conference room and game rooms were silent. "Got a minute?"

She looked dubious. "I guess so."

"Good." I pulled the wooden chair that sat next to her desk around to the opposite side so I could look directly into her eyes. "Were you having an affair with Philip?"

The blood drained out of her face. It was weird to watch.

"Wh . . . what?"

"Listen, Maryjake. I'm not in the greatest mood, and I don't have time nor inclination to pussyfoot around. Besides, I already know the answer. I guess the question I should be asking is, how much did James know about the affair?"

I hadn't thought she could lose any more

color, but it turned out she could.

"The point here is not that I'm a snoop," I continued. "Well, maybe it is, a little, but it shouldn't be. The point is that someone killed Philip on purpose by giving him botulism, and it could very well be your husband because you were having an affair with your boss."

Her swallow was audible. Maybe this whole trying-for-subtlety thing was a bust. Getting straight to the point seemed to work perfectly well. I'd have to remember that.

Then her eyes welled up with big, glossy tears that spilled over onto her cheeks, and she grabbed at my hand lying on the desk between us.

Crap.

"Is there something you want to tell me?" I asked. "Something about James?"

She shook her head, sending the saline flying. At least she wasn't sobbing hysterically. Yet.

"How about the money that's gone missing here at HH?"

"What?" She looked more confused than she had in response to any question so far.

"What are you hiding?"

She made a little hiccupy sound. "Nothing! I just don't want James to get in trouble. He was furious when he talked to

Philip, but he wouldn't actually hurt him. He's not that kind of guy."

"When did it start?" I asked. "Between you and Philip?"

She sighed. Sniffled. Reached into her desk drawer and took out a tissue and blew into it. "James and I were having problems before I even started working here. Then I met Philip, and it was, like, zing! I can't describe it. He was sexy and kind and so confident, like he believed he could do anything. It was irresistible."

Ew.

"I would have left James for him. I told him that. But he said he wouldn't be responsible for breaking up my marriage. I don't know how James found out — maybe because I talked about Philip sometimes at home. But James is always thinking that other men are interested in me — kind of the jealous type, you know what I mean?"

Speechless, I nodded. Swallowed. "Are you leaving James now?" I finally managed to ask.

She looked horrified. "Of course not. I'd be alone then. I don't want to be alone."

"Ah," I said as noncommittally as I could manage. I felt slightly nauseated. "What if James was the one who poisoned Philip?"

"That's ridiculous. Huh uh. It was an accident. Ruth is wrong. They were her beets, and no one did anything to Philip. It was just a horrible, awful accident. I mean, come on, who would use botulism to kill someone?" Her voice had gained strength the longer she protested. "Besides, James is a straightforward kind of guy, not some weird sneak poisoner."

"Did you love Philip? Don't you want to know what really happened?"

"I know what happened," she insisted.

"He was going to get a restraining order. And no matter how many times you say otherwise, Ruth didn't can the beets that killed him. Someone orchestrated his death, and he knew who it was." I paused, searching her face. "And I think you know who it was, too."

Her head swung back and forth. "No. No, it couldn't be my husband. James was out gathering field data in New Mexico for two weeks, and he only got home the afternoon of the preserves exchange. Even if you were right about someone murdering Philip, and you're not, he couldn't have had anything to do with it."

She stood, grabbed her bag out from under the desk, and began backing toward the door.

I held out my hand. "Maryjake, wait."

"I've heard enough of this." She turned and fled.

It would be easy enough to find out if James was indeed out of town until right before Philip died, but he was still at the top of my list. After all, he could have given Philip those beets before he left.

Right? I sat and toyed with a pen and tried to think of a way to trap him, ignoring the little voice in the back of my head that said James was probably innocent.

Jude came out of the newly furnished game room with a screwdriver in his hands. He looked at me, then down at the tool as if it were a strange insect. He wasn't exactly the rough and ready type.

"Where's Maryjake?" he asked.

"She had to go."

"Gosh darn it! Now I don't have anyone to cover the phones. Can you . . . ?"

"Nope. Sorry." I had way too much work to do at home, and besides, I wanted to get back and see how Barr had recovered from his dizzy spell earlier. Never mind figuring out how to check James' alibi.

"What about Meghan?"

"She's got clients all day," I said.

He threw the screwdriver in a corner, leaving a gouge in the wall. He came over to the phone and started punching in numbers, presumably forwarding the Heaven House calls to his cell phone. "I guess I have to do everything myself in this place."

"I'm sorry I can't help you out right now," I said.

"What did you say to Maryjake that made her leave?"

"Nothing," I lied. "She said she had some things to do, is all." Like go warn her husband that he was a murder suspect.

He took a deep breath and seemed to get himself under control. "I'm sure she'll be back soon. She's very responsible."

"Uh huh," I agreed, gathering my coat up.

"Say, is that offer of your pickup still good?"

"Sure."

"How about tomorrow morning?"

I did some mental juggling. "How long do you think it'll take?"

"Couple hours."

"Just the two of us?"

He shuffled his feet. "I'll get some other people to help. Kelly should be free. And maybe Bette."

"What about the Chase brothers?" I asked.

"I'd have to pay them," he said. "I was hoping to get over here on the cheap. Besides, I don't have much stuff, I really don't."

"Okay then. Get some folks together, and we'll get you resettled tomorrow in the a.m. Say, ten o'clock?"

"Thanks, Sophie Mae."

"Sure. See you later." I raised my hand in farewell.

On the way home I wondered why he hadn't said anything about calling Ruth to come answer the phones. If he knew she was in the hospital he would have told me, wouldn't he? Then again, he hadn't told us Philip was dead that night at the preserves exchange. Didn't want to upset morale, he'd said. And he knew about my stalker, so maybe he hadn't wanted to scare me. Probably best not to put too much stock in his omission.

But still.

TWENTY-FOUR

Barr had taken a quick nap but was awake again when I got home. I filled him in on my encounter with Maryjake. Now that it was done and over, he didn't seem quite so upset with me for wanting to talk with her in the first place. Funny how that worked out.

While I was gone, Kelly had dropped by with the letter James had written Philip. Thinking back, he must have been in Philip's office shortly before I let myself into HH with Meghan's key that night. He was the one who'd left the light on. Scared the flip out of me, finding that light on. Probably left the door to Philip's apartment unlocked, too. Didn't say much for Kelly's attention to detail, but he still seemed like a good-enough guy.

I bent over the page and puzzled over James' awkward scrawl. Luckily, it was more of a note than a letter, so there wasn't much to decipher.

Philip,
You don't love Maryjake, and you'll hurt her if you keep this up. She deserves better than a fly by night playboy who waves a bunch of cash around and then moves on to new meat.

Stay away from my wife.

The missive wasn't signed, but there was no question who'd written it. It wasn't half as angry as either Ann or Mandy's emails had been. Instead it struck me as almost poignant.

"I expected something more . . ."

"Fire and brimstone?" Barr asked.

"Exactly. This hardly seems like a threat at all."

"Hard to tell," he said, all noncommittal.

"Not that that proves James innocent."

"No." Barr was still thinking about it, and until he was done, I wouldn't get much more of an opinion than that.

Returning the note, I told him I had some work to do. He settled in on the sofa to do a little telephonic maneuvering of his own. Having something to do seemed to give him more energy, and I left him happily punching numbers into the cordless handset.

Downstairs, I started on the air fresheners. When I originally experimented with the formulation for them, I used half-pint canning jars because the rubber-rimmed lids sealed the scent in so nicely and kept them from drying. Since beginning to market them, however, I'd discovered a supply of pretty blue jars with chrome lids that worked just as well and looked nicer on a table or shelf.

The fresheners were basically essential oils suspended in a simple gel created with plain old gelatin. As they dried, they released the scent into the air, exactly like commercial gel air fresheners do, except mine contained aromatherapy blends: a bright wake-up scent with peppermint, tea tree oil, and eucalyptus for the office — also great for beside the bed if you had a cold. For the bedroom, either clove and cinnamon if the customer was looking for something sensual, or lavender, chamomile, and orange if they were looking for a good night's sleep. Those three were my biggest sellers, but I also had a balsam fir scent nice for the living room as well as a blend with clary sage, lavender, and rose geranium.

I started water boiling and set up the jars to fill with the gel mixture. Then I began melting gelatin and adding scents and finally poured the fresheners, blend by blend. Then I started on a new batch. The intense bouquet of all those volatile essential oils filled my nose and brain. A sense of calm and focus settled over me as I mixed and poured, a cherished side benefit of my work.

As I finished the last of the order, a knock sounded on the door leading to the back yard. Luke stood with his hand up to the window glass, shading his eyes as he tried to peer inside. As usual, Seth stood behind and to one side of his brother.

I walked over and opened the door, smiling broadly. "Hello, boys. Would you like some money?"

Luke stepped eagerly inside. "Meghan called. Said you had a check."

"It's upstairs. We could've sent it, or dropped it by your house if you didn't want to wait."

"We're out and about. No trouble coming by to pick it up."

"All right. I'll just run and get it." I went up and grabbed the check off the corner of the kitchen counter and returned downstairs.

Seth had finally crossed the threshold and stood looking around wide-eyed. When I handed his brother the check, I heard him inhale deeply.

"Kind of strong in here, isn't it?" I asked, watching him.

"It's nice. Really nice."

Luke rolled his eyes. "C'mon. Let's get going."

Seth looked away, embarrassed.

"I think it's nice, too," I said. "You want one of these air fresheners?"

Luke gave a little laugh, not unfriendly at all, but certainly conveying the opinion that real men don't need no stinkin' air fresheners.

"Wait," I said. "Give me a chance."

I walked over to the table and grabbed one of the balsam fir-scented jars off the table. It had been one of the first I'd poured, and now it was gelling up nicely. I waved it under Seth's nose.

His eyes brightened, and his mouth turned up. "Smells like a pine tree. Only, you know, better. Luke, take a whiff."

I was pleased as punch to hear him say that. For one thing, he seemed so darn shy that getting him to say anything at all was a kind of victory, and for another, if I could get men interested in more of my products, I'd have a whole new marketing demographic.

Luke took a token sniff. "Nice. You ready?"

Seth held out the jar to me.

I shook my head. "Take it. You can always stick it behind the seat of your truck or something. At least it's better than those little cardboard thingies people hang from their rearview mirrors."

Seth gave Luke a look. "Yeah, lots nicer than those." He directed another small smile my way. "Thanks."

"No problem. Thanks for all the work on the chicken coop, you two. It looks great, and you did a fantastic job. Any reference you need, just have them call us; Meghan and I will be happy to vouch for you."

That put a big grin on Luke's face. "Glad to hear it. And don't think we won't take you up on the reference, either."

They were nice kids, I thought, as they closed the back door and headed off down the alley, Seth once again a few steps behind his older brother. He held the little blue pot of air freshener in front of him like a vase. I was sure they both missed their mother, but I couldn't help but wonder whether Seth missed her more.

I went to check out the chicken house, imagining how the hens would like it. Meghan and I had discussed it ad nauseam, and finally decided on a black-and-white barred Plymouth rock, a classic Rhode Island red, and two Araucana, or Easter egg chickens. The first two laid brown eggs, and the second two would lay light green or blue eggs.

I was half tempted to go buy the chicks that afternoon. The first eight to twelve weeks we'd keep them in the mudroom, so they'd be plenty warm. At the very least, I could set up the nursery for them.

The mudroom is where Barr found me, hanging a heat lamp from the bare beam above so it would shine directly down on the pen in the middle of the floor. The pen was a thirty-six-inch square box, cut down to eighteen inches tall, and overlaid with a wire lid created from the side of Brodie's old dog crate. The lid was removable for easy cleaning, would keep the girls in when they started thinking about running, jumping, and flying, and would support old towels as a roof to keep the temperature in the nineties while the chicks were still tiny. Three inches of fine pine shavings lined the floor, and the waterer and feeder sat up on bricks so they wouldn't get gunky.

He came and stood in the doorway, taking in my cobbled-together chick nursery. "That'll work pretty well."

"You think so?" I could hear the worry in my voice as I surveyed my work. "Neither Meghan nor I have done this before, and I'd hate to kill the little things just because we do — or don't do — something out of ignorance."

"We had chickens the whole time I was growing up. You'll be fine. They're not that tough to take care of."

Barr had grown up on a ranch in Wyoming, once a working cattle outfit, but for years now a dude ranch of the first order. Guests came to ride horses and work cattle, go fly fishing, hang out on the river, hike, camp, or cross-country ski in the winter.

"I'm grateful for any suggestions. Don't hold back because you don't want to hurt my feelings," I said.

He smiled. "Oh, don't worry, I'll speak up. If you're done with this little project here, though, why don't you come into the kitchen, have a cup of something, and I'll tell you what I've learned about James and Kelly so far."

I obeyed with alacrity.

Settled in at the table with a cup of Bewley's Irish tea for me and a cup of Earl Grey for him, he brought me up to speed.

"Kelly O'Connell is indeed who he says he is. Has a private investigator's license in

New Jersey, and is well enough thought of by the authorities there."

A wave of relief washed over me. Meghan's bad luck with men might be turning after all. I hoped so. I really hoped so. I was even starting to like Kelly myself, after his frank admission the other night, and his obvious devotion to Meghan, even after such a short time.

"And James Dreggle? Did Owens find out anything about him?"

"Not Owens."

"You did ask him, didn't you? Or is the favor bank getting low? Can you ask Officer Dawson?"

"I could, but didn't. Just because I'm not on active duty at the moment doesn't mean I'm not still a cop, you know."

Being in the hospital and now house-bound was making him cranky. I couldn't blame him. I'd be the same way.

"Of course," I said. "So you called his work?"

"I did. And his supervisor confirmed James Dreggle was out of the state for a couple weeks, in New Mexico doing some count or other — the supervisor kept calling it "ground truthing," but I finally gleaned it had something to do with finding out how many of a certain species of bird there were in a given area."

"Sounds tedious."

"He was with a team of two other people the whole time. They didn't return until the afternoon of the preserves exchange."

"Great." I took a noisy sip of tea. "He could have given the beets to Philip before he left, right? Then he'd have an alibi if there was any suspicion, and Philip would be out of commission and unable to cuckold him while he was on his business trip. Maybe he didn't even intend to kill him."

He looked doubtful. "It's possible."

I slumped in my chair. "But not very probable. He'd be leaving an awful lot to chance."

He nodded, thoughtful. "Yeah. Could have been a hopeful shot in the dark, I suppose."

I said, "Maryjake made a good point today. James is a pretty straightforward guy. Botulism poisoning is, well, anything but."

"And yet," Barr said, "he's a scientist, and he'd know about botulism. And it's also possible that if Maryjake knew he did something to Philip in a, as you say, straightforward manner, it could so alienate her that he'd never be able to save his marriage."

"Yeah. Maybe. But how do you give a guy

something to eat when he knows you hate him?"

"You make him think it's from your wife."

I pointed a finger at him. "Right. Well, maybe it happened that way. But if it did, unless we can actually trace the beets to him, there's no way we could prove it."

Barr sipped his tea and looked his rueful agreement at me.

"Hungry?" I asked.

"Oddly enough, I am a little."

"Why oddly?"

"Uh, did you see the huge plate of food you set in front of me this morning? And I ate every darn bite of it, too, after you abandoned me."

I was pleased to hear his appetite was returning. "That was hours ago. How about a sandwich?"

"Sounds good."

"Egg salad? Tuna?"

"Do you have any peanut butter?"

Did we ever. I bought the stuff in the industrial-sized container. I got up and sliced off a couple pieces of bread from the loaf on the counter. Almost time to make more, I noted, as we'd plowed through both loaves Meghan had made last Tuesday. Erin's lunches used up a lot of it. I reached for the raspberry freezer jam, then saw the apricot jelly from the preserves exchange that Meghan had been eating on her health muffin.

I turned to Barr, a jar in each hand. "Would you rather . . ." But I trailed off, looking at the lovely amber of the apricot.

"What?" he asked.

"Did you see all those jellies Jude brought to the preserves exchange? All backlit with the little white Christmas lights? There must have been five different kinds."

"I guess."

"No, really, do you remember?" I needed him to recall that scene the same way I did.

"I wasn't feeling so hot, if you'll recall." He squinched his forehead in concentration. "But, yeah, I think so. He had them set up next to Maryjake's stuff."

"Does Jude strike you as someone who'd make jelly?"

"Not so much. But I could see him in a kitchen more easily than, say, driving a backhoe."

"Hmmm. True enough. But he hasn't lived here very long, and I know he lives with a widower Thaddeus Black introduced him to. Maybe they hang out and make jelly in Mr. Oxford's kitchen."

"You're so fond of asking questions, Sophie Mae. Why don't you just ask him if he made the jelly?"

"Because if he didn't, then he got it from someplace else, and that means there's some other source for home-canned food that we don't know about. Maybe things besides jelly."

Comprehension dawned. "Like, say, beets?"

"Exactly. But if he killed Philip, we don't want to tip him off. I can find out more without asking him."

"I don't like the sound of that."

"Don't worry. I'm going over to help him move tomorrow. I can check out where he lives, maybe ferret out a little more info about his tendency to cook, that sort of thing."

Barr's voice was flat. "I still don't like it."

"Oh, please. I'm not about to go by myself. He asked me to help him move because I have a truck, but Kelly and Bette are going to be there, too. Now, which do you want on your sandwich: raspberry jam or apricot jelly?"

He made a face. "For some reason, the raspberry sounds a lot better after that conversation."

Twenty-Five

Back down in my workroom, I concocted a facial mask. I felt ragged and tired, and a nice little boost to my skin seemed like a reasonable self-indulgence. Blending colloidal oatmeal, dried goat's milk and neem powder together with witch hazel created a green paste that would have frightened the Wicked Witch of the West. Oh, but it made my skin feel lovely, and mixing the ingredients together, fussing to get the right consistency, proved soothing in it's own right.

My confident assertion that I'd be able to find out something useful about Jude as I helped him move didn't quite reflect the way I actually felt. For days I'd been trying to figure out what happened to Philip, asking impertinent questions with little success. I knew more about everyone associated with Heaven House by now, but I didn't seem to be any closer to finding Philip's killer. The victim had turned out to be a real jerk, and lots of people disliked him. Still, no one I'd suspected so far had panned out.

Jude felt different, though. He had plenty of motive, the poor relation now in a position to take over the kingdom of the favorite grandson. Sneaky, maybe a little passive-aggressive — I could totally see him poisoning someone. If he had opportunity as well, in the form of some beets gone bad, then it made all the sense in the world.

But did any of that matter?

Meaning, who cared? Other than me, no one was willing to follow up, make things official. Meghan would have preferred that I drop the whole thing, Maryjake wasn't interested in finding her lover's killer, the police didn't want to admit Philip's death might have been a homicide, and I had the feeling that even Barr was indulging me because I was his girlfriend and because he was bored. Once he got back to his regular cases his interest would likely wane as well.

So why should I bother? Even if I had my best suspect yet, why should I put myself out there, maybe even put myself in danger, in order to prove it? I had my own life, a busy life I'd partially put on hold, and for what? Nothing, that's what.

Tootie had mentioned a similar situation,

a murder committed by deliberately exposing someone to botulism. The killer had never been prosecuted. Maybe she could tell me more.

I put the green paste in a jar and screwed the lid down tight. Time enough to indulge in the facial goop later. Right now, I wanted to hear more about that other case of botulism poisoning.

I found Tootie in the activities room at Caladia Acres. It was way better than the one at Heaven House, brand new dart board at the latter not withstanding. A series of dings and whistles echoed out to the lobby, but when I turned the corner a bell started clanging and lights flashed in the corner.

Someone had won at the Whack-A-Mole game. A wiry little guy with a shock of wild gray hair that looked like he combed it with an egg beater swung his arms around like an orangutan. He whooped as if he'd just picked the winning lottery numbers. Everyone else in the room seemed pretty darn excited, too.

"That'll show you, you rotten little varmints!" he cried and made a punching motion in the air.

Tootie, serene approval on her face, saw me in the doorway and made her way over with the use of her silver-headed cane. "You'll have to excuse us," she said. "Felix takes his mole whacking quite seriously, and he just beat the house record."

I laughed. "Honest to Pete, Tootie. What will that activities director come up with next?"

"I don't know, but I'm anxious to find out. Things have certainly livened up around here lately. Did you hear about the area she set up so we can practice our croquet shots for next summer?"

I listened while she filled me in on more of the new doings around the place. I had to smile at her unaccustomed sprightliness. I hadn't seen her use her wheelchair for weeks, and I wondered whether the increased activity at the nursing home had anything to do with it. As she spoke, we walked over to a round table in the corner and sat down.

"Our new poker table," she informed me. "We play Texas Hold 'Em every Saturday night. I won eighteen dollars off Felix last week. That man will bet on anything."

"You're playing for money?"

"Don't be such a stick in the mud."

I laughed again.

"Now, why are you here?" she asked.

"Can't I just come visit?"

"Of course you can. But you have something on your mind. I can tell."

I sighed. "You're right."

She waited.

"I . . . well, I guess I'd like your advice on something."

She raised an eyebrow. "Really. You're not usually one for asking advice."

I chose not to take that wrong. "I know."

"Does this by chance have anything to do with that young man of yours?"

"What? Oh. No. Nothing like that." But naturally my mind immediately veered to the question Barr had posed about whether I'd thought about getting married again, and his hints about how much he liked living with me.

I tried to concentrate. "You remember the story you told us at dinner the other night about the woman who killed two brothers by poisoning them with botulism? Your cousin, wasn't it?"

Her face turned grave. "This is about Philip Heaven."

I nodded. "How did she do it?"

She leaned back stiffly in her chair and studied me. "I don't know for certain. Only what I heard my older sister say."

"Okay," I prompted.

"Hmm. Well, I think it was quite straightforward. She killed them by serving them food she knew had gone bad, and she timed it so it was unlikely they'd be able to get help."

I leaned forward. "Do tell."

"My cousin, or rather second cousin — her name was Edna Louise — worked in the kitchen of a good-sized boarding house for men in the early nineteen-twenties. This area was all thick forest then. Huge Douglas firs everywhere. Anyway, the two brothers, twins actually, were lumberjacks and stayed there when they weren't out working the surrounding hills."

"Why did she do it?"

"For the sake of her daughter. Women didn't have many options then, including with the law, but Edna Louise made her own options. She had some preserves that showed all the signs of having 'turned.' "

Elbow on the fancy poker table, I rested my chin in my hand. "What kind of preserves?"

"I don't know, but people canned everything back then if it couldn't be used fresh, dried, or kept in a root cellar. Soups, stews, whole chickens, all sorts of things. But she served it to them on purpose, and didn't give it to anyone else."

"Wasn't she still running a risk that

someone else would get sick?"

"Of course she was. And I dare say she knew it. She must have thought the risk was worth it."

"That's ridiculous," I said.

"Passion makes for some unusual ethical decisions."

That was an understatement. "How did she make sure they wouldn't be able to get help?" I asked.

"She gave it to them the day they were leaving for a job located far from town," she said. "It probably wouldn't have mattered much anyway; there wasn't much help available for a good dose of botulism in those days."

Even the modern hospital hadn't been able to help Philip. I wondered what his killer would have done if the doctors had been able to save him. Thank the powers that be they were able to diagnose and treat Barr.

"The twins had hurt your cousin's daughter?"

Tootie closed her eyes for a moment and nodded. In a tight voice she said, "Yes." There was a finality to the word that kept me from pursuing any more details.

Instead, I asked. "Do you think Edna Louise should have been punished for what she did?"

"No one deserves to have their life taken away from them."

"That's what you told Erin. But it sounds a little too pat."

"You're right," she said. "Reality is a lot more complicated than that. If I'd been on a jury, I'd have had a difficult time convicting her."

"So sometimes what's legal isn't necessarily just," I said.

Tootie's narrowed gaze bored into me. "What is this all about?"

I took a deep breath. "I'm pretty sure someone killed Philip intentionally with botulism toxin. I have a fair idea of who it might be, but it'd be so hard to prove, and no one seems to be all that interested in finding out for sure. Philip wasn't the nicest or best guy around; he was, in short, an embezzling, cuckolding, trust-fund baby who made promises to everyone that he had no intention of keeping."

"I'm surprised at you, Sophie Mae. You know better than that. If what you say is true, you can't just let it go. You're talking about someone who solved a problem by killing someone else."

Not to mention beating up Ruth, I thought.

"Who is this killer?" Tootie demanded.

Reluctantly, I told her. Every time I'd told someone I had a good suspect, I'd ended up being wrong. Now it seemed like bad luck to say it out loud.

"Hmm. Jude Carmichael. The cousin. He certainly did resent Philip."

I leaned forward. "He did? How could you tell?"

"It was obvious in their interactions. Philip was the top dog, Jude the poor relation. It's a story told a million times over. Where do you think he got the preserves?"

Befuddled by her easy observations, I answered absentmindedly. "I can't be sure."

"Did he can them himself, or get them from someone else? Does he have a lot of friends? Women? Older? I'm sorry to sound both sexist and ageist, but those are your best bets for finding the source of home-canned food. Not many people do it anymore."

"He doesn't seem to know that many people in town." A memory tickled my brain. Ruth talking about her friend who had canned beets, her friend who was now dead. Something clicked into place. "Hang on. Let me make a phone call."

I went out to the reception desk and asked to use the phone. Thaddeus answered the phone in Ruth's room. Several voices murmured in the background.

"How's our patient?" I asked.

"The doctors said she's going to be right as rain, just has a bit of healing up to do."

"That's terrific news." I'd been concerned about the effect the blood thinners would have on her recovery. "Is she available? Sounds like she has some visitors."

He snorted. "I'll say. She's had a whole bevy of them camped out in the room, knitting and chanting."

"Chanting?"

"Praying or something. I leave 'em to it. Hang on, I'll get her."

The background voices paused, and Ruth came on the line, her voice strong.

"You sound like you feel better," I said.

"Much. I have some friends here to help me out."

"Well, I don't know what they're doing, but as long as it works, I'm all for it."

I liked hearing Ruth laugh at that, though I wasn't sure why it was so funny.

"I have a question for you."

"Shoot," she said.

"The other day you mentioned a friend of yours who did a lot of preserving. In fact, I believe you said she canned beets."

"Yes." Tentative. Curt.

"I seem to remember that she's passed on. Can you tell me who she was?"

There was a very long pause, and then Ruth said in a wondering voice, "Her name was Hannah. Hannah Oxford."

"Oxford — isn't that the name of the man Jude lives with?"

"Indeed. George Oxford. Hannah was his wife."

"I see."

"Yes. I think I do, too. Sophie Mae, be careful."

"Believe me, I will."

We said goodbye, and I turned to find Tootie had followed and was leaning on her cane behind me.

"Did you hear that?" I asked.

"Enough. You didn't tell me Ruth was in the hospital."

I rubbed my eyes, suddenly tired. "I'm sorry. I should have. She told me some things and asked me to keep them quiet. I guess I've been a little too quiet."

Bafflement settled across her face. "I don't understand."

I inhaled. "She was attacked last night. She doesn't know who attacked her, but whoever it was mentioned the beets and wanted her to stop talking about them. It must have been Philip's killer."

306

Jude Carmichael? Hitting Ruth? That didn't fit with the sneaky picture I had of Philip's poisoner.

"What did the police say?" Tootie asked.

"She didn't tell them. That's what she wanted me to keep quiet."

She thumped her cane on the carpet. "That doesn't make any sense!"

"He threatened Thaddeus."

The wrinkles around her mouth deepened as she considered this. "What are you going to do?"

"I'm not sure. What if I'm wrong about Jude? Sometimes I feel like I'm tilting at windmills."

Tootie's jaw set. "You know you have to follow up on your suspicions. If you hadn't followed your instincts about what happened to Walter, I'd have gone to my grave thinking he'd committed suicide. You're smart, and you have moxie. I know you can solve this. It's important. And it's right."

Her words energized my fading resolve. "I'm helping Jude move tomorrow. I'll take a look around."

"Now, don't do anything rash. This is someone who beat up a seventy-year-old woman. He wouldn't hesitate to hurt you."

Jude seemed so dull. I tried again to imagine him hitting someone. "I have no intention of being alone with him. Both Kelly and Bette will be there. And Kelly is a rough-and-tumble kind of guy. Did you know he and Meghan are dating?"

For a moment Tootie looked pleased. "She mentioned him. I'm delighted she found someone she's interested in."

"Me, too," I assured her. "Me, too."

Concern settled over her features again. "You promise to be careful?"

I held up my hand. "Believe me, I'm not interested in playing the hero."

The sooner I could hand a workable clue over to the people who should have been investigating Philip's death, the better.

TWENTY-SIX

"You can come, can't you?"

"What?" I'd been distracted by my thoughts and hadn't heard what Erin was saying.

"The bee. It's tomorrow night. You'll be there, right?"

"Wouldn't miss it for the world, Bug. I'm proud of you for going ahead and competing even though Jonathan bailed." Meghan, Erin and I had just trooped back in from where I'd shown off my cobbled together chick nursery in the mudroom.

"That's not a name we're uttering out loud in this house right now," Meghan said.

"Oh. Right. He-who-must-not-be-named, then."

Erin rolled her eyes. "God. You're so weird."

Okay, maybe I was a little weird. I was at least willing to consider the idea as I stood in front of the bathroom mirror and slathered green goo on my face. Mmmm. Felt heavenly. But definitely looked . . . weird.

After dinner, Meghan had taken Erin to the library to exchange the books she'd read in the past week for a pile of new ones. Barr was watching some basketball game on television. I finally had a chance for a little private self-indulgence.

So, with a heavy hand, I slathered on the oatmeal mask and perched on the edge of the tub to deal with my ragged nails and rough cuticles.

The doorbell rang.

I paused, orange stick in hand.

It rang again.

I opened the bathroom door and shouted down the stairs. "Barr? Can you get that?"

No response.

The doorbell rang again, bing-bong, bing-bong. And then the knocking started. Cautiously, I ventured down a few steps. More knocking. Loud.

"Hello?" The voice on the other side of the door was a woman's.

"Coming," I yelled. "Barr?"

He didn't answer. I'd reached the bottom of the stairway, when he came barreling out of the kitchen and opened the front door. Detective Lane walked in.

"Detective Ambrose," she said, then stopped, staring at me. Barr turned around, and his eyebrows climbed up his forehead.

"I didn't think you were going to get the door," I said, sounding less than gracious.

"Sorry. I was downstairs on your computer. Didn't hear it at first."

"What *is* that on your face?" Detective Lane asked, eyes wide.

I touched my cheek, and my fingers came away with green on them. At least I'd put it on thick enough that neither of these two could see how red my face had turned underneath.

"Oh, come on," I said. "With your beautiful skin I bet you apply a regular mud mask."

She shook her head, making that thick auburn hair sway like a shampoo commercial model's. "Never thought about it."

I glared at her. "I'll be right back." I turned and stomped up the stairs to the bathroom.

Barr and Detective Lane were murmuring in the living room when I returned downstairs, face scrubbed and the hair damp around my face. I still wore my sweats.

He stood when I walked in and held out a cup of coffee to me. The dark circles under his eyes offered testimony to how hard he'd been driving himself to get back up to speed in the last couple of days, but his eyes were calm and his smile bright as he greeted me. I took the coffee and sat down, thanking him.

"To what do we owe this pleasure?" I asked Lane. Just because I looked like a slob didn't mean I couldn't behave with a little class.

Barr answered me. "Robin caught the guy who's been terrorizing women in Cadyville. The one they've been calling the Creep."

Robin? I buried my desire to bristle. He hadn't given me any indication I needed to worry about this woman — this incredibly beautiful woman he had so much in common with. Then again, he'd been sick as a dog most of the time he'd known her. My eyes flicked between them, but they only looked at me, pleased as punch.

And who could blame them? "That's great news," I said. "How did you manage it?"

Lane proceeded to tell us how she'd interviewed over a hundred people in the neighborhoods where the attacks had taken place, then cross-referenced information she'd gathered about cars parked on the street. In this way she'd tracked down the Creep's car and put him under surveillance. In the end she'd caught him red-handed, just as he was about to attack another woman.

"You did all that? By yourself?" I realized how condescending the words sounded as they left my mouth. Oops.

"I had a lot of help. This is a great department. And I've really come to like your little town here."

I showed some teeth. "That's nice. We always like to hear from the converts."

"Robin likes it so much she's going to stay," Barr said.

"Stay," I said.

"She'll be a great addition to the department."

Lane was watching my reaction with a glint of amusement in her eyes. Not mean, though. More like we were both in on the same joke. And the joke was somehow on her. In a lot of ways it was hard not to like her.

I turned to Barr. "So you won't have to work so hard? Chief Maher found the funding?"

"Yep. Just needed the right incentive, I guess."

A glance at Lane rewarded me with another amused look, this time the joke being on Andrew Maher. How did she do that?

"Well, I'm all for it," I said. "Less work

313

for you, so you can have a real life."

"Bingo. I knew you'd be pleased."

"What an understatement. And what a relief that the Creep is off the streets."

"Well," Lane said, "it's both good and bad for you."

"What do you mean?"

"He's not your stalker."

I sat back against the arm of the sofa. "You're sure?"

"Yes. I have phone records, and he gave a full confession. I'm not exactly surprised, since your stalker behaved differently from the very beginning. But it does mean someone else is still interested in you."

"But not the scary guy. Not the violent one."

"Hard to tell. Just because he's not the violent one we caught doesn't mean he's not violent at all."

I sighed. "Great."

Barr looked concerned all over again. Almost like nothing had changed. I was getting sick of feeling like I was spinning my wheels on all fronts.

So I couldn't help sounding cranky when I said, "Now that you've caught your major bad guy, are you going to investigate Philip Heaven's death?"

Lane looked at Barr. He said, "Robin, it

314

really does look suspicious."

Her forehead wrinkled. "Have you talked to the Chief? Or to Zahn?"

He grimaced. "Of course. Neither want to deal with it. As far as they're concerned, unless the Health Department tells them there's something fishy with Heaven's death, everything is copasetic."

"I can't investigate something like that without their buy-off," Lane said.

"What about justice? Does that enter into the equation at all?" I asked.

She looked upset. "I have to stick with the assignments I'm given."

I stared at her. All that glamour and so by-the-book. Barr and I exchanged looks. We weren't getting anywhere with this.

But I couldn't help trying one more time. "What if there's actual evidence? Something you could show your bosses, something they couldn't ignore?"

Her expression was momentarily hopeful, until she realized what I might be implying. "What did you have in mind?" she asked, her tone full of warning. "I know you have a tendency to go do things on your own. I can't let you do that."

"Oh, I didn't have anything in particular in mind," I said. "I was just curious about what it might take to open a case that's been deemed closed. Or, rather, never open in the first place."

"Ms. Reynolds," she began.

But Barr interrupted her with, "Maybe we could go over some of the other cases that are still pending? I'll be back in a week or so, but I'd sure like to keep up with what you're doing in the meantime."

One last wary look at me, and she turned back to him. "Sure. After all, we're partners now."

I pasted a smile on my face and took a sip of my rapidly cooling coffee.

Partners. Great.

Detective Robin Lane had been gone for an hour, and Barr was back watching his basketball game, looking more content than ever. I'd called the references Mandy Koller had given me, and had decided to take the plunge and hire her. Feeling a little giddy at the notion that I'd soon have more time to do what I thought of as "the fun stuff" for Winding Road — playing with recipes, cooking up batches of soap, and figuring out creative ways to sell my products — I folded a pile of laundry while Meghan worked in her office and Erin plugged away at her math homework.

I was happy Barr would have help at work,

and I'd finally get to spend more time with him, but it was tempered with a vague sense of unease at the thought of him working with that gorgeous, smart woman day in and day out. She didn't wear a ring, and she seemed to be footloose and fancy free enough to make the decision to move to Cadyville from Seattle without having to consider the effects on her family.

I didn't have to worry about Barr. I knew that. He was a good guy, an honest straight-shooter who'd never been anything but affectionate.

Still. Day in and day out. Bleah.

The phone rang. Adding a towel to the mounting stack of folded laundry, I went out to the hall to answer it.

"Sophie Mae. It's me. Allen. Don't hang up!"

Gawd. "Why not?"

"Are you really scared of me?"

"Is that what this is all about? Some power trip you get from trying to scare me? Because I've got to tell you, that'd really make mad."

"No! I just wanted to talk."

"I know you're not the Cadyville Creep. I know you're just some guy who likes to push buttons on the phone. And I'm going to get the police to track you down, just like they did the Creep. When they do, they're going to throw your butt in jail so fast you won't have time to say 'death threat.' "

"What? Death threat? Who's this Creep dude? Are you okay? You sound really uptight."

I kind of lost it then. "I sound uptight? Really? Did it ever occur to you that you're the one making me 'uptight'? That you're driving me nuts, not because I'm afraid, not because you're scary, but because you and your stupid phone calls are a real pain in the patootie!"

The phone made a nice loud crashing noise when I slammed it down on the cradle.

"You have to hit the Off button," Barr said from the doorway to the living room.

"What?"

"It's still on."

I looked down. Slamming the phone down hadn't disconnected it. Allen could still hear me. How embarrassing. Barr picked up the receiver.

"Don't call here anymore. She really will go to the police. In fact, I am the police." A pause, then, "Hello?"

He turned off the phone and returned it to the cradle much more gently than I had. "Hmmm. Seems to have hung up. I'd be surprised if you heard from him again."

"Good," I said, and rubbed both hands over my face. "I'm going to bed."

"Want some company?"

I looked up at him and grinned. "Of course. But it's probably not a good idea."

"Erin."

"Right."

"I'd like to put a suggestion on the table."

"What's that?"

"I'd like you to consider a living situation that wouldn't involve Meghan and Erin."

My breath stuttered in my chest. Carefully, I asked, "You mean a living situation that would include you?"

"Oh, absolutely it would include me. And there would be no reason for us to be in separate beds. Ever."

Wow. The idea thrilled me. Terrified me. But I'd have to give up living with Meghan and Erin, and over the years they'd become my family. I was so confused I couldn't speak.

He seemed to understand, gathering me into his arms and resting his chin on the top of my head. "Just think about it."

Mute, I nodded. I doubted I'd be thinking about anything else all night.

I did, though. Think about something else, I

mean. After everyone had gone to bed, I slipped out from under my warm covers and went to the closet. Fumbling around in the dark, I finally felt the pint canning jar in my hand. By the streetlight coming in the window, I could see the vague outlines of the preserved beets inside.

Ruth's beets, saved from destruction by the Health Department. Maybe they'd come in handy some day. I could only hope.

Was I being an idiot, going to help Jude move? Was he really dangerous? He seemed so . . . innocuous. It would probably be a boring morning spent hauling boxes.

No reason to make it into a big deal. Just be careful.

And if I did come across some information that could help convince the powers that be in the Cadyville Police Department that there was a case worth investigating, so much the better.

Tootie was right. I couldn't walk away from this.

Twenty-Seven

Erin had left for school, Meghan was working at the hospital, and Barr had dozed off. I thought about waking him before I left, but that just seemed mean. All that sleep seemed to help him regain his strength and wind. He knew where I'd be, plus I'd leave him a note downstairs to remind him, so he wouldn't be worried when he awoke to find me gone. Still, I couldn't help myself. Brushing aside a lock of chestnut hair from his forehead, I kissed the fine web of wrinkles at the corner of his eye. He stirred and made a snorting sound. I tiptoed out and shut the door softly behind me. Downstairs, Brodie toddled over to the foot of the stairs and lay down in habitual guard mode.

My mood bordered on giddy. The Winding Road invoicing was done for a while, and I'd found a wholesale order for a full display rack of soaps — a gross in all — waiting in my email inbox that morning.

Mandy Koller would soon be dealing with a significant portion of my bookwork. The Cadyville Creep was no longer a threat. I'd given Allen what-for the night before on the phone, and maybe this time it had taken — I almost felt bad about hurting his feelings — but not quite. Barr's health was steadily improving, Erin was going to compete in her spelling bee in spite of Jonathan Bell's defection, and Meghan had gotten over being mad at me for investigating Kelly O'Connell. And even though the thought made me crazy nervous, Barr obviously wanted to take our relationship to the next level.

Outside, the sun peered through a clear blue hole in the clouds, and the air smelled green. A big grin split my face as I strode down the front sidewalk to my little truck parked by the curb.

Detective Lane and I would never be best friends, but after her visit last evening I felt I had a good chance of convincing her to investigate Philip's murder. She'd caught the Cadyville Creep and proved she could do the job. Now I just needed the smallest piece of evidence to push her over the edge. In the cheerful light of morning and my present state of mind, all my doubts from the night before had vanished. I would be very careful, I'd find something for Detective Lane to run with, and I'd happily hang up any notions of investigating on my own forever.

Jude's little car hugged the curb in front of Heaven House, but the place looked empty when I walked into the main room from the street. I squinted in the comparative dimness after the bright sun outside, waiting for my eyes to adjust. A banging noise issued from the game room, followed by a yelp. Then silence. Curious, I crossed to the open doorway.

Inside, Jude stood with a hammer in his right hand and the index finger of his left hand in his mouth. His face was pinched with pain and his eyes were closed. A nail protruded at an angle out of the freshly painted wall just above his head, and a framed black-and-white picture of an elderly, white-haired gentleman in garb from a century earlier leaned against the floor molding.

"Who's that?" I asked.

Jude jumped and opened his eyes. "Gosh, you startled me."

"Sorry. I thought you heard me come in."

"Not with the racket I was making," he said, sounding quite proud of his lame handiwork. Still, pounding a nail in the wall was more than I'd ever seen Philip do for Heaven House. He glanced down at the picture I'd indicated with my question.

"Don't you recognize him? That's Edgar Cady."

"As in, Cadyville?"

"Of course."

I shook my head. "I never knew why it was called Cadyville."

"That's exactly why I decided to put his picture up. Maybe it'll inspire some of the kids who come in here to read about our little town. I've already acquired some materials from the historical society."

"That's very laudable," I said, taking a good look at the old gent. Mr. Cady had been a severe looking man. I looked back at Jude and changed the subject. "When will Kelly and Bette be here?"

"Oh, they'll meet us over at my place." He turned and hung the picture, fussing with getting the angle right. "We can go now, if you want."

"Um, okay. I'll follow you."

He walked past me and I heard the clank of metal hitting metal behind me as he returned the hammer. "I can't fit much in my car. I'll just ride with you in your truck, if that's okay."

But that wasn't okay. "You'd be surprised

at how much you can fit in your car." Ol'
Edgar's stern gaze seemed to agree with me.

"Nah. It'd be awkward getting things in
and out. Anyway. It's only a two-door." He
walked past me, toward the front door.
"Let's go."

His insistence surprised me. It seemed out
of character. But did I really know that? I
mean, it wasn't like I'd spent a lot of time
with the guy. Perhaps he had a stronger
personality once he started getting past his
shyness with people.

Turning and walking out to the main
room again, I still didn't like it. I scrambled
for a reasonable excuse to make him take
his own car. He had no reason to imagine I
thought of him as a threat, or that I hoped
to find proof he'd been involved in Philip's
murder. At the front door, I hesitated.

"They're probably waiting for us." He
looked bewildered. He looked bewildered
better than anyone I'd ever met. "What's
wrong?"

My reluctance could make him suspicious.
I made a decision and stepped outside. Jude
turned to lock the door.

"Nothing," I said. "What if somebody
comes by?"

Waving his hand, he said. "It'll be fine.
Anyone who sees it's closed will try again

later. Phones are already forwarded."

He sure seemed to forward those phones a lot.

"Why isn't Maryjake here?" I asked.

"She has Sunday and Monday off."

But she'd been in yesterday, Sunday, when I'd stopped by, and Jude had been upset when she'd left, so he must have expected her to be there.

Or she'd been covering for Ruth.

"When does Ruth answer the Helpline?" I asked.

One shoulder lifted and dropped. "The schedule for the volunteers changes all the time."

He opened the door and slid into the passenger seat of my pickup. His look through the window was expectant. I went around to the other side, got in and started the engine.

As I pulled away from the curb, I asked, "Where to?"

"Starling Lane."

It was a little cul-de-sac off 8th Street. A series of old, Craftsman-style two stories marched neatly around the perimeter. I didn't know anyone who lived there, but Cadyville was small enough that I still knew where it was.

Turning left on Maple, I accelerated to

twenty-five. "I'm really impressed you know so much about Cadyville history. I've lived here for years, and you know way more than I do. How long have you been in the area?"

"About six months. I like to know about where I live."

A little jab there. Fine.

"Turn here," he said.

I did as I was told, and Jude directed me to a white house at the end of the cul-de-sac. I parked in the driveway, and we got out.

"I don't see Bette's car," I said. "And doesn't Kelly drive an SUV?" None of those parked in the cul-de-sac, either. The various late model sedans and inexpensive mid-range cars indicated that retirees made up most of this little neighborhood.

"They'll be here soon enough. We're probably a little early." He went up the front steps and let himself inside with a key. "Coming?"

We weren't early. But maybe they were late. If I refused to go inside with Jude, I'd look foolish and paranoid and probably insult him. Now, I've seen Oprah, and I've read the books, and I know I should follow my instincts, and my instincts told me not to go into a house, alone, with someone I thought might be dangerous. Besides, I'd sworn — to Tootie, to Barr, but mostly to myself — to be careful. I scrambled for a rational reason, or even a fair excuse, not to go inside.

A large form filled the doorway. "Jude! There you are. I was hoping we could talk about — Oh, you have a friend with you. Welcome, my dear."

With a whoosh of relief, I recognized the deep baritone of Jude's landlord. He'd answered the phone when I'd been trying to find the errant beet canner for Ruth. He was tall, with a face that looked like slabs of granite overlaid with well weathered skin. He wore brown slacks, a yellow-on-beige checked shirt, and a light tan polyester jacket that zipped up the front.

I held out my hand. "You must be Mr. Oxford. I'm Sophie Mae Reynolds. It's very nice to meet you."

He gracefully took my hand and, instead of shaking it, turned it over and raised it to his lips. His palms were warm, the skin like a dry leaf, and his fingers were long and tapered, giving him a sensitive air despite the rest of his chiseled appearance.

"Likewise, making your acquaintance. Please call me George. What a charming young lady, Jude."

And what a charmer this lovely old man

was, I thought as I murmured, "Thank you." He'd be snapped up by some age-appropriate widow as soon as he was ready. Maybe even before. And maybe not even age-appropriate, now that I thought about it.

Jude reddened at the implication that he might have had anything to do with my being charming. But I was so happy to see George Oxford. Knowing I wouldn't be alone in the house with Jude until Bette and Kelly showed up made me feel way better.

"There should be two more people coming to help Jude move," I said.

George looked at Jude with surprise. "You're moving today?"

Jude looked more uncomfortable than I'd ever seen him before, which was saying something. "I was going to tell you this morning, but we missed each other."

"I see. Well, you did say you expected to be taking over your cousin's apartment a few days ago, so I guess I should have been expecting it. Sure will miss you, son — you've been a real life-saver, being here. And with Hannah gone . . ." George swallowed loudly and cleared his throat. "Sure will miss you." He turned and went inside, I suspected to pull himself together.

The house interior was dark and smelled

like dust and burned tomato soup and that curious effluvium of old man. Deep green carpet, worn threadbare in spots from decades of traffic, stretched into a living room on the left and a dining room on the right. Beyond, yellow light spilled from the kitchen doorway, and I saw the dull gleam of real Linoleum and the chrome edging of old, yellow Formica counters. The edge of the refrigerator visible from the front door was round, a shape I hadn't seen for years.

Jude glanced at me as if to see what I thought, but I didn't know whether to feel nostalgic or creeped out by these surroundings.

"I live downstairs, in the basement," he said.

Oh, good. Well, in for a penny, in for a pound.

The sound of rattling dishes came from the kitchen. Beside me, Jude sighed and pinched the bridge of his nose between his fingers. Ruth had said he helped George Oxford out around the house, and that she thought the older man appreciated Jude's company as well, but I hadn't realized how important Jude's role had apparently become.

"Do you want to go talk to him?" I asked.

He shook his head. "He's proud. I'll check

in with him later, assure him that I'm not abandoning him." He beckoned me to a doorway on the left, and I followed him down a set of old wooden stairs very similar to the ones that led from our kitchen down to my workroom.

Jude continued. "It's hard for him to take care of this place all by himself, and he gets lonely. I'll still visit."

We stepped into a large room paneled in dark wood. "That's awful nice of you," I said.

He whirled and put his hand on my shoulder, not seeming to notice how violently I flinched.

"No, it's just human," he said. "I mean, everyone ought to be nice to each other, don't you think? I believe if we were just kind to one another we wouldn't have so much crime and hate and violence. In fact, that's one of the new tenets of Heaven House, to promote kindness everywhere. I don't think it would hurt to have a few core values to structure the thinking behind the programs and the way the volunteers interact with the HH clients, do you? More like a mission statement than the Ten Commandments. Of course, some of the directives will overlap. I mean, they would, wouldn't they?"

I nodded, silent.

He continued. "Now, don't think I have any problem with religion-based community organizations, because I don't. Heaven House just doesn't happen to be one. But a lot of them work miracles, especially with the homeless and the addicted. I don't know if we're ready to take on some of the big problems like that yet, but someday I want the chance. It has to build, one program upon the next, contacts and networking, like a web of support within the community, putting the energy out there and then letting it come back, synergistically, holistically." His eyes widened. "Heaven House is going to be a perfect example of what a community center is supposed to be. You'll see, Sophie Mae, you'll see."

TWENTY-EIGHT

Wow.

And . . . wow. I'd never heard him put that many words together at one time before. In fact, I was pretty sure I hadn't heard him utter that many words, total, since I'd met him. I'd certainly had no idea he was so passionate about Heaven House. It was beyond passionate; it was almost obsessive.

Attempting nonchalance, I carefully backed away from his touch. "You're so right. Look at how much you've already done with the place since you've been in charge."

How it must have rankled him to see Philip screwing it up. Did Jude know his cousin had stolen money meant for Heaven House programs? If he did, it would have added insult to injury, and for all he knew the foundation's board hadn't done a darn thing about his cousin's transgressions.

Maybe Jude had decided to do something about it himself.

As these thoughts crystallized, I'd been looking around the room to see how much work faced us. Now I focused on the contents: a sofa and chair, a coffee table and an end table, one ancient bookshelf packed with books, leaning dangerously away from the wall.

I turned to find Jude staring at me. "Is all this going to HH?"

"What? Oh. No. The books, yes. But that's all. This stuff all belongs to George. I rented it furnished."

That seemed odd, considering he'd been so insistent about needing my truck in order to move. My discomfort, temporarily banished by George's presence upstairs, came slinking back.

"Will you keep the furnishings Philip put in his apartment?"

He looked disgusted. "That stuff is overpriced, pretentious garbage. I'll sell it all, buy something more practical, and donate the difference to a good cause. Maybe fold it back into Heaven House."

Wow again. It seemed the foundation was willing to support Heaven House programs, and I couldn't see it needed money from selling Philip's fancy fixtures. Then it dawned on me: maybe Jude was trying to pay the foundation back for some of the money Philip had taken.

"What about in the bedroom?" I asked, growing increasingly uneasy at the absence of Bette and Kelly, especially since he didn't seem to have enough to warrant their help, anyway.

"Some clothes."

"Is anything boxed up yet?"

He shook his head, but didn't look at all sheepish, like I would have. Great. This wasn't so much about moving him as it was about packing up his books and undies.

I straightened my shoulders. "When are Bette and Kelly going to be here?"

Now he looked sheepish. An awkward pause, and he said, "Well, they might not come."

I took a deep breath. "Really. Why not?"

"I, uh, didn't exactly get a hold of them."

My heart did a little skippity-thump, and a spasm of anxiety made my hand fly up to my mouth. I coughed into it to hide my fear, then crossed my arms and tried to look stern.

"You lied to me. That's not very nice."

He looked at the floor. "I'm sorry."

"Why did you tell me they were coming?" And why had I believed him? I wanted to smack my forehead. Stupid, stupid, *stupid.*

His shoulders lifted once and then fell back into their familiar slump. "I was afraid you wouldn't help me."

"But you don't really need my help, do you?"

"Of course I do." He looked around. "Well, maybe not. But I *want* your help."

He sounded a little like Allen when he said that, and my ears strained to make a connection between their voices.

The flimsy arm of the sofa wobbled as I gingerly perched on it. "I still don't understand why you lied."

"I thought you might not want to be here with me all by yourself."

Carefully, I said, "Is there a reason I wouldn't want to be alone with you?"

An embarrassed smile flickered on his face and then was gone. "Well . . ." The smile again, just a flash. "I know I've been kind of flirty."

I stared at him. *Flirty?* Jude?

"But I'm not going to make a pass at you, I promise. I wouldn't want you to be uncomfortable."

Launching to my feet, I briskly walked to the bookcase. Good Lord. This guy had so many problems they overlapped each other. I didn't have time to spend all day futzing with his various obsessions and anxieties. If I had a chance, I'd sneak upstairs and ask George about Hannah's beets. Otherwise, I just wanted to get this over with. Peeve had replaced my apprehension.

"Since it's just the two of us, we'd better get this show on the road, or we'll never get done," I said. "Do you at least have boxes?"

I knew I sounded impatient and rude, but I felt impatient and rude. Who did he think he was? Nice, having all those great plans to help people he didn't even know, but it was downright obnoxious to fool me into helping him move without even bothering to pack first. If I hurt his feelings, too bad.

Wide-eyed, he pointed toward the bedroom. "In there."

No, there wasn't anything frightening in the bedroom. No, he didn't attack me or lock me in. And no, I didn't pack his underwear for him. I set him to work filling boxes with the contents of George Oxford's hand-me-down dresser and went out to the living room to pack books. They were mostly novels, mostly science fiction, and mostly authors I'd never heard of. Jude hauled each box to my truck as I finished filling it.

He grabbed the last box of books and tromped up the stairs. The sink, filthy and rust-stained, in Jude's little bathroom downstairs was too gross to use, plus there weren't any glasses. Dusty and sweaty and thirsty, I figured I had a good excuse to take a break and seek out George to beg a glass of water.

And while George played host, I could find out more about what preserves Hannah had left behind when she died.

George wasn't in the living room or the kitchen.

"Mr. Oxford? George?" I called. Through the front window I could see Jude rearranging the boxes under the topper that covered the back of my pickup. We'd be on our way soon.

"George?"

The house was silence except for the loud tick tock of the huge grandfather clock. I went in the kitchen and opened cupboard doors until I found a glass and then let the tap water run for a few seconds to chill. No ice needed.

It tasted like ambrosia.

As I drank a second glass, I spied a closed door that looked like it might belong to a pantry. I padded quietly over to it and opened it. Shelves marched down the walls of the small space, full of cans and cans of red-and-white labeled soup and boxes of breakfast cereal.

Bachelor food.

No preserves.

I wandered out to the living room, ignoring the pull to go back downstairs and get the last box packed so we could leave. I trailed my fingers along the surfaces of side tables, picking up less dust than I would expect. George was a better than average housekeeper for a widower.

The upright piano held several pictures. George and his wife, mostly. No children. Sad, I thought.

A crewel embroidery sampler hung over the piano. The stitches were exquisitely executed: French knots and lazy daisies and some lovely couching. The Home Sweet Home design named the inhabitants of the home: George and Hannah.

Where was George?

His absence raised the hairs on the back of my neck. This was exactly the situation I had been determined to avoid, and yet it appeared I was here alone with Jude.

Had he killed Philip? He was definitely strange. But did that make him dangerous. I hadn't felt any danger while we'd been together downstairs. Maybe he was just a big, shy, kind of weird guy with bad social skills.

Taking a deep breath, I shook my head at my rationalizing. Didn't matter. He was the best suspect for Philip's murder so far, with a possible motive plus Hannah Oxford's theoretical preserved beets. I was leaving. Whether it made him suspicious or not, I would tell Jude I'd called home and had to leave right away. Meghan needed me. For what? An emergency massage call? Lame. So what? I'd figure something out. I'd meet him over at Heaven House with his stuff in a couple of hours, or even come by and pick him up here, get the last box or two. Only I'd be sure to bring reinforcements the second time around.

Just one last check for those beets, and then I was gone.

A quick glance out the front window showed Jude still shoving boxes around. I hurried back into the kitchen and began opening cupboards. Nothing of any interest whatsoever. Stumped, I set my water glass in the sink and stared out the small window in the back door. The narrow driveway that ran beside the house, half obscured by overgrown rhododendrons, led to a detached one-car garage. I darted a look toward the front door as I slipped outside.

The breeze picked up a few stray raindrops from a holly bush and flung them against my bare neck. I ducked my head and trotted to the long horizontal window in the garage door. Palms cupped around my eyes, I pressed my forehead to the glass.

Too dark to see.

With my fingertips, I rubbed at the dirt that partially obscured my vision and tried again.

No luck.

Around the corner, a small door accessed the garage from the side. The wobbly round knob turned easily enough, and I was inside.

"George? Are you in here?"

The smells of old motor oil and dust, mildew and ancient wood shavings assaulted my nose from the dim shadows. Most of the space was taken up by a champagne-colored Monte Carlo. A lawn mower crouched in the corner. A vast assortment of hand tools arranged with precision on pegboard hooks covered one wall. A shelving unit in the corner held jars of . . . wait a minute. I edged around the car and inspected the contents.

False alarm.

Each canning jar held a specific size of nut or bolt or nail. Shaking one in my hand like a giant rattle, I sighed.

Wait a minute. I squinted in the darkness. There. On the bottom shelf.

Bingo.

Excited, I squatted on my haunches and rearranged the dusty remains of Hannah Oxford's preserves. All the jars were unlabeled, but the contents were easy to ascertain. Cucumber pickles. Picallilly relish. Green tomatoes. Marinated mushrooms. Green beans. Jellies and jams.

No beets.

But there wouldn't be any beets. Jude wasn't an idiot. He'd have disposed of them.

Okay, enough was enough. I rose to my feet. Time to get the heck out of Dodge. I turned.

And froze.

Jude stood in the doorway, face obscured, utterly silent. He leaned one shoulder against the door jam, arms crossed, blocking my exit.

"Hi!" I said. "Ready to go?"

"What do you think you're doing?" His voice was so soft I had to strain to hear.

I licked my lips. Then I jammed my fists onto my hips and demanded, "What kind of a question is that? I was looking for George, and I couldn't find him in the house. Thought I'd check the garage to see if he was out here."

"He left."

"Really." I approached him, all Miss

Chatty. "Without his car? Sure hope it doesn't rain."

Now I could see Jude's eyes. The cold gaze was less than encouraging. He didn't budge, so I couldn't get out the door without physically pushing him aside. He was a lot taller than I'd realized. I smiled up, a big friendly grin.

I was so tense I could hardly swallow.

Then he looked down at the ground and shuffled his feet. The familiar gesture was oddly comforting. "George is a hardy soul. He doesn't mind getting a little wet."

Once again, I wondered about Jude leaving George so abruptly, and with such little notice. Anyone who would beat up Ruth wouldn't stop at hurting George.

Jude reached for me then, and without thinking about it, I drew back. His gaze probed mine, and I tried another breezy smile. I could feel it waver on my face, lips twitching. Fear radiated from every pore, coming off me in waves. His eyes flicked to the shelving unit in the corner.

He suddenly looked unbearably sad. "So you know."

"Know what?" I asked, too quickly.

He shook his head. "Don't even try, Sophie Mae. I can tell. I knew it was too good to last."

That comment threw me. "What was?"

"Finally having what I wanted. What I deserved. And I really liked you a lot. If you weren't dating that cop, I'd have asked you out."

I crinkled my eyes and tried to look accessible. "Barr and I aren't that serious, you know."

"Stop it. I'm not an idiot."

I held my hand up. "I'm only saying. Don't think I haven't noticed you're a pretty good-looking guy."

"Shut up!"

I shut up. Which was just as well because I'd started shaking in the cool air of the garage, and I had to clench my teeth to keep them from chattering.

Every nerve was tuned to a sudden move from Jude while my mind worked over the walls and windows, searching for a way out. The garage door wasn't an option; I'd never get it open before Jude managed to stop me. Again, I noted how big he was.

Funny how I'd never really noticed that before.

He backed out of the doorway, and I wanted to throw myself past him. "Come on," he invited. He didn't sound very friendly, though.

"Where?"

"I have to pick up something at HH."

"You can take my truck, if you want. I'll finish packing."

He looked at me, and I knew there would be no more packing. "Come on," he repeated. "You're driving."

Fine. Just get me into the open air, and I'd run like a deer. I ducked as far away as I could as I passed him in the doorway, but it wasn't far enough. His hand shot out, fingers hooking into the sleeve of my sweater, twisting until the grip started to cut off my circulation.

"Ow. Stop that."

His grip loosened an iota, and suddenly his other hand was in the pocket of my jeans.

"Hey —" I protested, trying swing away. God, what did this weirdo have in mind?

He removed his hand and jingled my keys in my face. "We're going out front, and you're going to behave. We're getting in your truck. You're going to drive me to Heaven House. Park in the alley. We'll both go in, and I'll get what I need, and then we're going to leave again."

"And go where?"

"You'll see. Let's go."

"And if I don't?"

He yanked my arm. It felt like my shoulder was going to twist out of the socket.

"Ow. I mean it: knock that off!" I yelled.

He yanked again. "Get in the truck."

Fear stabbed through me. Something horrible would happen if I got in the truck with this nut bag. I began to fight, twisting and trying to pull away while kicking at his knee. He instinctively turned his hips away, or else I'd have had a chance at his gonads. I jammed the heel of my palm toward his face, hoping to connect with his nose, but he jerked his head out of range.

This was a guy who couldn't pound a nail in a wall? I pulled my arm back again.

His hand came out of nowhere. When it connected with the side of my head, my vision filled with little dancing sparks of light.

"Get in the truck, or I'll have to hurt you." So much for shy and awkward.

"Like you did Ruth?" The thought of what Jude had done to her made me so mad my vision cleared.

"I didn't mean to hit her that hard," he muttered.

"Right. And George? What about George? Is he lying in some closet inside, all beat up because you're such a tough guy?"

It was such an incredibly stupid thing to say, but if he hit me some more, so be it; all I knew was that whatever Jude had in mind with this little trip to Heaven House was going to be very, very bad.

But he didn't hit me again. He looked . . . upset. "I would never do anything to hurt George. He's my best friend in Cadyville."

"So where is he?"

"Over at his friend Marvin's house. He goes over there to watch *All My Children.* And I think he's kind of upset about me leaving. Didn't want to watch. You know?"

I stared at him. He sounded like the same old Jude, a little odd, seeking approval.

Nice as pie to his landlord.

"George is fine," he said. "Now let's go."

He started pulling me toward the street. I continued to resist. He stopped and looked at me, considering.

"If you don't stop being a pain in the ass, I'm going to have to hit you again."

I shoved my chin into the air. "Go ahead. I'll fight you with everything I've got. And somebody in this neighborhood is bound to notice. Lots of nice retired folks who stay home all day, I bet."

What was I waiting for? I opened my mouth to scream.

"I'll hurt the little girl. Meghan's kid."

My mouth snapped shut. I hadn't thought I could be any more scared.

Turned out I could.

TWENTY-NINE

The rain was back, spitting out of a mercury sky onto the windshield of the Toyota. There were times when the precipitation of the Pacific Northwest got to be too dang much. I craved sunshine and warmth and air that sucked the moisture right out of your nasal passages in only a few breaths. I wanted high desert. I wanted to be anyplace where it wasn't so verdant, so green, so dank and damp and dark. The earlier blue sky and sunshine had been a tease, a glimmer of summer snatched away after only an hour or two.

That may have had something to do with my bad mood, but the real explanation was probably the killer sitting in the passenger seat beside me.

"What are you going to do?" I asked. Meaning what are you going to do *to me?*

Jude didn't answer, appearing to concentrate on the road in front of us. His eyes flicked over to the speedometer, which was pegged at exactly twenty-five miles an hour. I should have been speeding, should have tried to get pulled over by one of Barr's buddies at the cop shop, but stupid me, I hadn't thought of that. I was still trying to get my mind around the fact that Jude had threatened Erin. What kind of bastard did that? I had a new appreciation for Ruth's fear that he might hurt her uncle Thaddeus. My attitude toward her dilemma had been too cavalier by far.

I asked again, "What are you going to do?"

He sighed and pinched the bridge of his nose between thumb and forefinger. "I'll work something out."

A carton shifted in the bed of the truck as I went around a corner. "There's no real evidence against you in Philip's killing," I said. "The Health Department is sure they have the real culprit, you know, beetwise. No one even thinks it was murder."

He got a little pale when I used the word "murder." Kind of sensitive for a killer, in my opinion.

"But you know," he said. "You'll tell."

"Tell what? I've got nothing. And anything you told me is hearsay. Even if I took out a sandwich board advertising what you did, you'd get off in court. Never see any jail time. I bet it wouldn't even get as far as court."

"My reputation would be ruined."

"Jude, you don't have a reputation in Cadyville."

"But I will. If I don't ruin it, then I will."

"If you hurt me, then you'll get caught. People wouldn't think much of that, now would they?"

"I won't get caught if you can't tell them."

I didn't like the sound of that at all. "There are people who know I'm helping you move."

"Good."

"But they'll know you're responsible if anything happens to me."

"No. They'll know you helped me out. Then you left. I don't know where you went. Gosh, I'm sure grateful she helped me move, I'll tell them. George saw you there. I don't know what happened to you after we unloaded the truck. I wish I did."

"You're banking on no one seeing us."

"Monday is Maryjake's day off. Heaven House is closed up."

"Barr will know. He knows I suspect you, and he's not the only one."

Fear and anger infused his face, and he ran a shaking hand through his hair. Then he dropped it into his lap. His eyes took on a speculative gleam. "Does he also know you have a stalker? Because you know how those situations can get out of hand, Sophie Mae. It's on the news all the time."

"Are you . . . you're not . . ." Nah. I'd recognize the voice. Wouldn't I?

"Allen?" I asked.

"Allen? That's the name of your stalker? Isn't that the guy from your first night on the Helpline?"

Jude had been standing right in front of me when I'd been on the phone with Allen that night at Heaven House. Of course he wasn't my stalker.

He continued. "Oh, that's perfect. No, I haven't been following you. God, you're full of yourself."

"Hey, wait just a tootin' minute there," I protested. "It's not my fault someone targeted me."

"Well, it's working out pretty well for me." His lips turned up in an unpleasant smile.

"Not really," I fudged. "They caught him, last night. The Cadyville Creep. So blaming him isn't going to work."

"This Allen guy was the Cadyville Creep?" More of that smile. "So why did you wonder if I was this Allen character just now? Maybe they got the wrong guy. Maybe you're still in danger after all. Everyone will be so sad they didn't do more to catch him. I could tell you were scared when you were talking about him today. How he was contacting you all the time, and how you'd see him on the street, but you didn't want to tell anyone, your housemate or your boyfriend, because you didn't want to worry them."

He was really getting into his story now. It was coming together a tad too well for my taste.

"How did you do it?" I asked. "How did you get Philip to eat the beets?"

Jude grimaced. "He was a pig. Ate all the time. He liked beets. Heck, he never met a food he didn't like. When I was looking through the preserves George's wife had put up, looking for something for the exchange, I saw the jar those beets were in. Foam. Funny color. Bad seal. Next thing I knew I'd put them on my dear cousin's desk. Off they went to his kitchen, and then down his gullet."

"But didn't he see they were bad?"

"I put them in another jar, all clean and pretty. It wasn't vacuum sealed, but he didn't know any better. His mother never had to can their food. My mother did, but not his. His mother had a cook to make little Philip's grilled cheese, a maid to make his widdle bed." His obvious bitterness rode under every sarcastic word.

"How could you be sure they'd kill him?" I couldn't let it go.

"Nothing is certain. Except, as I said, he was a pig. If it didn't work, he never knew where they came from. I was still safe."

"And if he served your poison to someone else? Did you think about that?"

His eyes were stony as he gazed at the rain falling on the other side of the windshield. "Collateral damage."

Astonishing. He truly didn't care who he hurt in his bid to take over Heaven House and wreak revenge on Nathaniel's favored grandson. His dismissive attitude infuriated me. My fingers gripped the steering wheel so hard they turned white. I felt as if I could rip it right off the column

Jude pointed. "Turn here. Go down the alley."

He'd threatened Erin, and I had no doubt he meant it. Could she be protected? With enough warning, yes. Meghan would be furious, but that was better than letting Jude kill me. Better than letting him get away with killing his cousin and hurting both Barr and Ruth.

I turned.

Halfway down the alley, I screeched to a

stop, opened my door and ran like my hair was on fire.

I'd be able to outrun Jude, non-athletic, bumbling, foot-shuffling Jude. Footsteps pounded on the pavement behind me, and I glanced over my shoulder. He was a lot faster than he looked. I veered between two buildings, determined to hit the street in front of HH before he caught up with me. There would be people there.

I panted like I was hauling a pack of rocks. I really needed to get more exercise. Maybe take up jogging or get a stationary bike or something. Six more steps. Almost there.

My head jerked back, and my feet left the pavement. The sight of buildings reaching up to the gray sky filled my vision.

Jude had grabbed my braid and pulled, really freakin' hard.

I landed on my butt in the damp muck of the alley. For a moment I couldn't breathe. Panicked, I flailed my arms and forced in a wheezing lungful of air. Pain shrieked up my neck.

He firmed his grip on the base of my braid and hauled me upright. Handling me like a rag doll, he forced me to stumble and trip into the back entrance of Heaven House.

"You just have to keep fighting me, don't you?" he muttered as he pushed me over to

Maryjake's desk and began rooting through the drawers. My head was pulled back at an awkward angle. I had to arch my back and neck in order to stay upright. A sad state of affairs, that staying on my feet had become the best case scenario.

"What did you expect?" I grated out through my humiliation. "That I'd meekly cave? Is that what you expect from women? Or is that what you expect from everyone? And if they don't give you what you want, you poison them, or beat them up, or —"

"Shut up." His tone was curiously flat, but I complied because I didn't know how to finish the sentence.

In his pocket, his cell phone rang. He fumbled it out, looked at the display, then answered.

"Heaven House Helpline."

I opened my mouth, and he yanked on my braid. "Help!" I yelled.

But he flipped the phone closed and put it back in his pocket. "Too late. They hung up. Must not have been important."

The phone rang again. This time Jude ignored it altogether.

So much for community service.

Back to the desk drawer. "There it is," he said under his breath. I craned in his grasp, slewing my eyes to the right. He held up a key so I could see it. "Philip's apartment."

"Are we going to unload your things now?" Couldn't quite keep the sarcasm out of my voice.

"Yes. At least I am. Somehow, I don't think you'd be much help." He went back to rooting through Maryjake's junk. "I saw it right here the other day . . ."

I swung my fist behind me, but my unseeing aim was off. I hit his leg.

"Damn it!" He grabbed my wrist and let go of my hair, swung me around, and grabbed my other wrist. It was fast. I fought again, as I had in the driveway at George's, but he was just too strong. I opened my mouth and screamed as loud as I could.

A tiny smile quirked up the left side of his mouth. This old brick building was well sealed and insulated. We might as well have been in a tomb. No one would hear me, and we both knew it.

And then he was wrapping scotch tape around my wrists, over and over again.

I laughed, and pulled. Stopped laughing. Like Jude, the thin transparent tape was a lot stronger than it looked.

He grabbed my braid again, let go of my hands, and turned me to face away from him. At least my hands were in front of me.

The drawer slammed shut, and I found

myself being steered to the far side of the room. Jude stooped in front of a red metal box, tools spilling out of it onto the painted concrete by the back wall. I had no choice but to bend, too, my hair still firmly in his grip like a rope handle.

Then I saw the small hammer he'd used to pound the picture hanger into the wall of the game room. It lay diagonally across the top tier of neat metal compartments.

My hands crept toward it.

Ever so slowly.

Jude muttered under his breath some more. Whatever he was searching for continued to prove elusive.

My fingers were only inches away.

"Where the hell is it?" His voice cracked with anger. He gave my head a slight shake, as if I were keeping something from him.

"What are you looking for?" My fingers touched the handle of the hammer.

With a sudden movement, he upended the entire contents of the tool box onto the floor. Wrenches clanged and bolts traced crazy circles.

The hammer slid away before I could curl it into my clumsy grip.

But there: a big fat adjustable wrench. I lunged for it, but Jude had seen it already and jerked my braid. My head snapped back so hard I thought my neck would break.

"Ow!"

He didn't respond, simply stood, pulling me up with him, and started marching toward the stairway to the top floor. Only now he had a roll of silver duct tape in his hand.

Staying on my feet was about to become a thing of the past.

Fear spurted through me. I couldn't let that happen.

I twisted in his grasp, pain shooting through my shoulders, then dropped my head and let my legs buckle. For a moment my weight was suspended from my hair. Then I was on my knees. He lost his balance and his right arm propellered as he let loose with a stream of obscenity that under other circumstances I would have found quite impressive.

But he didn't let go.

He did, however, turn to face me.

As hard as I could, I brought my clasped fists up between his legs. He grunted. Doubled over.

And loosened his grip enough for me to pull away from him.

I rolled onto my back and aimed a kick in the exact same spot I'd just punched. The first blow had connected directly, but I only had so much strength in my arms. I wanted to hurt him for good.

I wanted to hurt him forever.

He saw it coming, threw his hips to one side, and I only kicked him in the behind. The look on his face when he turned back was one of naked fury. A tsunami of adrenaline washed through me, and I was up on my feet and running.

Jude was right behind me.

Front door: locked. Back door: too far away. Upstairs: trap. Only option: game room.

I veered inside and swung the door shut. It closed with a satisfying *snick* in his face, and I fumbled for the lock.

No lock.

Right. Okay.

Panting, I held the knob while Jude rattled it. It began to turn in my hand. There, at the new table — a metal folding chair. I let go and lunged for the chair. The door began to open. I slammed my shoulder into it, closing it again. Jude swore some more. I jammed the chair under the knob, mashing one of my fingers in the process. It's hard to be graceful when your wrists are bound together.

He pushed and he pushed, but the chair held fast.

I gradually backed away from the door. Had to find a way out. My gaze swept the room. No phone. Nothing on the bookshelves. Nardella and her Treasures blinking over in the corner. Three more metal folding chairs. One of those would make an awkward weapon.

Why didn't I carry a cell phone like normal people? If I could just get out of here, I promised, I'd join the twenty-first century. I'd get a cell phone, an mp3 player, and any other technology I could find. I'd renounce my neo-luddite ways, I really would.

The picture of Edgar Cady was framed behind glass. Maybe I could do something with that.

Speaking of glass . . .

The three south-facing windows let in a decent amount of light, even at this time of year, even with the sky returned to its typical winter dinginess. On the ground floor, they stared out at the ugly painted teal cinderblock of the building next door. Though not very big, I should still be able to wiggle through one of them. Excited at the prospect, I hurried over to them.

Unlike the ancient painted-over window frame in Philip's office upstairs, these windows had been replaced with modern security frames. Obviously designed not to open. Disappointment weighed like bricks in my stomach.

But windows are made of glass. Glass breaks. I eyed the folding chairs again.

Near them, the Chase brothers had installed the dartboard Maryjake had been so thrilled about. It was made of concentric rings of cork, painted red and green, black and white. On the floor below was a package of steel-tipped darts.

I wrestled them open and managed to extract one of the sharp pointy parts. It quickly perforated the transparent tape binding my wrists, allowing me to pull it apart and remove it.

The door shuddered as Jude kicked it.

I jumped.

"Careful," I called out, trying to sound confident. "If you make too much of a mess then the authorities'll know you have a very nasty temper."

The obscenity was even more creative than before. But the kicking stopped.

I finished screwing together the darts and added the flights. I couldn't hit the side of a barn with one of those things on a good day, but that wasn't going to stop me from trying if I had to.

A small door at the end of the game room

revealed a small storage closet. In Jude's idealized community center it would no doubt contain sports equipment and games within a week. Now all it contained was a vacuum and . . . a jar of pickled asparagus. I recognized the label. This was the jar I'd left for Maryjake Friday evening. She must have stuck it in there yesterday, meaning to take it home, and forgotten it.

I took it out and hefted it. The quart jar fit nicely in my hand. I would have preferred a hardwood baseball bat, believe me, but I took it over to the table and set it next to the darts.

I picked up one of the chairs. Time to break a window.

Boy, I didn't want to do that. Sure, it made sense: break the window, scream my head off, get the hell out of there.

Except if I could get out, Jude could get in, and I didn't know where he was.

I heard voices out in the main room of Heaven House.

"Help!" I yelled at the top of my lungs. Lightheaded with hope, I grabbed the folding chair and swung it at the glass. Hard. The window cracked a little

God, what a wimp.

I shouted again. "Help! Please help me!" And swung again. The glass shattered with a loud, satisfying crash and tinkle. I considered the gaping hole, lined with sharp glass teeth. The opening seemed small. Winter blew into the game room, and I shivered.

"Sophie Mae? Sophie Mae! Where are you?"

"In here. I'm in the game room," I shouted. That voice was familiar, but at the same time, not. Who was out there? "Hello?"

Conversation again. I edged to the door and put my ear against it. They'd moved closer, but I strained to make out what they were saying.

"What are you doing to her?" The strange voice demanded.

He wasn't yelling now. Recognition dawned. It was my good friend, my buddy.

My stalker.

"Allen?"

Scuffling sounds then, and a shout, then another, and a grunt, then an even louder yell, suddenly cut short. And then only the sound of my panting breath against the silence.

I snatched the jar off the table, hauled the chair out from under the doorknob and swung the door open, brandishing the pickles. I heard a gurgle from my right, and in the dim light from the front windows I saw Jude, face red and jaw clenched, kneeling over Seth Chase, hands around his throat. Seth still struggled, but weakly.

Fifteen feet away, Jude was killing the poor kid who had come to rescue me.

I ran up behind him, lifting the jar above my head. He heard me coming, and whipped around at the last minute. His gaze locked on mine. I brought the heavy jar down, and he crumpled to the floor.

The flash of resignation in Jude's eyes right before I bashed him over the head would stay with me for very, very long time.

THIRTY

Eyes closed, Seth rolled onto his side in a fetal position, hands moving protectively to his neck as he coughed and gagged air back into his lungs.

I knelt beside him. "Are you okay?"

His eyelids fluttered, and then he was looking at me. He nodded weakly, and his lips moved.

"Don't try to talk. I'm going to call the police. Stay here." Like he was in any shape to go gallivanting off.

His fingers curled onto my arm. "I'm sorry," he croaked, wincing at the effort.

I brushed back a piece of dark hair that had flopped into his eyes. "Don't worry."

"Are you going to tell them?"

"Stop talking. I mean it. Just trust me, okay?"

After a few seconds, he nodded and closed his eyes again.

I left him and went to the telephone on

Maryjake's desk. I dialed the police station and asked for Detective Lane. She was out.

"Well, track her down. Tell her Sophie Mae Reynolds is at Heaven House and that someone just tried to kill me. He's still here but could regain consciousness at any time. And while you're at it, send a patrol car and an ambulance over here."

Guess what? It turned out I should've called 911 instead of the Cadyville Police station. There was quite the hullabaloo as the cadet on the front desk tried to figure out what to do, and then I was talking to Sergeant Zahn, and then finally to Detective Lane on her cell phone. By then the sirens had arrived. Lane showed up soon after.

I thought she'd be spitting nails, but she took one look at the situation and — get this — she apologized to me.

Like I said, it was kind of hard not to like her.

Jude was still out, which scared me. I hadn't wanted to kill him; I'd only wanted to stop him. An ambulance whisked him off, and another set of paramedics stayed to work on Seth.

He was feeling better by then, and in a whispery voice told Lane how he'd come by Heaven House to pick up some tools he and his brother had left there the day before. He had a key, which Jude had given the brothers for easy access since he planned for them to complete several handyman projects over the coming weeks. When Seth came in, he'd found Jude trying to get into the game room and me calling for help from the other side of the door. He'd confronted Jude, who had attacked him and tried to strangle him.

His eyes locked on mine. "Sophie Mae saved my life."

"That makes us even, then," I said. "Because you saved mine, too."

Okay, granted, Seth's rescue wasn't as, um, hands on, but I had no way of knowing whether I could have escaped out that window or not. If it hadn't been for him, Jude might have very well killed me by now. The thought made me shiver, and Detective Lane's forehead wrinkled with concern.

I smiled, big and bright, and she seemed to relax. When she went to talk to one of the patrolman, I crouched next to Seth's chair.

"Was that you on the telephone? Did you hang up when Jude answered?"

He nodded. "I saw your truck in the alley." He looked down, embarrassed. "It wasn't that I was following you, but I had my eye out. I wanted to talk to you."

I harrumphed.

He rolled his eyes. "Only to apologize. Only because I know I've been bugging you, and I never really meant to do that. The first call? It was stupid. I was just bored. But then you seemed so nice. I knew who you were. I guess I got a little obsessed. I'm real sorry. It's just, well, since we moved here it's been . . ." His whisper trailed off, and he blinked away the welling tears.

"Here. Drink this." I handed him the bottle of water the paramedic had given him to sip.

"Thanks."

"Seth, you might have been bored when you called Heaven House that first time, but you were also depressed. And lonely. And you know what? That's okay. That's what the Helpline is all about. I wasn't very good at getting you what you needed, but I'll make you a deal."

A stubborn expression settled on his face.

"Just listen. If you'll contact one of the free counseling services I can put you in touch with, I won't tell Lane you were the one calling me."

Alarm replaced the stubbornness.

"Yes, she knows someone has been stalking me. I know you don't like it when I call it that, but you have to admit that it wasn't exactly normal behavior."

Sheepishness across his features now. "Yeah. I know. I really am sorry."

"I believe you. So that's the deal: you talk to a professional about the stuff you wanted to talk to me about — life, death, and maybe, if you want to, about your mom dying — and I'll keep mum. You stop calling me all the time like you were, and we can be friends."

"Friends?"

"Friends. And friends talk to each other. So you'll be able to talk to me, too. But no more being weird about it."

He considered, then shook his head. "I can't. My dad, Luke —"

"You don't have to tell them, at least not at first. It's your business if you talk to a therapist. They'll deal with what's happened to your family in their own way, but they don't get to tell you how to do it."

Hesitation, a glance at Lane scribbling in her notebook across the room, then a single bob of his head. "Okay."

I had to fill out paperwork and give my statement at the police station. It seemed to take forever. Lane came over to the desk where I was rechecking my written statement one last time and put her hand on my shoulder. I looked up, wondering what she wanted from me now.

"Just got a call from the hospital. Jude Carmichael is awake and lucid. And, from what I hear, has a heck of a headache. He's complaining left and right, but he's confessed to everything."

Sighing in relief, I said, "I didn't kill him, then."

"Nope." Her grin was wide. "You wielded those pickles with exactly the right amount of force."

I gave her a look, and she left to talk to George Oxford, who was waiting pensively on the other side of the room. She was still grinning as she walked away.

Taking a deep breath, I used one of the desk phones to call home. Meghan answered.

"Is Barr around?" I asked. What a coward. I wanted him to tell her what had happened.

"He's asleep upstairs."

"Still?" I tried to keep the worry out of my voice.

"No, again. What's wrong?"

"Nothing. Just tell him I'm done with the stuff at Heaven House, and I'll be home when I can. I'll probably be late."

"But, Erin —"

"I know. I'll get there as fast as I can."

"Sophie Mae, what on earth . . ."

"Fill you in later."

"But everything's okay?"

"It is now."

I hung around until someone returned from George's house with the rest of the Hannah's preserves. George had confirmed that Jude had taken several of the jars to Heaven House, but he didn't know exactly what he'd removed. At one point, he said, there had been beets out in the garage with the rest of his wife's home-canned goods.

No telling whether they'd be able to prove the beets Jude had pilfered to give to Philip were from the same batch. For all I knew, the jar the Health Department had taken from Philip's apartment had been summarily destroyed and wouldn't be available for comparison. But between Jude's confession and my statement, the prosecutor wouldn't need the beets to make his case. I didn't know if it would do any good, but I'd told Lane about the jar of Ruth's beets I'd hidden away.

By the time the police were done with me, it was pitch dark outside. I hurried home, took a quick shower and changed my clothes. The day was not yet done.

Two kids remained on stage when I got

there, and tension in the room was high. I excuse-me'd my way down the row of seats to the empty one next to Barr, causing grumbling from the spectators as I went. Kelly sat on the other side of my housemate, his hand on her knee. Meghan craned around Barr to spare me a questioning look, then redirected her attention to where Erin sat alone on a stool under the bright spotlights. A carrot-topped kid stood in front of the microphone stand, looking terribly serious. The spray of freckles across his nose was visible from a third of the way back in the auditorium.

"Where have you been? I was getting worried," Barr whispered in my ear.

I smiled and turned my head slightly, glad that in the dim light Barr couldn't see the bruise blossoming across my cheekbone. I'd pay for not telling him and Meghan right away about my near deadly encounter with Jude, but I'd had enough on my plate at the police station. Dealing with Detective Lane, Sergeant Zahn and Chief Maher had taken all my energy. The last thing I'd needed was to worry about my boyfriend rushing from his sickbed and yelling at me for being stupid.

Ditto for Meghan, minus the sickbed. And probably double the yelling.

"I'll tell you later," I said.

"Is it good news?"

Meghan nudged Barr's arm. "Ssh."

"The best," I whispered. "You look fabulous, dahling." I was changing the subject, but also telling the truth. Dressed in jeans and a button-down shirt and cowboy boots, he looked almost like my old, reliable Barr. A big blue hunk of turquoise decorated the string tie around his neck this evening.

He pointed up front.

"Fluorescent," droned an adult voice through the sound system. I spied the speaker holding a microphone off to the side and below the elevated part of the stage.

"Fluorescent," repeated the red-haired kid. "F-l-u-o-r-e-s-c-e-n-t. Fluorescent."

"That is correct."

Applause, even from the kids already eliminated and now sitting in the front row.

Carrot-top and Erin switched places. She licked her lips and squinted against the bright light, eyes searching the audience. Her gaze settled on our row, and she gave a little smile.

"Serendipitous," intoned the judge.

Erin licked her lips again. "Serendipitous. S-e-r-e-n-d-i-p-e-t-o-u-s. Serendipitous."

"I'm sorry. That is incorrect."

Her face fell, and I heard Meghan groan.

Then the whole place erupted in applause, people standing and clapping. The judges got everyone settled back down for the awards ceremony.

Later, as we were all filing out to the cars, Erin said. "Well, at least I still get to go to regionals."

"Really?" I asked.

"Yep. Top two."

Behind me, Meghan made a small noise, too low for her daughter to hear, but enough that I turned around and looked at her. She gave me a weak smile, and Kelly laughed.

Of course, all hell broke loose when we got home and I told them what had happened. Meghan cried, and Barr kept hold of my hand and wouldn't let go. Kelly listened carefully, and I had the feeling he wanted to take notes for the foundation.

"I can't believe you went off with him alone like that," he said at one point, though he sounded oddly admiring. Barr frowned. Probably afraid I'd feel encouraged to do something that stupid again.

Fat chance.

"Well, I did think you were going to be there," I said.

"What? Why?"

"Jude told me he'd asked you and Bette

to help him move, too. Then you weren't there, and he said you were running late. Then he finally told me you weren't coming at all. And by then —" I shrugged, "— I thought George was upstairs."

He shook his head and started asking more questions, most of them about the money

Finally, I held up my palm and pointed toward the living room. Erin sat on the sofa, acting like she was watching television, but I could tell she felt upstaged.

"Listen. Seth is fine, and he's not really a stalker after all. He agreed to go see a professional, as long as we don't rat him out to his brother and father, and I agreed to be a friend when he needs one. The kid just misses his mom and wanted someone to talk to.

"Jude has a nasty concussion, but he's a hard-headed s.o.b., and he's going to be fine, too. Except for the going to jail part. Detective Lane is sure she can work with the county attorney to put a good case together against him for Philip's murder. I'm sure Ruth will agree to help, now that he can't hurt Thaddeus."

"What about Heaven House? And the foundation?" Meghan wanted to know.

"No clue. And you know what else? I

don't really care. Philip's killer has been caught, the Cadyville Creep won't hurt anyone else, and even my own personal stalker mystery is solved. I'm perfectly happy to put this all behind us and celebrate Bug's victory."

So we all trooped into the living room and Meghan broke open the sparkling apple cider and the single malt Scotch, and we toasted our resident spelling expert in as many creative ways as we could think of. Finally, we called it quits, and Meghan pointed Erin toward the stairs to put on her pajamas and brush her teeth. Before she obeyed, she came over and put her arms around me.

"I'm glad you're okay."

"Thanks, Bug. I'm glad you get to go to the regional bee."

A big grin split her face. "Me, too. 'Night everyone."

After she'd gone to bed, Barr said, "That agreement you made with Seth Chase? I don't like it."

"You sure say that a lot. Let's see how it goes. If he breaks his word, or if he still seems to be acting strangely, I'll be the first one to take action."

Meghan said, "I think it was a compassionate and kind thing to do. Sometimes you have to give people the benefit of the doubt."

Kelly, beside her on the sofa, was all goo-goo eyed as he watched her. Oh, he had it bad, too, I thought.

"Thank you," I said, directing a triumphant look Barr's way. "When are you going back to work?"

"In another week or so. I've found I kind of like the time off. And the TLC I've been getting here. Doesn't seem right to be in too much of a hurry to end it." His eyes said more, reminding me of his suggestion the night before. For some reason, after having my life threatened, the idea of making a major step forward in our relationship didn't seem quite so scary.

"To family," I said

Barr smiled, and Meghan and Kelly raised their glasses. "To family, and to friends."

RECIPES

Winding Road Saltea Bags

These have it all! Like other bath tea bags, this recipe includes dried herbs long used to benefit the skin. However, you'll also find Epsom and sea salts, essential oils to soothe your skin and your mood, and a slight fizzing action that disperses a light, softening bath oil.

Makes four teapot-sized bags.

1/8 cup dried green tea (gunpowder green if available)
1/4 cup dried calendula
1/4 cup dried chamomile (loose leaf chamomile tea is fine)
1/4 cup dried lavender flowers OR dried spearmint OR dried rosemary OR dried lemon peel
1/2 teaspoon of one of the following essential oils to match the dried herb above:

lavender, spearmint, rosemary or 1/4 each
of lemon and orange
1/8 cup baking soda
1/16 cup citric acid
2/3 cup Epsom salts
2/3 cup sea salt
2 full teaspoons light oil such as hazelnut,
jojoba, almond or wheat germ

Combine all dry ingredients thoroughly.
Combine oils separately, then drizzle over
the top of herbal/salt mixture. Mix thoroughly. Divide into four large (teapot sized),
heat-sealable tea bags (available online, or
in specialty bulk tea shops). Wrap in cellophane or package in a glass jar to preserve
scent.

Toss one bag in the bath. First it will puff
out and fizz, dispersing the oils (don't
squeeze!), then it will float in the water. The
longer you leave it, the more the herbs will
steep, tinting and softening the water.

AIR FRESHENERS Á LA SETH

The essential oils in these keep them fresh
for a long time, but you can also add a drop
of vitamin E oil to each one as an added
preservative. Just as with commercial gel air
fresheners, the scent is released as the gel
dries. Each one contains a lot of essential

oil, so they are quite fragrant.

Makes four fresheners (4 ounces each).

1 packet of unflavored gelatin
3/4 cup boiling water
1/4 cup cold water
Coloring (food coloring is fine, or you can skip the color altogether)
4 teaspoons essential oil or essential oil blend

Dissolve gelatin in boiling water. Stir in cold water, coloring and essential oil. Pour into 4-ounce glass or plastic containers with lids — avoid using tins, as the oils may corrode the metal. Once the liquid is no longer steaming, five minutes or so, cap the containers and allow to cool at room temperature. When ready to use, uncap and enjoy!

Some nice scents for these are lavender, cinnamon with clove, rosemary with peppermint, or fir needle.

MEGHAN'S WINE JELLY

This jelly can be made anytime, and provides a special accompaniment to meat. Earthy red wines like Cabernet Sauvignon or Shiraz are particularly good with lamb or beef; a sweet Chablis or dry Chardonnay is nice with chicken. Add a little Sherry to the mix for an interesting twist.

Makes four 1/4 pint jars.

2 cups wine
3 cups sugar
2–3 ounce foil pouches liquid fruit pectin

Mix wine and sugar in the top of a double boiler placed over boiling water. Stir four to five minutes, until sugar is dissolved. Remove from heat and immediately stir in pectin. Mix well. Skim off any foam. Pour hot jelly into heated 1/2 pint canning jars, leaving 1/4 inch of space. Apply jar lid and ring, twisting tightly.

Process jars for ten minutes in a hot water bath (190° F). Remove jars from boiling water and allow to cool at room temperature.

SOPHIE MAE'S FAVORITE WATERMELON RIND PICKLES

These are sweet and sour and utterly delicious. They make a great addition to a holiday relish plate, and are yummy with cold roast beef . . . or eaten out of the jar by the light of the refrigerator at midnight. You might have to hunt for watermelon with a thick rind; so many recent hybrids have eliminated the light green or white interior rind as well as the seeds. Any heirloom variety should work. If you can't find a watermelon with a thick rind, keep a little of the red flesh on when you trim the pieces. They won't be quite as crisp, but the lovely color will make up for it.

Makes four pints.

8 cups watermelon rind cut in 1-inch cubes, dark green skin removed
1/2 cup pickling salt
4 cups cold water
5 teaspoons whole cloves
4 cups sugar
2 cups cider vinegar
2 cups water

Combine salt with cold water and stir to dissolve. Pour this brine over the watermelon rind, adding more water if needed in order to cover. Weigh down with a plate to completely immerse the rind. Allow to stand for six hours. Drain and rinse thoroughly. Drain again. Combine vinegar, sugar and water. Tie the cloves in a cloth bag and add them to the vinegar mixture. Bring to a boil; simmer for ten minutes. Pour vinegar mixture over watermelon rind and let stand overnight. It's a good idea to use a plate to weight the rind down again.

The next day bring all to a boil; check consistency of rind. If still hard and crunchy, cook until rind is translucent, five to ten minutes. This may not be necessary, depending on the thickness and kind of watermelon rind. Be careful not to overcook or your pickles will be mushy. Take out the bag of cloves, and pack the watermelon rind into hot, sterilized pint jars. Add enough hot syrup to leave 1/2 inch of room at top of jar. Apply jar lids and rings, twisting firmly. Process jars in a boiling water bath (185° F) for ten minutes. Remove jars from water and allow to cool at room temperature. When cool, check to make sure jars have sealed properly.

ABOUT THE AUTHOR

Cricket McRae has always enjoyed the kind of practical home crafts that were once necessary to everyday life. Her first Home Crafting Mystery, *Lye in Wait,* focuses on soap making; the third in the series, *Spin a Wicked Web,* features spinning and fiber art.

The employees of Thorndike Press hope you have enjoyed this Large Print book. All our Thorndike and Wheeler Large Print titles are designed for easy reading, and all our books are made to last. Other Thorndike Press Large Print books are available at your library, through selected bookstores, or directly from us.

For information about titles, please call:
 (800) 223-1244

or visit our Web site at:
 http://gale.cengage.com/thorndike

To share your comments, please write:
 Publisher
 Thorndike Press
 295 Kennedy Memorial Drive
 Waterville, ME 04901

12/08